HAVE SWORD WILL TRAVEL

Garth Nix & Sean Williams

Piccadilly
PRESS

First published in 2017 by Scholastic Press,
an imprint of Scholastic Inc., New York, USA

First published in Great Britain in 2018 by
PICCADILLY PRESS
80–81 Wimpole St, London W1G 9RE
www.piccadillypress.co.uk

A CIP catalogue record for this book is available from the British Library.

ISBN: 978-1-84812-652-7
Also available as an ebook

1

This book is typeset by Perfect Bound Ltd
Printed and bound in Great Britain by Clays Ltd, Elcograf S.p.A.

Piccadilly Press is an imprint of Bonnier Zaffre Ltd,
a Bonnier Publishing company
www.bonnierpublishing.com

To Anna, Thomas, and Edward,
and to all my family
and friends
- Garth Nix

To my instructors at the Tai Chi
and Chi Kung Institute in
Adelaide, masters of the sword
- Sean Williams

CHAPTER
ONE

Odo and Eleanor did not set out to find their destiny. At best, they were hoping for eels.

'I've never seen the river so low before,' said Odo as he climbed down the banks and began to trudge through the thick, reddish mud. He'd walked along and waded in the same stretch of the Silverrun for what felt like every single day of his life. Like his days, the river was always much the same. But now, there was a lot more mud and a lot less river.

'Father says it never *has* been so low,' said Eleanor absently. She was already a few steps ahead of him – but that was no surprise. She was *always* a few steps ahead of him, he felt. Odo watched as his best friend stopped and looked intently at one of the puddles next to the narrow, knee-deep stream that was all that remained of the once-rushing river. Before Odo could say anything else, she lunged with her spear and lifted out a writhing eel firmly stuck on two of its three sharp prongs.

'Got it!' she cried.

'I noticed,' said Odo. He was impressed, but it was more

fun to make Eleanor think he wasn't. He took the snapping eel off the spear, his strong fingers holding it firmly despite its slime. Then he put it in the wicker basket he held and strapped the lid back on. There were already four eels inside awaiting the fifth.

'When the river is this low, it's very bad for the mill,' Odo went on. 'There's not enough water to turn the wheel. We're grinding with the small millstone now, turning it by hand.'

'I wondered why you sneaked away,' said Eleanor. She headed downstream. 'Let's go to Dragonfoot Hole. All the eels will be gathering there, I reckon.'

'I didn't sneak away!' protested Odo. He was the seventh child of the village miller – and even if there had been *seventy* more kids in the family, there would always be work to do. 'I did my share this morning!'

'I know – you're *very* good,' said Eleanor with a grin, in a way that made *good* almost sound like an insult. Her father was the village apothecary, and though she did help him with some things, he by and large let her do what she liked. What Eleanor liked the most was looking for adventure. In the village of Lenburh, this meant spearing eels, shooting rabbits with her bow, or scrumping apples from the bad-tempered Wicstun family. Which was fun for about three minutes . . . Eleanor wanted more. Her mother had been a soldier knighted on the field of her last battle, and Eleanor planned to follow in her footsteps, if she could find someone to train her. In the becoming a knight part, not the dying in battle.

Odo didn't know what he wanted to be. He would be thirteen next spring, and at that age most people were already doing whatever they would be doing for the rest of their lives. He had to decide soon if he wanted to apprentice with someone other than his mother, the miller.

'Do you reckon we'll all have to move?' he asked Eleanor, eyeing the shallows and the mud. 'I mean if the water dries up completely?'

'Yep!' said Eleanor brightly, spearing another eel. She quite liked the idea of heading off into the unknown.

'The river will come back though,' said Odo, basketing the eel without even thinking about it. 'It's been raining lately.'

'But isn't that what makes it all so strange?' Eleanor asked as she peered around the edges of the biggest sinkhole on the river. 'It's been raining and the river is still drying up. Look, what's that?'

Odo looked. Dragonfoot Hole was a deep depression that exactly resembled the imprint of a mighty clawed foot. Odo had never seen it so clearly before. Normally he would have had to dive down to the river bottom holding his breath, but now the water hardly flowed over his large bare feet.

Odo could see three eels swimming just below the surface where Eleanor was pointing. Then he caught the faint gleam of something shiny sticking out of the muddy riverbed.

'Metal,' he said. 'Probably an old horseshoe or something. I'll get it.'

He knelt and reached down into the water.

Eleanor could make out a long silver shape through the murk. 'Doesn't look like a horseshoe,' she commented.

'Well, I know that *now*. Ow!' He pulled his hand back and looked at the thin line of blood on his finger. 'It's sharp!'

Eleanor knew she should tend to her best friend's wound. But she couldn't take her eyes off what they'd found.

'It's a sword,' she said breathlessly. She started to reach for it herself, but Odo grabbed her wrist.

'Careful!' he warned. 'I only just touched the tip of the blade, and look!'

He held up his injured finger, showing Eleanor the cut. A single drop of blood welled up and slid across his flour-stained fingernail, falling into the water above the submerged weapon. For a moment the drop stayed together, then it broke apart and swirled away.

'Press on it; that'll stop the bleeding,' said Eleanor, unimpressed. She'd helped her father sew up many really serious wounds, like last week when Aelbar the farmer had run over his foot with a plough. 'I'll just lever this out.'

She reversed her eel-spear, pushed it into the mud under the silvery blade, and heaved down.

The sharp, pointy end of the sword came out of the mud with a loud squelching sound.

'It's not even rusty!' exclaimed Eleanor in wonder. She moved the spear shaft further along, eager to free the rest of the weapon from the mud. 'Can I have it? You've never wanted a sword.'

'I guess so,' said Odo. He'd been pressing on his cut finger, but stopped to have a look and see if it was still bleeding. It was, and another big drop of blood fell. This time, it didn't fall in the water. It fell on the tip of the sword and ran down the narrow gutter in the middle of the blade.

Blood.

The single word was not spoken by either Odo or Eleanor, but by a deep, male voice that was a little scratchy, as if it belonged to someone woken from a very deep sleep.

Eleanor and Odo looked around and then at each other. They were alone in Dragonfoot Hole. There was no one standing on the high banks on either side and no one upstream or downstream either, and this was a straight stretch, at least fifty yards of empty river.

'*Blood.*'

The voice was stronger now. More awake. It sounded like it was coming from someone right next to the two children. Someone they couldn't see.

Odo stepped back and clenched his fists. He was very big for his age, and strong from all his heavy work in the mill.

Eleanor reversed her eel-spear again, holding it ready. She wasn't big, but she was very, very quick, as the eels knew to their cost.

'*BLOOD!*'

Odo and Eleanor screamed as the sword erupted out of the water. It shot into the air as if wrenched from the mud by some invisible warrior, and hung there unsupported, water cascading from its golden hilt and sharkskin grip, the sun making the huge emerald in its pommel gleam.

'*Who has woken me from my rest?*' roared the voice.

There was no doubt where that voice was coming from now. *The sword.*

Eleanor struck at the weapon, catching the blade between the prongs of her eel-spear. Twisting, she forced the sword back down into the river with a huge splash.

'Run, Odo! I'll try to hold –'

The spear juddered in her hand, moving violently despite her best efforts to keep it still. Odo grabbed hold as well, but that only seemed to make the sword angrier. It suddenly twisted in the water, broke free, and chopped up the shaft of the eel-spear, reducing it to six-inch bits in a flurry of lightning-fast blows.

Eleanor flung the last bit of the spear away and turned to run. Odo threw the basket of eels at the sword, but the sword dodged it easily. It bashed Eleanor with the flat of its blade, knocking her down to the mud, then whisked around in front of Odo, hovering there with its incredibly sharp point a finger-width from the hollow of Odo's throat.

Odo stood completely still, his eyes wide in terror.

'Did you wake me from my rest?' The sword wasn't shouting now. It almost sounded normal, like someone stopping at the mill to ask Odo when they could get their wheat ground.

'Um, I'm not . . . not sure,' said Odo. 'We were hunting eels and we saw your . . . you . . . shining there . . .'

'Blood woke me,' said the sword. 'The blood of a true knight, for naught else could raise me from my slumber. I have need of such a knight. Whose blood has awoken me?'

Odo knew the answer to this question. And if there was any possible way to get out of giving the sword the answer, he would have. But he had a feeling the sword already knew.

'Ah, well, I suppose that was my blood,' said Odo. 'But I'm not a knight. I'm just one of the miller's children –'

'Do you mean to kill us, sword?' Eleanor interrupted, sitting up in the mud and wiping at her face. Odo sent her an urgent 'don't give it ideas' look, which she ignored.

'I do not make war upon innocents,' said the sword, sounding faintly affronted. It backed up a little, still hovering in the air like a huge, shining, and frighteningly dangerous wasp. 'What is your name, miller's son?'

'Odo. And this is my friend Eleanor.'

'And you are not a knight.'

'Er, no.'

'But your blood woke me, and only a true knight's blood could have done so,' mused the sword, as though working through a difficult problem.

'If you say so.' Odo made a slight gesture with his fingers to Eleanor. She knew this meant *run away while the sword's talking*. But she ignored him again, stood up and faced the sword, her hands on her hips.

'You're one of those magic swords, aren't you?' Eleanor wasn't afraid now the sword was just talking, not attacking. 'Like in the stories. Sir Wulfstan had one called Bright Talon. What's your name?'

'𝕳ildebrand 𝕾hining 𝕱oebiter,' said the sword proudly. '𝖄ou might know me better as 𝕭iter. 𝕹o doubt you have heard the many stories told of me. 𝕸ore than this so-called 𝕭right 𝕿alon, I'm sure.'

Odo and Eleanor exchanged a quick glance. Eleanor gave a slight shrug. She'd never heard of Hildebrand Shining Foebiter, and she was much more interested in old legends than Odo was.

'We live in a small village,' said Odo. 'We don't get to hear many stories. Uh, can we go now?'

'𝕹o,' said Biter. '𝕴 must think. 𝕸y rest could only have been broken by the taste of a true knight's blood. 𝖄et you say you are not a true knight. 𝕬re you *sure*?'

'Yes,' said Odo. 'I'm not any sort of knight.'

'Does it have to be a proper knight?' Eleanor asked. 'What if it's someone who's going to be a knight one day? The daughter, say, of a knight. Wouldn't that be enough?'

'𝕴 . . . slept for many years,' said the sword. '𝕸y memories are somewhat clouded. But I am sure . . . *fairly* sure . . . about the detail of the true knight.'

'Fine.' Eleanor couldn't help sounding a little miffed. 'If you need a "true" knight, there is old Sir Halfdan at the manor. We could take you to him, I suppose.'

'No,' said Biter. 'I can only be *woken* by a true knight. Yet you are not a knight. This situation cannot be allowed.'

Odo didn't like the sound of *that*. 'Why don't you just go back to sleep and forget we ever found you –' he pleaded.

'Kneel!' ordered the sword. He rose higher in the air and angled back, as if to strike at Odo's neck.

'At least let Eleanor go.'

'And go too while you're at it,' added Eleanor urgently.

'Kneel, I say!'

Odo knelt down in the mud, babbling.

'Please, spare Eleanor. It was my fault you got woken up –'

The blade came whistling down, slowed at the last moment, and turned sideways, slapping Odo on the left shoulder. Odo flinched, but the killing blow didn't fall. Instead, the blade whipped up above his head and then tapped him on the right shoulder.

'Rise, Sir Odo!' called out the sword, pulling away and hanging dazzling in the sunlight.

'Sir . . . what?'

'Now you are a knight,' said the sword. 'All is properly in order.'

9

'What?!' Eleanor cried out, her voice high and tremulous in her throat. 'This is so unfair! *I'm* the one who wants to be a knight. I'm a better fighter than Odo too.'

'She is,' Odo agreed. He started to stand up, then stopped as he realised his legs were shaking and might not hold him. His neck still felt bare and cold where he'd expected the sword to slice.

'𝔜ou can be 𝔖ir 𝔒do's squire,' said Biter to Eleanor, which didn't make her feel any better at all. '𝔈very knight must have a squire. 𝔅ut enough of this chatter. 𝔇oubtless 𝔍 have been awoken to combat great evil or dire threat. 𝔗ell me what it is.'

Eleanor helped Odo up. Neither had any idea what to say. Just moments ago they had been hunting eels, and now one of them was a knight and the other a squire . . . and a talking sword had got it completely the wrong way around.

'𝔜ou are too afraid even to speak of it,' Biter pressed. '𝔖ome fell beast creeps at night and steals children and livestock? 𝔄 sinister steward in midnight-dark raiment demands tributes beyond endurance? 𝔠ome, 𝔖ir 𝔒do, when you wield 𝔅iter you need fear none of these!'

'It's not that,' said Odo. 'We . . . that is . . . there's simply no great evil threatening us.'

'Or dire threat,' said Eleanor. 'Least I can't think of one . . .'

'𝔗here must be something,' said Biter in an aggrieved voice. '𝔗ake my hilt, 𝔖ir 𝔨night, we will sally forth and essay the matter. Your hand, Sir Odo. To me.'

Odo gingerly held out his open palm. The sword flashed up and around in a circle, the sharkskin grip slapping against the boy's hand. Odo closed his fingers around it and held the sword away from his body as if it was an actual shark.

'Hold tighter!' called Biter. Odo gripped harder and felt even more worried than he had a few moments before.

'What does "essay the matter" mean?' Odo said out of the corner of his mouth to Eleanor.

'*Look into things*,' replied Eleanor. And as soon as she said it out loud, she thought, I like the sound of that. Her whole life, she'd been waiting to *sally forth*. More than anyone else in their town, she was ready to *essay matters*. All these actions led to a much bigger, brighter, and very attractive word . . .

Adventure.

Immediately, Eleanor's mood turned surprisingly cheerful, despite the mud all over her and the presence of the magic sword that was straining in Odo's grip like a dog on a lead.

'This isn't good,' whispered Odo. 'How am I going to get rid of this sword?'

'Why would you want to, you big saddle-goose?' asked Eleanor, her eyes bright. 'This is an adventure! At last!'

Now Odo didn't know what scared him more – the bizarre sword in his hand or Eleanor's even more bizarre enthusiasm.

'But I don't want an adventure!' he protested. 'Or to be a knight!'

Eleanor slapped him on the back. He took a step that turned into a stumbling run up the riverbank as Biter pulled him forward.

'But you've got both!' Eleanor called out. Then she laughed and added, 'Lead on, Sir Odo!'

CHAPTER
TWO

Odo had no illusions as to who was leading who. The sword pulled him along the path so hard he almost overbalanced, reminding him of the time the rival team of shepherds' children had almost beaten the miller's children during the annual tug-of-war competition on the Lenburh green. Then, as now, he felt that at any moment his feet would slip out from under him and deposit him on his backside in front of the whole village.

The first witnesses, it appeared, would be Aaric and Addyson, the unbearable twin sons of Lenburh's baker.

'Look here!' Aaric scoffed, sauntering over. 'It's Odd Odo and Eelanor playing soldiers – and they've stolen Sir Halfdan's sword to do it!'

Eleanor flushed in anger and embarrassment. Aaric and Addyson had doughy skin and hair as white as flour – they looked like loaves brought out of the oven too soon – and their favourite occupation was taunting Eleanor and Odo, knowing full well the two friends had been forbidden to fight them.

'We're not playing,' she told them. 'And that isn't Sir Halfdan's sword. It's . . . he's *Sir* Odo's . . . and he doesn't take kindly to the likes of you.'

'Sir *who*?' The twins clutched their bellies and howled with laughter. 'You'd better take that sword back before Sir Halfdan or the reeve sees you with it.'

'𝔇𝔦𝔰𝔯𝔢𝔰𝔭𝔢𝔠𝔱𝔣𝔲𝔩 𝔨𝔫𝔞𝔳𝔢𝔰!' Odo felt the words vibrate up the sword and along his arm even as Biter lunged forward.

Aaric and Addyson fell backwards with cries of fright.

'Odo!' Aaric shrieked. 'What are you —?'

The sword slashed the air in front of Aaric's nose and would have cleaved his skull in half if Odo hadn't yanked the weapon back with his entire body weight. Setting his heels deep, he kept Biter at bay as the twin bakers stared in shock.

'No, don't hurt them!' Eleanor called out. 'They're just stupid, not dangerous.'

If the sword murdered the twins, that would bring their brief adventure to the worst imaginable end. Eleanor and Odo would be outlawed at best, if not hanged from the justice tree on the hill above the village. She wanted to be remembered as a famous knight, not as an infamous murderer of dull-witted baker boys.

Aaric stood up, face red in outrage. 'You could've killed me!'

'Wait till Da hears about this!' said Addyson.

'𝔄 𝔨𝔫𝔦𝔤𝔥𝔱 𝔥𝔞𝔰 𝔞 𝔯𝔦𝔤𝔥𝔱 𝔱𝔬 𝔡𝔢𝔣𝔢𝔫𝔡 𝔥𝔦𝔪𝔰𝔢𝔩𝔣 𝔣𝔯𝔬𝔪 𝔞𝔩𝔩 𝔣𝔬𝔯𝔪𝔰 𝔬𝔣 𝔪𝔬𝔠𝔨𝔢𝔯𝔶,' said the sword, slicing a figure eight through the air despite Odo's efforts to keep him grounded. The baker twins retreated a few more steps and looked at each other as they slowly realised Odo wasn't somehow faking the sword's voice, and that he was honestly straining to keep the sword back from them.

Biter was a real enchanted sword — and he apparently wanted to kill them.

'Or *herself*,' said Eleanor.

'𝔄nd any who fall under his protection,' added the sword in a magnanimous tone.

'Or *her* protection.'

'We don't need protection, Biter,' said Odo. He smiled nastily at the twins. 'They're just a nuisance. Like gnats.'

Aaric opened his mouth to utter a cutting retort, but closed it after Addyson pulled at his arm. Neither of them took their eyes off the shining silver sword that quivered in the air, only barely restrained by Odo's powerful arms.

'𝔚ell, Sir Odo, if they are not your true enemies, let us go find them and dispense justice!'

Biter surged forward, dragging Odo along the path. Aaric and Addyson screamed and bolted back towards the village.

'Skelpie!' called Aaric.

'Murder!' shouted Addyson. Their cries of protest were plaintive bleats that did not slow them down one jot.

'That showed them,' said Eleanor, seeing the possibilities now that shock had turned to amusement. 'What about Old

Master Croft? He yelled at us once for stealing his fennel even though we didn't steal any.'

'Lead me to this Old Master Croft,' ordered Biter. 'He will trouble you no more!'

'No, no,' said Odo, struggling in vain to control the sword. Biter was swinging from side to side, reacting excitedly to anything that moved, which included Pickles the ginger cat, who had stopped by on her way to inspect a den of field mice and a branch swaying in the wind. Cat, mice and branch all narrowly avoided being sliced into several pieces.

Meanwhile, Eleanor had years of injustices to make up for. 'Reeve Gorbold spent our tithes on a blue linen dress with beads for his daughter once, remember?'

'Sir Halfdan made him pay it all back,' said Odo patiently. 'Being beheaded isn't going to teach him any lessons. Or do us any good.'

'What about the Wicstuns? They're too tall anyway.'

'Yes, take me to the wicked Wicstuns!'

'Stop it! Both of you!' The loudness of Odo's shout startled all three of them. Biter drooped at his side and Eleanor bit her lip. Odo had never shouted at her before, not seriously.

'Don't even joke about chopping heads off, Eleanor,' he said more calmly, although his hands shook with more than just physical exhaustion from trying to control the sword. 'We have no enemies here, Biter. Just annoying people, and thoughtless ones, but no one who deserves what *you* want to do to them.'

'I am no mere executioner's skewer,' said the sword sullenly. 'I am also skilled in the art of poetic justice –'

'There's no need for your justice!' Odo could feel his voice rising again and struggled to keep Biter under control. 'We have a reeve, and the village moot, and even old Sir Halfdan. If there *was* a problem, they would take care of it.'

'Well, there *is* the river,' Eleanor pointed out. 'No one's taking care of that. If it stops running, there won't be a village or any people. Annoying, thoughtless or otherwise.'

Biter twitched.

'The river isn't flowing?' he said. 'It must be blocked by something.'

'Probably just a rockfall upstream.' Odo had heard his mother tell his father this more than once. 'It'll wash away in the spring rains.'

But the sword wasn't listening to him.

'Blocked by something . . . or someone! Sir Odo, it is no coincidence that you woke me this day.'

'Sure, because no one would even have seen you at the bottom of the river –'

'Our quest lies before us. We must seize the chance to save the helpless villagers of . . . ah . . .'

'Lenburh,' Eleanor supplied.

'Lenburh! It is our destiny. Sir Odo, let us depart this minute!'

'No, wait!'

The sword dragged Odo several feet along the path again, but this time Odo really dug his heels into the ground and bent his knees. He was getting the hang of it now. The trick was not to let Biter get him moving. Once he was off balance the sword had all the power. 'We can't just leave without telling anyone!'

'Without telling anyone what?' asked a voice from behind them.

Eleanor spun around. Her father, Symon, was looking at them with a rather bemused expression on his face, his overflowing gathering basket evidence he was returning from the huge clump of nettles that grew around the standing stone further along the path.

'We're going on an adventure!' she said.

'I see. Right now?'

'I hope not –' Odo started to say even as Biter swung him around to present his shining blade in Symon's face.

'State your name and allegiance!'

'Ah, I *thought* I'd heard someone else,' said Symon. He did not seem unduly perturbed and did not back away. 'An enchanted sword. It has been a long time –'

'State your name and allegiance!'

'But you are the visitor here. Is the obligation not yours to introduce yourself first, according to custom?'

'Er, yes, I suppose so,' said the sword. 'Please pardon me, for I have been long asleep. I am Hildebrand Shining

Foebiter and I think I used to also be called the Scourge of . . . something or other . . . something quite terrible, I'm sure . . .'

Eleanor's father bowed, losing some of the nettles from his basket in the process.

'My name is Symon. I am healer, herbalist and apothecary of Lenburh, and my allegiance first and foremost lies with my daughter, Eleanor.'

'Squire Eleanor,' said Biter. 'Now in service to Sir Odo.'

Symon looked at Odo and raised one eyebrow. Odo shrugged unhappily.

'We found Biter in Dragonfoot Hole,' Eleanor explained excitedly. 'He knighted Odo and now he's taking us to find out what's happened to the river upstream!'

'I see.' Symon set his basket down and cupped his chin thoughtfully.

'It is a noble quest, Master Symon,' Biter said. 'Though we may perish, we must not quail.'

'I think that two children would perish more easily than an enchanted sword,' said Symon. 'But it is true someone should investigate what is happening with the river. Is there no one more suitable?'

'They may be young, but Sir Odo found me and awoke me. The mighty quest is his,' said Biter. 'By the same token, your daughter is small but seems valiant, and my knight must have a squire.'

19

'Don't try to stop me,' said Eleanor mulishly.

'Oh, I can see there's little point in me doing that,' Symon said with a glance at Eleanor that she couldn't read. Was he angry or sad? Or both at once? 'Minds have been made up, plans made . . . You have made plans, I assume? Gathered supplies . . . a map at least?'

'Um, not yet,' Eleanor admitted. 'That's . . . that's exactly what we were going to do next.'

'It's all happened so quickly,' said Odo. He gave Symon a beseeching look, hoping that the herbalist could somehow make the sword let them go so they could get back to their ordinary lives.

'I know what knights are like,' Symon said, putting a hand on Eleanor's shoulder. 'Always rushing off on quests, never thinking of the things they might have forgotten. But there's no stopping them, not once they've set their hearts on a particular path. And you have your mother's heart, Eleanor.'

Definitely sad, she thought. For an instant her resolve wavered.

'Promise me,' Symon said, looking away from her, 'that my daughter will come to no harm.'

'𝔖𝔦𝔯 𝔒𝔡𝔬 𝔴𝔦𝔩𝔩 𝔨𝔢𝔢𝔭 𝔶𝔬𝔲𝔯 𝔡𝔞𝔲𝔤𝔥𝔱𝔢𝔯 𝔰𝔞𝔣𝔢,' Biter replied.

Odo gulped. Symon wasn't seriously thinking about letting Eleanor go, was he?

Symon looked from the sword to Sir Odo and back again. 'Swear on it.'

'A knight's word is –'

'I'm asking *you*, not the boy.' There was sudden steel in Symon's voice. 'Swear on it. By your blade.'

'By my blade!' Biter came upright in a salute, painfully wrenching Odo's wrists.

'Good.' Symon reached out and ruffled Eleanor's hair. It was blonde and cut short like his, so stray strands wouldn't foul his potions. 'You have my blessing.'

She beamed up at him, even though her eyes were suddenly full of tears. Where had they come from? Eleanor hadn't cried since her mother's vigil, when she and her father had sat alone overnight before the procession through Lenburh the next morning. For all that she had dreamed of leaving the village, it did not truly strike her until now that it would mean leaving him too.

'Thank you, Father,' she said.

'Come, Sir Odo and Squire Eleanor,' said Symon. 'You have much to do, starting with getting that mud off you both.'

CHAPTER
THREE

Eleanor and her father lived in a thatched cottage just over the boundary of Sir Halfdan's lands, within a short walk of the manor. The knight was old and had many ailments, and his squire, himself in his sixties, was a frequent caller at the cottage, seeking unguents and remedies that Symon patiently supplied, knowing that many of them provided relief more for the mind than the body.

'I've been expecting this day,' he told the children, 'though it has come sooner than I . . . hoped. I have supplies for you, Eleanor, enough for three days. I traded an ounce of yarrow leaves for this leather jerkin, and this bedroll is the finest down from Enedham . . .'

The list was long, but the pile collapsed neatly into a pack that Eleanor could just about lift. Odo volunteered to carry it for her, knowing that he would have nowhere near as much.

But Symon did have something for him, unexpectedly.

'In here, I think,' Symon said, rummaging through a deep chest. 'I'm sure of it . . . Ah!'

With a clatter of discarded odds and ends, he produced a long, black shape attached to a leather belt. 'This belonged to your mother,' he told Eleanor, presenting it to Odo.

The scabbard was the perfect size. Biter was larger and heavier than any weapon Odo had ever seen before, much larger than the hunting hanger Sir Halfdan wore, and his arms ached as much from holding him as from trying to control him. But would Biter allow himself to be contained?

'May I?' Odo asked the sword.

'I insist upon it,' Biter replied. 'Fine steel such as myself must be cared for and protected. In addition, I will require sandpaper and tung oil, and a sharpening block, and . . .'

His demands went on, but with a twinkle in his eye Symon returned to the chest and produced everything Biter required. He also added a small leather pouch, which upon investigation proved to contain sixteen silver pennies, five ha'pennies and some copper farthings.

'Do you have another sword in there, Father?' asked Eleanor hopefully.

Symon shook his head. 'Your mother's sword was buried alongside her in accordance with her wishes.'

Eleanor nodded. She had only the faintest memories of her mother, who had died when Eleanor was a little girl. Once a year she and her father visited the grave, which was in a dense copse on Sir Halfdan's lands inhabited only by sheep. Her memorial read, *Rest, brave Sir Quella, a true knight, beloved of husband and daughter.* Eleanor had traced those words with her fingers a thousand times, wondering how Quella had been brave, imagining the glorious moments of her knighting during her last battle, while shying away from the fact she had died at the end of it. Eleanor had to imagine the details because her father talked very little about it.

Now there were other things Symon wasn't saying – this time about Eleanor's departure, and how it was destroying him. Symon still had that sad, resigned look. It made Eleanor feel guilty, but there was no way she was changing her mind.

'Thanks, Father,' she said, hugging him.

'It's a parent's duty to let go,' he said. 'Speaking of which, Odo . . .'

Odo had been dreading this moment. As they headed down the hill to the mill, new scabbard banging against his legs with every step, he tried to find the words to tell his mother. Mertice the miller was a big woman with blunt features that matched her tone. She operated the small millwheel without pause or complaint; her arms were strong, and it was her turn.

'Fixing the river, you say?' She regarded her middle child with a distracted eye.

'Yes, Ma.'

'Will it take long?'

'I don't know, Ma.'

'And you say that's an enchanted sword you have there?'

'Yes, Ma.'

'Can't you just sell it? It might fetch a goodly sum —'

'No, Ma,' replied Odo hastily as Biter harrumphed in his scabbard.

'Ah, well, and so it knighted you.'

'Yes, Ma.'

'Don't suppose you can stop being a knight then.'

Odo was silent. He had been wondering about that.

'It's in the blood,' said Mertice, rather surprisingly. 'Your great-grandfather was a miller who became a knight.'

'He did?'

'Oh, yes — we used his old helmet as a flour measure when I was a girl. Don't know where it went. Worked out all right for him on the whole. He liked the life, wandering about and so on. Came back when he was old to tell his stories. I knew him a little, although he died when I was six. Maybe seven. You take after him a bit . . . in the eyes mainly.'

'I do?'

'Yes. Anyway, you'll be doing some good if you can fix the river, and Hedley can take your turn at the wheel. If a knight's what you have your mind fixed on being, best to get started young.'

Odo was far from sure he wanted to be a knight at all, but he knew better than to argue, with Eleanor nudging him in the side with one bony elbow and his mother actually giving him permission.

'Thanks, Ma.'

'Take Barton's pack from his room and Aldwyn's hat. You can have the loaf and sausage you see on the counter there, plus the flask of cider in the pantry. And your da's put aside thirteen silver pennies for you, one for each birthday. Take it from the strongbox. That should do you.'

It was a far cry from what Eleanor's father had given her, but Odo was glad for that much. His family would miss the provisions more than they would miss him most likely, with the river so low and the mill practically at a standstill.

Eleanor watched him collect his supplies. She knew that Odo had never dreamed of leaving home so soon. He probably never wanted to leave Lenburh at all. But he had the sword, and she couldn't leave without him. They were a team when it came to adventures, as they were in the catching of eels.

She saw him dart into the room he shared with two of his older brothers and collect a small memento, which he tucked into his pack. It was a wooden duck called Enid that his father had carved for his fifth birthday. She opened her mouth to tell him to save the weight, then closed it.

'I suppose I'm ready,' he said, standing on the upper landing with a pack on each shoulder.

'Then let us depart!' Biter's voice rang out clear and unmuffled despite his new home within the scabbard.

'Promise me one thing.' Odo was talking to the sword, but he looked at Eleanor so she would know the message was for her too. 'One quest, and then I retire.'

26

'A knight never retires,' said Biter.

'Well, I'm going to. When the river is fixed, we find a proper knight, someone more suitable to give you to. I never asked for this, and I don't want it.'

'So you want to be a miller?' asked Eleanor.

'It's all I know.'

'That doesn't answer the question.'

A commotion from outside drew their attention: raised voices, growing nearer.

'I know he's in there! No one fights my boys without fighting me as well!'

Eleanor recognised that gruff voice. It was the baker, no doubt with twins Aaric and Addyson in tow.

'We've got to get out of here,' she hissed.

'Not until you promise.'

'Come on out, you reeky coward!'

'No man calls a true knight a coward and lives!'

Odo put both hands on the sword's hilt, trapping it in the scabbard.

'Promise!'

'Oh, all right,' said Eleanor, tugging him towards the mill's back entrance. 'If that's what you want.'

'A good sword always obeys his master's wishes,' said Biter.

That would have to do, even though Odo was aware, like Eleanor earlier, that this didn't really count as a promise.

FOUR

It was perfect weather for an adventure, Eleanor thought as the three of them walked along the old sunken road out of Lenburh, bordered on both sides by high ramparts of blackberry bushes, and from there to the path by the river. The sun had passed its afternoon peak but still cast a heavy, autumnal heat across the river, which seemed, if possible, more sluggish than before.

Their eel basket remained exactly where Odo had been knighted. Neither volunteered to venture back out into the mud to rescue it. Someone else could do that, someone without a magic sword.

They would follow the river path upstream, along the riverbank, through undergrowth and the occasional stand of willows or alders. Eleanor didn't hesitate, setting off without a backwards glance. After one last look across the mud at Dragonfoot Hole, Odo followed. *Sooner started, sooner finished*, his father liked to say. That probably applied to adventures too.

'How long do you think this will take?' he asked, wondering how soon he could be rid of the sword.

'Depends on where the blockage is,' said Eleanor, flicking at dandelions with a thin stick. 'Might be days away. Weeks, even.'

Odo swallowed a sudden lump in his throat. 'It'd be much quicker if we had a horse.'

'Or maybe we should grow wings and fly instead?'

'No need to be sarcastical. I just thought . . . I mean, *weeks* . . .'

Eleanor looked back over her shoulder. Her oldest friend was downcast, but she refused to let him spoil her mood. Which meant finding some way to cheer him up.

'It probably won't be weeks. Biter, what do you think?'

The sword's emerald suddenly flashed as it caught the afternoon sunlight, uncannily as though it had turned its attention to her.

'A laden knight will travel four leagues per day on foot by good path or road. As we progress, we will naturally uncover information regarding the location of the river's trouble. That will allow Sir Odo to determine the length of our journey and our quest.'

'Ain't that right, Sir Odo?' Eleanor asked him. 'No point being all gloomy until we know something about anything.'

Odo nodded. A shadow passed over him, making him

blink and look up. They were walking under the Big Bough from which Lenburh children had dropped into the river for generations. All they would drop into now would be stinking mud.

Fix the river, he reminded himself. *Then you can retire.*

'I guess we should start looking for people coming the other way,' he said. 'They might know where the blockage is.'

'We're bound to come across someone soon,' Eleanor said, squinting up the path to where it vanished around a bend in the river. There could be dozens of people beyond that point, for all she could tell.

Only there wasn't anyone there either, just another stretch of river she had explored many times before. Although beyond the boundaries of the village, it still fell under the patronage of Sir Halfdan. The ageing knight didn't own it, but in theory he would defend it from attack. Not that he had been doing much defending of late, Eleanor thought. All he did was raise a toast at the harvest festival and hand out the mostly edible or drinkable prizes. To be fair, though, there hadn't been any attacks in living memory for him to guard against. Lenburh was a peaceful place.

She wondered if a drought counted as an attack. It probably depended on the cause. If it did, she swore she would do her best to help Odo overcome it, and thereby prove her worthiness as a knight in her own right so she could have Biter when Odo retired.

They turned another bend. Still no travellers to be seen, just a stand of weeping willows that Eleanor knew slightly less well than those closer to home. Their long, slender fingers swayed from side to side as though seeking the river that now lay out of their reach.

'Can I ask you a question, Biter?' Odo said.

'Ask away, Sir Odo.'

'Why didn't you know the name of our village?'

'Good question,' Eleanor said. 'Were you washed downstream from somewhere else, or were you just not paying attention when you went into the water?'

'Hard thing to miss, an entire village,' said Odo.

The sword shifted minutely in the scabbard, making a small grating noise like the clearing of a throat.

'The exact circumstances of my submerging are . . . unclear to me,' Biter said.

'Does that mean you don't remember?' asked Eleanor. *Clouded*, he had said of his memories when they had found him. It struck her as strange that a sword could be forgetful, but no less strange than that a sword could talk.

'It is possible the knowledge was taken from me,' the sword said, 'by means of darkest sorcery.'

'Why?' asked Odo. 'How?'

'That I do not know.'

'More likely you just forgot,' said Eleanor. 'How old are you anyway?'

'If I knew how long I slept in the water, I could tell you the answer,' said the sword.

'Well, what's the last year you remember?'

'Year four seventy-nine in the Calendar of Nobles.'

Neither Odo nor Eleanor knew what that was.

'Year seventeen of the rule of King Sherwyn?' Biter tried again.

'Do you mean Sherwyn the Seventh?' asked Odo, who had learned a little history from his oldest brother's books. King Sherwyn the Seventh had gone steadily madder and madder until he'd ordered his army to march off a cliff, at which point the soldiers turned around and had him deposed. Armies didn't usually depose kings, Odo had learned from that story; Sherwyn the Seventh was the exception.

'There was no seventh,' said Biter. 'He was the first of his name.'

'But obviously not the last.' Eleanor asked Odo, 'How long between the First and the Seventh?'

Odo shrugged, making the packs on his shoulders move up and then down. 'I don't know. I think Sherwyn the Seventh was about three hundred years ago.'

They walked in silence for a long moment, but not as long as three centuries spent at the bottom of a river.

'There were eels. So many eels,' said the sword. 'My sleep was very deep, and my dreams only of eels.'

'Lenburh probably didn't exist more than three hundred

years ago,' said Eleanor. 'That would explain why you don't remember it.'

Odo wasn't so sure. Lenburh had always existed, in his mind, and always would exist unless the river stopped running for good. Another possible explanation for Biter's amnesia that no one had raised was that Biter was lying. But why would a sword lie about how it had come to be imprisoned in mud, far from its rightful owner? Out of embarrassment?

Or perhaps something more sinister.

'I believe your explanation is correct, Squire Eleanor,' Biter said, prompting a look of combined satisfaction and resentment from the girl. It was one thing to be praised by the magic sword, another to be reminded of her place in the order of things. At least, she reassured herself, it was only temporary. 'Let us move on to more practical matters. Sir Odo, I am keen to know the details of your training. Clearly you lack experience with a sword of my repute, but what about the arming sword or riding sword? And the lance — let us not forget that. How progressed is your tilting?'

'Ah,' said Odo, shifting the packs again. He was starting to feel their weight now. 'Progressed? Not as such. Not progressed at all, to be honest.'

'The short blade? Dagger wielding? Shieldwork at least?'

'Biter, you dullwit,' said Eleanor, 'we keep telling you: you've got the wrong person. Odo's good at numbers, sewing and lifting heavy things, whereas I —'

'Then we have much to do!' The sword shot out of the scabbard with the sound of a razor across a strop. 'We will commence with blocks and move on to parries. I will demonstrate the motion as we walk. Later, while your squire makes camp, we will practise in earnest. Attend!'

Eleanor ground her teeth as the sword darted and stabbed in a series of elegant moves that Odo did his best to follow. But Eleanor didn't look away. Patiently and methodically, fingers twitching with every imagined move, she committed the feints and blocks to memory.

Soon, she swore, it would be her turn.

FIVE

Odo didn't know exactly when they left the purlieu of Lenburh and entered unknown territory. The river wound more or less northward through an unchanging landscape, home to birds, badgers and a variety of placid snakes. It wasn't until the sun dipped low into the trees on the opposite bank and Eleanor suggested finding a clearing off the path for the night that he wondered how far away home lay.

And then there wasn't time to think at all.

'𝔇emonstrate the five 𝔏ethal 𝔣orms,' the sword ordered him while Eleanor set up the camp, 'as 𝔍 instructed you earlier.'

The sword swung him bodily from side to side, supernaturally strong and impossible to resist, crying '𝔥ave at you!' and '𝔄vaunt!' to imaginary foes as he went. Odo tried to keep up, but really there was little more he could do than hang on and hope he didn't hurt himself.

When Eleanor could take it no longer she said, 'If you're

going to swing that thing around, make yourself useful and cut some firewood.'

'Do not mistake me for an axe, squire. My edge must not be blunted upon timber –'

'I'll see what I can find,' said Odo. 'Come on, Biter. We can at least collect kindling together.'

He nodded at Eleanor in gratitude for the chance to catch his breath, but she had already turned away and was moodily sorting through their supplies.

'Squires kept a civil tongue in my day,' grumbled Biter as Odo rummaged through the undergrowth in search of fallen logs.

'Oh, you remember them, do you?'

'With perfect clarity. There was one belonging to Sir Wylie, who had an extraordinary nose for bandits. She could sniff them out clear across a forest, allowing her master to ambush them long before they bothered her holdings. A splendid young woman. Shame about that crossbow bolt . . .'

Odo soon learned that most of Biter's reminiscences ended rather bloodily, as did life for a hare that happened to cross their path. The sword moved in Odo's hand and neatly severed the small animal's neck before Odo even noticed it was there.

'Dinner!' Odo told Eleanor as he staggered back into the clearing under an armful of wood with the small corpse balanced on top.

'Good work,' she told them. 'I'll clean it. You cook.'

'Done.'

'I will need cleaning also,' said the sword, sticking itself point-first into the earth near where Eleanor had cleared fallen leaves for the fire.

'I'll get to you in turn,' said Eleanor, pretending gruffness although she didn't mind. She had yet to touch the sword and was looking forward to examining it more closely. Its steel had an opalescent quality that warranted study, and there were swirling patterns in the metal.

While Eleanor skinned and gutted the hare, Odo lit the fire and laid out the cooking utensils Symon had given them. Soon he had the animal roasting on a makeshift spit over a steady flame, with a pot of root vegetables stewing on coals nearby. He had often cooked for his family, but somehow this smelled better than anything he had made before. For the first time that day he felt something like contentment, a feeling mirrored on Eleanor's face as she sharpened and oiled the sword. She was thinking about the adventures that lay ahead, once they fixed the river and she became a knight. *Sir Eleanor* had an excellent ring to it.

Biter emitted a low hum of contentment, like a cat. 'A little higher . . . no, below the cross-guard . . . perfect!'

'Do you know how many people you've killed, Biter?' she asked him.

'None,' said the sword.

'What?'

'I have killed no one. The knights I have served, however, have slain many.'

'Oh.'

'A sword cannot kill of its own volition. We are the wielded, not the wielder.'

Odo filed this away for future reference. If he had known this when they'd first found Biter, he wouldn't have been so afraid of having his neck cut through.

'So tell us about your knights then,' said Eleanor, eyes gleaming with the same light as the newly polished sword. 'Who was your last one? What happened to her?'

'Sir Nerian was his name. He was strong of heart and mighty of arm. Together we quelled a rebellion against King Sherwyn in the north . . . or was it the south? The finer details of the campaign elude me for the moment . . . As to his fate, I'm afraid I can't remember anything at all . . .'

Out in the darkness surrounding their campfire, a twig snapped.

Biter swept out of Eleanor's grasp and through the fire, scattering the hare and spit in a shower of sparks. Odo raised a hand to defend himself, and found himself holding the sword instead. It yanked him to his feet.

'What —?'

'Who goes there?' the sword called.

'A humble traveller who smells your dinner,' came a reply from the shadows.

'𝔄𝔭𝔭𝔯𝔬𝔞𝔠𝔥!'

The bushes parted, allowing a rumpled, grandfatherly figure to step into the light. Dressed in sun-bleached garb that had seen more than its fair share of the road, the man had a long salt-and-pepper beard tied in decorative knots. He carried a pack that towered high above his head, adorned with elaborate needlework.

'Didn't mean to startle you,' the apparition said. 'I have acorns and some dried apple if you're willing to trade.'

Eleanor lowered only slightly the paring knife she had scooped up from the cutlery by the fire. 'What's your name? Where are you from?'

'Call me Firman. I'm headed south from Nægleborg and hoping to find better fortune on the way.'

Neither Eleanor nor Odo knew the man's hometown, but both noted Firman's direction. He came from the north, so might have news of the river.

'I guess we can spare some hare,' Odo said, tugging the sword down, or trying to. The sword resisted.

'Come on, Biter,' he hissed. 'Be reasonable.'

'𝔄𝔡𝔳𝔞𝔫𝔠𝔢 𝔱𝔴𝔬 𝔭𝔞𝔠𝔢𝔰,' the sword ordered Firman. '𝔜𝔬𝔲 𝔪𝔞𝔶 𝔰𝔦𝔱 𝔱𝔥𝔢𝔯𝔢. 𝔠𝔬𝔪𝔢 𝔫𝔬 𝔠𝔩𝔬𝔰𝔢𝔯 𝔬𝔯 𝔶𝔬𝔲 𝔴𝔦𝔩𝔩 𝔣𝔢𝔢𝔩 𝔪𝔶 𝔰𝔱𝔦𝔫𝔤.'

'Argh!' The traveller nearly jumped out of his skin. 'That sword . . . it talked!'

'It's enchanted,' Eleanor explained. 'It can move on its own too, if you give it reason to.'

'I won't.'

Watching Biter the whole time, Firman warily did as he was told, busying himself first with the unfastening and lowering of his pack, then with sighing and rubbing his shoulders. 'Who else do I have the pleasure of meeting on this long and winding road?'

'Sir Odo,' said Biter, 'and his squire, Eleanor.'

Firman's eyebrows went up. 'A knight, eh? That explains the sword. But where's your pavilion? Your coterie? I thought knights ate stags on spits, with sugared swans for dessert.' He smiled.

Biter made a sound that might have been a wistful sigh. Eleanor decided she would trust Firman for the moment. Slipping the knife into her boot, she reconstructed the spit, brushed the dirt from the partially cooked hare and put it back over the fire.

'What do you do?' she asked.

'I'm a forester,' Firman said. 'If ever you go to Nægleborg I am sure they will speak well of me there.'

Again, that smile. Odo couldn't tell if Firman was laughing with them or at them.

'Sir Odo is a knight-errant,' said Biter, 'pursuing his first campaign.'

'Well, good luck to you,' said the man, before Odo could

add, 'And last campaign'. Firman pulled a cloth bag from his pack and unfolded it to reveal the promised acorns and dried apple. 'You'll find plenty to do the way you're headed.'

'Do tell,' said Eleanor, leaning forward and cupping her hands around her knees.

'It's the river,' he said. 'It's drying up.'

'Yes, we noticed. We're going to fix it.'

'It's going to get worse. There's no more water coming down at all — this is just the dregs. It must be completely blocked somewhere north of here. Already people are guarding the few wells about as if they gave gold, not water.'

'Do you know what's stopped the river?' Odo asked. 'And where?'

'No. North, that's all. I've heard something's happened in the mountains, but I haven't been there myself. Why would I? I'm heading for greener regions. Trees die where there's no water. A man's got to earn a livelihood, and all along here will be a desert in a few years.'

Odo and Eleanor looked at each other, both thinking of dying trees and the land turning dead and brown.

'How far are the mountains from here?' asked Odo.

Firman shrugged. 'I never went there. A few weeks, afoot. I suppose you don't have a horse tied up somewhere?'

Odo shook his head and tried not to look disappointed. He had hoped for a destination closer than the mountains.

'Trees won't be the only things that will die with the

river,' he said. 'We want to save our village, along with all the others in danger.'

Firman smiled. 'That is a noble quest, Sir Knight. May good fortune find you. You'll need it.'

The hare was ready. Eleanor cut it into pieces, speared each one with a broken stick and handed them around. They ate in silence, wrapped up in their thoughts as the fire crackled and popped, casting light that danced across the sword's newly polished steel. Eleanor wondered if Biter was thinking about the pavilions he might have enjoyed in his past life, perhaps resenting the privations he was forced to endure now. Odo worried at the scab that had formed over the cut on his finger, hoping it wouldn't fester.

'There's one other thing,' Firman said when the meal was done. 'I've been wondering if I should tell you, but it would be remiss of me not to, given where you're headed and what you attempt. There's a rumour . . . no, not even that. A *name* . . . a name I keep hearing whenever anyone talks about the river, as though it could be connected to the blockage, perhaps even the cause. It's an old name. You probably don't know it . . .'

'Tell us the name,' said Eleanor.

'Quenwulf.'

Biter's emerald flashed in recognition. '𝔔𝔲𝔢𝔫𝔴𝔲𝔩𝔣 𝔱𝔥𝔢 𝔡𝔯𝔞𝔤𝔬𝔫?'

'Yes,' said Firman. 'The dragon.'

CHAPTER
SIX

Quenwulf the dragon!

Even Odo and Eleanor knew that name. Everyone knew it. Quenwulf was an ancient and terrible beast, and her name was one to frighten children with. She was a creature who had done almost every terrible thing anyone cared to mention. She had razed towns to the ground, eaten armies whole, defeated every hero sent against her. Not that anyone was ever very clear about where these things had happened, or when. Somewhere else and long ago, thankfully.

'I thought Quenwulf was a legend.' Odo gulped. 'Those stories . . . they can't all be true.'

'Why not?' asked Eleanor.

Odo didn't have a good answer to that.

'Though my memories are not . . . precise,' said Biter thoughtfully, 'I do remember Quenwulf. She was real enough. I think I even met her. A parley, perhaps? Something nags at my mind . . . I do recall a great creature, far bigger than your family's mill, Sir Odo.'

Everyone was silent as they thought about that.

'But why would a dragon want to dam the river?' asked Eleanor. 'I've never heard a story about a dragon doing *that*.'

'Perhaps the dragon breathes fire upon the water and boils it away,' Firman offered. 'Some fear Quenwulf wishes to dry out the lands surrounding the river, then to burn it all in some vast and unholy pyre. Dragons are said to worship flame.'

Odo imagined Lenburh burning, and shuddered.

'How are we supposed to fight something like that?' he asked, his voice sounding very small.

'Maybe you shouldn't,' said Firman. 'That's why I'm telling you.'

'We can't go back,' said Eleanor, although her voice was not as steady as she would have liked. 'We promised to save the river. And besides, we have Biter.'

'Is he going to be enough?' Firman asked.

They looked at the sword to see if he had an opinion on the matter. He was unusually silent. Maybe he didn't want to be melted into slag by a dragon's fiery breath, or crumpled to junk in a dragon's powerful claw.

'Hildebard Shining Foebiter,' said Biter, 'Scourge of something or other, but now that I think of it, also . . . Dragonslayer!'

'That does sound impressive, I'll admit,' said Firman.

'All right then,' said Eleanor. 'Wielding Biter the Dragonslayer, I'm sure you will succeed, Sir Odo. Nothing has changed.'

'Except for the dragon being the most famous, most powerful one anyone has ever heard of,' muttered Odo. As always, he was glad to have Eleanor's company, but now he was more worried than ever that this adventure would end up with one or both of them dead. Eleanor was just too brave. It would be sensible to turn back right now, but he knew he could never convince her to give up their quest. Or Biter, for that matter.

Besides, he also had a clear image of what it might cost Lenburh and all its people if they failed. He had seen fires in the forest, and the night that Swein Cow Drover's hut had burned. He imagined that on a greater scale, the whole village a writhing thing of red flame, black smoke across the sky, ash falling for miles around . . .

'Well, that's all I've heard, and now you know it too,' said Firman. 'My day has been a long one, and you have many long leagues ahead of you. Full belly cures faint heart – isn't that what they say? Let's sleep on it and see what tomorrow brings.'

The children agreed. Biter volunteered to keep watch, but Eleanor found it difficult to sleep. Her thoughts were full of her father and how he would feel if he knew she was going off to do battle with a dragon. Her mother, Eleanor knew, had died in a forlorn hope, assaulting a much stronger enemy. She wondered in the darkest hour before the moon rose if she was marching off to the very same fate . . . But her mind slid away from that thought, and soon Eleanor fell into a weary sleep.

For his part, Odo was exhausted from knightly training. He fell instantly into a deep slumber, disrupted only once, when he woke to the sound of shuffling footsteps along the river path.

Through bleary eyes he saw Biter scooping earth upon the dying coals of the fire, extinguishing the faint light from the embers. In the darkness the sword was visible only as a few disconnected glints of starlight reflected in his steel. Odo winced as Biter swooped down near his face.

'Firman is not the only traveller on this road tonight,' the sword told him in a whisper.

Odo raised his head and opened his eyes as wide as they would go. It didn't help, but in the dim starlight he could just make out a dark lump that was the forester and another that was Eleanor. He was about to lay his head back down when a sharp odour struck his nose. It was like the harsh smell of the wood-ash lye Lenburh's tanner used to clean her hides, but sweeter, somehow. Stranger.

'Urthkin,' whispered Biter.

Odo jerked up, alarmed, but the sword added, 'Fear not. There is no danger, provided we do not provoke them.'

'Really?' asked Odo. All the childhood stories, whispers, and rumours he'd heard about urthkin were bubbling up in his head, and he was now very much awake.

Urthkin lived in subterranean warrens, occasionally hollowing out mountains to make giant nests, like termites'. They hated the light and wore elaborate, shady costumes with enormous broad-brimmed hats when forced out into the day. They were prodigious miners, trading precious metals and gems for products grown or made on the surface. They were said to be savage fighters who never took prisoners.

Odo had never seen one before. No one he knew had. Briefly he wondered if he should wake up Eleanor to tell her what was nearby, but the strange smell slowly faded, and he could no longer hear the muffled footsteps on the path.

'They have gone,' whispered Biter.

'You're sure?' asked Odo nervously.

'I am sure,' said Biter. 'But I will keep watch. Sleep, my knight.'

Odo lay back down, doubting that he would ever get to sleep again. His mind was too busy with thoughts of a great dragon boiling away the river and urthkin emerging from the ground and swords flashing this way and that and . . . he fell asleep again.

When he woke the next morning, the near-encounter was pushed abruptly from his mind by Eleanor's angry shout.

'Firman's gone! And look – the ill-bred varlet took the last two pieces of hare!'

Odo shot upright, blinking sleep from his eyes. Every muscle hurt from the unfamiliar exercises Biter had been giving him, making him groan as he twisted around looking for the forester.

What Eleanor said was true. The camp was empty apart from the two of them and Biter, and the remains of the carcass were gone.

'I thought you were on guard,' Odo scolded the sword.

'I was.' Biter sounded offended. 'I told the artisan to take the meat. We will hunt more as needed.'

'I was looking forward to eating that!'

Eleanor resented the sword giving away meat she'd prepared, although Biter would probably have expected her to give her share to Odo anyway, or at least serve it to him. A squire's work was never done.

Odo was already laying out their supplies and meagre dishes. Firman had considerately cleaned up after himself before he left, filling in his toilet hole and burying his rubbish.

Maybe, she told herself, I should concentrate on the positives.

'So, a dragon,' she said, taking the chunk of hard brown bread Odo offered her, 'Quenwulf the dragon. Do we know what her strengths are? Does she have any known weaknesses?'

'Let's concentrate on finding her first,' said Odo, rubbing his aching calves while he chewed. In his mind, he was planning how to redistribute the weight in the packs so Eleanor could carry the smaller one.

'Do you think we'll get to keep her head?' Eleanor asked.

'I seem to recall the skull of the dragon Axcræfta measured

the length of five tall men from ear to chin,' said Biter, neatly slicing the wings off an unwary fly that chose that moment to investigate the sausage. 'King Ormod turned it into a boat and was burned in it when he died.'

'Are there ever any queens in your stories?' asked Eleanor.

The sword ignored her. 'There is no time to lose, Sir Odo. If even the urthkin are on the move, the situation must be truly dire.'

'Urthkin?' said Eleanor.

'The urthkin!' exclaimed Odo, suddenly remembering the strange smell and the soft footfalls in the night. 'We heard some coming down the road before moonrise. They didn't stop.'

'It's all happening, isn't it?' Eleanor's mind filled with of visions of dragons, night creatures and exotic travellers, in descending order of interest to her, but greater interest nonetheless than anything she had left behind in Lenburh. 'This really is an adventure now!'

'I guess it is,' said Odo, not very happily.

Eleanor wasn't discouraged by his lack of enthusiasm.

'An adventure,' she said happily, her eyes bright. 'Just what I've always wanted!'

SEVEN

It might be an adventure, but all the usual boring tasks of ordinary travel had to be completed too. Breakfast, toilet and repacking gear took up a good hour before they were on the road again, heading northward as before. After a few miles, the path veered away from the muddy trickle that had once been the river and joined a road, though it was mostly just a wider stretch of dirt. Every now and then there were sections of ancient paving, and even a milestone with an inscription so eroded it was impossible to tell what it said.

Eleanor and Odo were amazed. They had never known that Lenburh lay so close to a real road, a road that looked like it went somewhere important.

They passed an actual signpost an hour into their journey — another sign of greatness that Lenburh lacked. There, if you needed directions you had to ask someone. But here, between two small hills, the road forked and there stood a tall post that had once held two signs. Only one remained, pointing off to their right, the eastern fork. Despite severe weathering, it was still possible to read the deeply etched word *Ablerhyll*.

Eleanor had actually met someone from Ablerhyll once – a herbalist who came to learn healing lore from her father. He had been tall, shiningly bald, nervous of children and animals and had become the subject of intense curiosity after his departure. Apparently he was a very good herbalist but a poor healer, since he was frightened of his patients.

Eleanor looked along the eastern road and wondered what Ablerhyll was like and whether the bald herbalist was still there, refusing to look anyone in the eye. She'd like to go and see, but not until their quest was complete. She knew that as a knight, or even as a squire, duty came first, certainly before mere curiosity. When she was a knight herself –

'Concentrate, Sir Odo. I will repeat the Seven Certain Blocks for you while you commit them to memory.'

Eleanor switched her attention firmly back to where Biter was dragging Odo's hand around, and concentrated on learning the Seven Certain Blocks herself.

But before she could do this, another distraction arose. A group of people suddenly came over the crest of the hill.

'Ambuscade!' roared Biter, lunging forward towards the broad-shouldered man who had the misfortune to be closest. Odo, obeying his naturally peaceable instincts, did not follow the sword's movement, but instead tried to hold it back.

This was just as well, since this was far from an ambush. It was simply a shepherd and his family travelling along the same road. The man held a rather flimsy crook, not even a quarterstaff. Behind him trailed a perfectly harmless flock of sheep, with his wife and three small children bringing up the rear.

'Help!' cried the man, leaping backwards into his sheep, who scattered in all directions. His wife, clearly made of tougher stuff, drew a knife from under her kirtle and advanced, the children behind her.

'𝔖tate your name and allegiance!' boomed the sword.

'I'm a – I'm a – I'm a –' The man's sword-induced stammer was impenetrable.

'He's a shepherd!' said Odo, desperately failing to wrestle the sword back into the scabbard. 'He's harmless.'

'You leave us alone!' called the shepherdess, who was weaving her way between the sheep, her knife held high. 'I'll give you what for, robbers on the high road!'

'𝔥ow dare you, woman!' roared Biter. He whisked himself through the air, just missing a sheep. '𝔜ou stand before knight-errant 𝔖ir Odo and the mighty sword 𝔅iter the 𝔇ragonslayer, 𝔖courge of the . . . the . . .'

'Sheep?' muttered Eleanor as Biter cut the wool from the back of a ewe that tried to get past Odo. The ewe turned away in fright, bleated and jumped into a muddy hole by the roadside, where it promptly got stuck.

'Everyone calm down!' shouted Odo. Using both hands, he managed to force Biter's point down to touch the road. 'Please! We are not robbers.'

'Bet we're going to be shepherds for a while though,' said Eleanor, looking at sheep bolting in every possible direction. She had a low opinion of ovine intelligence. 'Now we have to catch them!'

By the time they had brought the flock back together, the shepherd had regained his voice and one of the younger children had fallen asleep on his mother's lap. The shepherdess was not impressed with being delayed by an apparently deranged magic sword.

'If it isn't one thing it's another,' the woman complained. 'First the dragon steals our sheep, now it's enchanted slicers –'

'A dragon?' asked Odo urgently.

'Where?' questioned Eleanor at almost the same time.

'Sheppy, two days north of here,' said the shepherdess. She looked at her husband and scowled. 'His village. I never liked it. We're going back to *my* family, down south at Wichslyn. They don't have dragons eating sheep there, I tell you. We won't stand for it *there*.'

'Might not have been a dragon in Sheppy neither,' said the shepherd, keeping a tight hold on his crook and maintaining a respectful distance from the sword. 'Could have been wolves.'

'If it was wolves, they were doing her bidding anyhow,'

said the shepherdess. 'Queen of the Wolves, ain't she? That's what her name means, don't it?'

'You mean Quenwulf?' asked Eleanor. It *did* sound a bit like *queen wolf*. 'I never heard she was queen of any wolves. I mean, why would a dragon –'

'All wild animals will obey a dragon,' said the shepherdess with certainty. 'She's made a nest in the Upper Valleys, they say, and when there's no sheep left to eat, she'll eat *people*. Leastways those not smart enough to get away.'

'I don't want to be eaten, Ma,' whined the oldest child.

'And you won't be,' his mother told him. 'Not at Wichslyn, where sensible folk live. No dragons or magicked-up toadstickers there.'

She shot Biter a sour look, and Odo judged it wise to keep moving.

'Again, I am sorry we . . . er . . . startled you,' he said.

'Are you really a knight, Sir Odo?' asked the middle child. 'You don't have any armour.'

Before Odo could answer, Biter shot half out of the scabbard, scaring the shepherd family yet again.

'𝔥e is indeed, for a knight is not known by his armour –'

'Or *her* armour,' interrupted Eleanor.

'𝔅ut by his sword!' continued Biter. '𝔎now ye that 𝔍 am 𝔥ildebrand 𝔖hining 𝔉oebiter, 𝔇ragonslayer and 𝔖courge of . . . er . . . 𝔑one but a true knight may wield me and live!'

His last words were delivered to the backs of people

54

and sheep as they hurried away, which rather lessened the awesomeness of his pronouncement.

'Nonetheless,' he added thoughtfully, 'the child does have a point. Armour. You are insufficiently equipped, Sir Odo, for an assault on any dragon, let alone one with the reputation of Quenwulf.'

'I don't see what I can do about that,' Odo replied. He was tired of failing to meet Biter's expectations. It wasn't helping him believe that he could actually succeed at their quest, even though he was relieved they would be walking only to the Upper Valleys, not all the way into the mountains. 'We haven't got anywhere near enough money to buy armour.'

'Never underestimate the value of a good deed, Sir Odo. Many a knight has been provisioned by those he has helped.'

'We rounded up those sheep,' said Eleanor.

'Yes,' Odo said, 'but only after we scared them off. Besides, what could they give us? Woolly vests? Good deeds or not, no one around here will even have any armour to give us.'

'Where there's a road, there will be a crossroads,' said Biter portentously.

'What does that mean?' asked Odo.

'Smiths can be found at crossroads,' said Biter. 'Just as divines at natural springs, or cider-makers by orchards.'

'I wouldn't mind some cider,' said Odo with a sigh. They'd finished all the cider in the flask his mother had given him.

'If there is a smithy ahead,' said Eleanor, 'they might give you armour if we promise to kill the dragon for them. Maybe they'll give both of us armour. And me a sword.'

'I suppose we can hope,' said Odo. 'But it seems unlikely to me.'

'If you never stand, you'll never fall, but never standing, you'll never be tall,' Eleanor said sharply, reciting a childhood rhyme she had often used to goad Odo into taking even the small risks of their adventures back home.

'Used to happen all the time in the old days,' said Biter. 'My knights and I were showered with gifts. Armour, horses, jewelled scabbards, hunting dogs, a special whetstone I particularly enjoyed . . .'

The sword continued to burble on about all the things he had been given as Odo and Eleanor started walking again. The miller's boy raised his eyebrows at Eleanor, indicating his doubt that anyone would give them such gifts. Or any gifts.

'Anything's possible,' whispered Eleanor, her voice hardly loud enough to be heard over Biter's continuing catalogue of presents. 'You never thought you'd be a knight, did you?'

'No,' said Odo heavily, and concentrated on setting one foot after the other, while not listening to the sword.

'A brace of peacocks, a bed in the shape of a swan, a very fine baldric, a sword-rest of black oak . . .'

Later that day, Odo wondered if Biter did know what he was talking about, at least as far as smiths and crossroads went. The road had meandered back down from the low hills to run along the river again, and Odo could see another road coming down to meet it somewhere up ahead, beyond the ever-present clumps of willow and alder. There, where the roads would meet, he saw a tall column of smoke. Darker smoke than from a typical cottager's fire, and much more of it. It could easily be a forge, though he doubted any smith would be as generous as Biter thought.

'Looks like there is a crossroads ahead,' he said. 'And maybe even a smithy.'

'*I knew it!*' exclaimed Biter.

Eleanor didn't comment. Her head was cocked, attending to another detail. She stopped and held up her hand for silence.

'You hear that?' she whispered.

Something was splashing in the mud up ahead, out of sight below the riverbank.

'It'll just be ducks,' Odo said. They had passed a flock of wild mallards earlier, their green-and-gold heads bright in the sunlight.

But it didn't really sound like ducks. There were regular splashes, and between them he caught a very human sound, the low sobbing of someone hurt or distressed.

'Is that someone . . . crying?' asked Eleanor.

'I think so.'

'*To the rescue!*' cried Biter. He leaped out of his scabbard and zoomed forward, with Odo hanging on as best he could. Pulled by the sword, he crashed through willow branches, trod down a huge clump of weed and came out on the riverbank.

The river was notionally the same width as it was near Lenburh, but now there was only a narrow channel of water barely two paces wide surrounded by an expanse of sticky, stinky mud. A decrepit wooden jetty stuck out twenty feet across the mud, a stark reminder that up until recently the river had been navigable for small boats. At the far end of the jetty, but under its boards, a forlorn figure crouched in the muck. It was a boy roughly the same age as Odo and Eleanor. He was dressed in a grey shift, weeping disconsolately and throwing rocks at the remaining rivulet in the middle of the river.

'Hello!' called Odo. 'Are you all right?'

The boy looked up in fright and went to stand. One foot shot out from under him and with a squawk he fell backwards into the mud.

'This is as bad as the sheep,' said Odo, hurrying to the jetty and running along it, Eleanor close behind. At the end, they climbed down a short ladder and dropped to the mud, sinking halfway up their shins. Biter allowed himself to be sheathed once he was certain there were no monsters or villains nearby. Mindful of their own balance, Odo and Eleanor wallowed over to the weeping boy.

He was sitting up and doing his best to wipe the mud off his clothes, but very clumsily. There seemed to be something wrong with his hands, as if it hurt him to use them.

'Are you all right?' Eleanor, the first to reach him, asked. 'We didn't mean to give you a fright.'

'It's not your fault,' the boy said. 'I'm just clumsy. That's what Master Fyrennian always says. Clumsy as a pig in a pantry, and he's right.'

Up close, Odo could see that the boy was pale-skinned and thin, with lank blond hair that had odd gaps here and there, as though random tufts of it had been cut away. His nose was long and narrow, with a blister on the end, and he had no eyebrows.

'Anyone could slip in this mud,' said Odo, reaching for the boy's hand to help him up. 'Up you come!'

'No!' shrieked the boy, falling back into the mud again. He held up his hands, showing the travellers that his palms and all ten fingers were badly burned. The skin was shining red and already beginning to peel away. From the pain in his eyes, Eleanor could tell it hurt terribly.

'Chaff and weevils!' Odo rarely swore, but this seemed an appropriate time to do so. 'How did you do that?'

'Pig in a pantry, remember?' The boy looked close to crying again. 'Not good for an apprentice smith.'

'I have some cream for burns in my pack,' Eleanor said. Her father had provided an unguent for every ailment imaginable.

She reached behind to swing her pack around, but stopped as the boy cried out again.

'I can't!' The boy's expression changed to one of alarm. 'Master Fyrennian will have my hide.'

'What?' asked Odo.

'I'm supposed to let my hands stay like this until they heal,' sobbed the boy. 'To l-l-learn my l-lesson.'

'Lesson?' rumbled Odo. 'Those burns won't heal on their own!'

'The m-mud helps,' sobbed the boy. 'And if I wash it off before I go back, the master will never know.'

'Come with us,' said Odo, picking the boy up and slinging him over his shoulder. He weighed surprisingly little, less than a full flour sack, and it wasn't too difficult for Odo to carry him ashore, even wading through the mud. 'I want to know more about this master who treats you so badly.'

On the riverbank, Odo and Eleanor introduced themselves. Biter was uncharacteristically silent, perhaps remembering the fright he had caused during previous encounters on the road, and Odo chose not to mention him.

'My name is Toland,' said the boy. 'I have to get back to the smithy. Master Fyrennian only gave me leave for an hour –'

'Not yet,' said Eleanor. She grabbed his shoulder and pushed him back down. 'I'm going to treat those hands.'

'No, you mustn't!' shrieked Toland again. 'He'll burn . . . that is, I must learn . . . I must learn my lesson.'

'We will talk to your master,' said Odo. He hesitated, then added with what he hoped sounded like confidence, 'I am a knight. It is my duty to help the defenceless, and you are certainly that.'

'So keep still,' said Eleanor firmly.

Toland looked up at Odo, then down to the sword at his side. He hesitated for a moment before slowly holding out his hands.

Eleanor applied one of her father's ointments as gently as

she could. Toland flinched every time she touched him, as much from fear as from actual pain, Eleanor thought.

While Eleanor applied the balm, Odo asked questions. They quickly learned that there *was* a crossroads ahead, and by it sat Anfyltarn, a village that existed solely to serve the huge smithy that had 'always been there'. Toland was just one of dozens of apprentices and smiths all indentured to the formidable Master Fyrennian.

'Tell us how you got burned,' said Odo, his voice gentle and encouraging.

'It was the fire.'

'Yes, we guessed that,' Eleanor said.

Odo nudged her, and she took the hint to let the boy talk at his own speed.

'I picked up a mould Master Fyrennian had been using before it was completely cooled down. I waited the normal time, but I forgot his forge is much hotter than the others.'

Odo felt Biter shift at his side, the sword edging half an inch out of the scabbard.

'Why is it hotter?' asked Odo, correctly interpreting Biter's move as interest.

'*Magic,*' whispered Toland. 'One load of coal will last a week, burning night and day, and it never needs the bellows. It melts iron in a minute, so you can pour it like water.'

Toland's expression was of wonderment as he described this marvel, but collapsed into a wince as Eleanor rubbed a

62

particularly sensitive spot. 'When he brands you, the fire is so hot you hardly feel it, at least not at first.'

'He brands you?' Odo asked, aghast.

'Sure. It's to bind us to the mystery, he says, but the older smiths say that's not true. I think it's to show we belong to him.'

He slipped one hand free and pulled up the arm of his shift. On his shoulder they saw a lumpy pinkish scar in the shape of an *F*, about the size of a hen's egg.

'We had to swear an oath of loyalty to him as well, when he took over from Master Thrytin. Even the senior smiths had to swear, though they didn't like it. No one ever had to swear an oath like that before. I crossed my fingers, so it didn't count.'

Odo and Eleanor exchanged a glance. This whole business of branding and oaths and refusing treatment for burns sounded not only very unusual but positively evil.

'Who's Master Thrytin?' asked Eleanor.

'He used to be the master of Anfyltarn. He was much kinder to us, particularly the little ones. Then Master Fyrennian came, and they had a contest of skill. Master Fyrennian won, but only because he had the magic fire. Master Thrytin has been locked up ever since, because he wouldn't take the oath Fyrennian demanded.'

'Did anyone else refuse?' Odo asked.

'No,' said Toland. He swallowed and smiled weakly.

'Master Fyrennian isn't so bad really.'

'So why won't he let you heal your burns?' Eleanor asked.

'To teach us to be more careful next time.'

'And what would happen if you tried to run away?'

'We can't. He's too rich and powerful. Everyone around here knows that he'll pay a reward for any of his branded servants. There was one girl, Scylle, she was two days' walk away when she was caught. The master branded her again, on the other arm.'

'*You must tell me more about the fire*,' said Biter suddenly, unable to remain silent any longer. '*The magic fire.*'

Toland jumped and cried out.

'Did that . . . was that . . . did that sword really just talk?'

'*I did,*' said Biter. '*I have a professional interest in fires such as the one your master uses.*'

'Only enchanted swords talk!' exclaimed Toland. 'That's how you can tell if they're enchanted!'

'*Indeed,*' said Biter. '*Though I have other marks of distinction.*'

'Even the master can't make an enchanted sword! Can I touch the blade?'

'*No,*' said Biter crossly. '*I keep my metal to myself, my knight and my squire, and the last only for maintenance.*'

'I get all the fun jobs,' said Eleanor.

'*Enough of this prattle,*' said the sword. '*The fire!*'

Odo pressed more gently. 'Can you tell us anything about

64

Master Fyrennian's magic fire, or is that part of the secret you're sworn to keep?'

Toland tore his eyes off Biter's hilt and shrugged.

'I'm sure it is, but I told you I crossed my fingers. The master never lets anyone see exactly how he kindles his flame.'

'What does he kindle it with?'

'I said he doesn't let anyone see . . . but he does *talk* about it sometimes, when he's angry and everything is waiting for the hot forge. Muttering to himself, about how if he'd found the crop himself he wouldn't have settled for just one firestarter. But I don't know what that means, or what crops have to do with fire. We don't grow anything. We don't even have any fields.'

At Odo's side, Biter twitched again.

'Maybe he's just trying to put you off the scent,' said Eleanor, not noticing.

'People talk a lot of nonsense when they're angry,' said Odo.

'Not in this case,' said Biter. 'He is a fool to speak about his secret fire in such a way.'

'But he didn't say anything!' said Toland, his face falling. 'Did he? Oh, he'll have me for ashes if I've said anything I oughtn't to!'

'It's not your fault,' Eleanor assured him, wondering what Biter was talking about. 'This "Master" Fyrennian of yours sounds like a real blackguard. Deposing the old master smith, branding and burning people, treating you like a slave . . .'

She'd noticed that Toland was not only thin and clearly underfed, but his shift was threadbare and burned in places, never patched or repaired.

'How are your hands now?' she asked.

Toland cautiously flexed his fingers. 'They feel much better.'

'Wait here for a moment. I need to talk to Odo. Uh . . . Sir Odo.'

They left Toland partly concealed under the gorse bushes, looking simultaneously relieved and worried, and walked thirty paces along the river path to be out of earshot.

'We have to help him,' Eleanor told Odo quietly.

'I agree,' he said with a firmness she hadn't expected. 'If I'm going to be a knight, I have to help people. I can't walk away from something like this.'

'Bravo, Sir Odo.' She grinned up at him. 'Now, Biter, what do you know about that fire? I want to hear everything before we go charging up that hill.'

'I cannot be certain,' said the sword, in something less than his usual bellow. 'But the boy's description is evocative: a fire that is both hot and pure, that consumes little coal or wood and is capable of melting iron so quickly. There is only one flame hot enough to do that, and that is a dragon's.'

'You think he has a dragon up there?' hissed Odo in alarm.

'No, I do not. They are impossible to hide, even in a smithy as large as the one Toland describes.'

'Then what?'

'Consider the goose,' Biter said. 'It eats stones to grind down its food, does it not? These stones it keeps in a special stomach, which is called –'

'A crop!' exclaimed Eleanor, before she remembered they were supposed to be whispering. 'You think this Fyrennian has something from inside a dragon's crop? The thing that makes its flame so hot?'

'I believe so. My recollections are somewhat vague . . . in places . . . but I do know that a dragon's fire is made in its crop, from the firestarters that gather there like the stones in a goose's crop. How this Fyrennian comes to have one, I do not know. Perhaps he stole it from a dragon's corpse, or found it buried under the site of an ancient battle. Either way, it is our duty to take it from him.'

'Agreed. Also, if we take away the source of his magic fire, then there could be a new contest of skill, which he would probably lose. Or we could give the firestarter to Master Thrytin –'

'No!' The sword's sudden bark made them both jump with surprise. 'No human should possess such a thing.'

'Why not?' asked Odo. 'It sounds incredibly useful.'

'And incredibly . . . dangerous,' Biter said. 'I cannot explain. I have slept too long; so many of my memories are obscured. But I know that such a power should not remain in human hands . . .'

The sword's voice trailed off and he made a curious throat-clearing noise.

'Not in human hands?' he resumed a moment later, sounding rather confused. 'What is a dragon's must remain a dragon's . . . ? No, no, that can't be right.'

'What are you saying?' Eleanor was confused too. 'If we get the firestarter we should give it back to a dragon? To swallow up for its own crop? How could we do that? I mean, it'd just burn us up before we could even talk to it, surely.'

'I . . . I can't remember,' said Biter. 'The important thing . . . I think . . . is that it mustn't remain in human hands. It should be . . . it should be . . .'

'Destroyed?' suggested Odo. There were lots of stories about evil magic things that needed to be destroyed. Often in very complicated ways.

'Yes!' answered Biter with some of his usual gusto. 'Destroyed! It is your duty to correct this wrong, Sir Odo.'

The sword slid out of the scabbard, flipped in the air, and slid his hilt into Odo's hand, as though to emphasise the importance of its conclusion. Neither Odo nor Eleanor found reason to argue. They wanted to challenge Fyrennian because of his cruel and tyrannical behaviour, as knights were supposed to do. Or at least that was what they did in all the heroic tales. Sir Halfdan mainly pottered about his house, complaining about aches and pains, but he was old and had presumably dealt with his fair share of petty tyrants in his younger days. No one told heroic tales about neighbours who were still alive.

'I've never done anything like this before,' Odo said, staring at the sword as though hypnotised.

'What, are you scared?' said Eleanor.

'Yes. Aren't you?'

'A bit.' She forced a fearless grin. 'But we'll have Biter. And it'll be good practice.'

'That it will,' said the sword. 'Remember everything that I taught you, Sir Odo, and you will be fine.'

'Really?' Odo said, surprised. 'I thought I had a lot left to learn.'

'You do,' Biter said. 'Fortunately, your enemy will be a smith and not a dragon. I am certain you will prevail.'

Odo frowned. He was not at all certain on this point. Something had to be done about Master Fyrennian, he felt this quite strongly, but the business of the firestarter worried him. Still, he supposed it was straightforward enough. Get the firestarter, depose Fyrennian, replace him with Master Thrytin . . .

They returned to the gorse to give Toland the good news, that they were going to come with him back to the smithy and liberate him and everyone else from Fyrennian.

But the gorse was empty.

The boy was gone.

CHAPTER
NINE

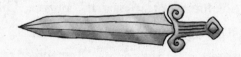

'Rancid oxgall!' It was Eleanor's turn to curse. 'Did Fyrennian find him and take him back?'

'I heard no sign of a struggle,' Biter said.

'I think he just slipped away himself,' said Odo, inspecting the ground for footprints and finding only Toland's.

'Why would he go back there?'

'Because he's afraid of what Fyrennian will do to him if he doesn't, I guess. We shouldn't have left him alone.'

'That makes no sense.'

Odo shrugged. It made sense to him. His father was by no means a Master Fyrennian, but when he was angry he got *very* angry. Often it was better to confess to some wrongdoing and take a lesser punishment rather than risk an explosion.

'If we hurry,' Odo said, 'we might be able to get there before he does.'

'Take only what you need,' Biter advised them. 'Light load makes fleet feet.'

They hid their packs and set off, Odo with Biter and

Eleanor clutching the paring knife. Toland's tracks led in a straight line uphill, away from the river, diverting to avoid the largest trees as the stumpy willows and alders gave way to more substantial oaks and beeches.

It soon became clear that they wouldn't catch Toland as they reached the edge of the sparse upper forest and Anfyltarn came into view.

It was not a typical village. It had a defensive earthwork mound built around it, topped by a wooden palisade. While there were a dozen or so of the usual small wattle-and-daub huts sprinkled about, the whole place was dominated by the great stone-built house in its very centre, a sprawling structure larger than any barn. It was twice the size of Sir Halfdan's manor house, which was the largest building either Eleanor or Odo had ever seen. Smoke billowed from seven tall chimneys, and the sound of industry rang from numerous open windows – the clanging of metal on metal, the roaring of giant bellows and the hissing of steam. It looked easily large enough to house fifty people.

Odo and Eleanor stopped to stay under cover of the treeline and look for Toland.

There was no sign of the fleeing boy.

'So what are we going to do?' Odo asked quietly.

'A frontal assault,' declared Biter. 'We will easily prevail against inexperienced smiths with the element of surprise on our side.'

'What surprise?' Odo countered. 'If Toland overheard what we were talking about and told his master that we know about the firestarter, they could already be waiting for us. Besides, people might get killed. *We* might get killed!'

'I think we should lie low until dusk and then sneak in,' Eleanor said. 'Find out where Fyrennian keeps his firestarter thing and steal it from him, then release Master Thrytin so they can redo their contest of skill. Master Thrytin will be grateful and give us armour. And me a sword.'

Odo nodded. This seemed a much better plan.

'Thievery is not among a knight's duties,' said Biter disapprovingly.

'Think of it as rescuing someone,' said Odo. 'Like a princess.'

'A princess who sets fire to things and used to live inside a dragon,' said Eleanor with a grin. 'That's my kind of princess.'

Biter grumbled something about squires remembering their place, but for once Eleanor didn't mind. Together they were righting wrongs and dispensing justice to those who needed it. This was exactly what she had always dreamed of doing.

Her grin turned to a squint of intense interest as she studied Anfyltarn. Eleanor had read all her mother's books about fortifications and defences, and the tactics to be employed by both attackers and defenders in a siege.

'See the way the forest suddenly stops here?' she said, indicating an expanse of empty ground between their hiding place and the nearest wall. 'It's been burned away so no one can sneak up too close. That palisade is newly built, and there are hides ready to be rolled down against fire arrows. Someone over there knows what they're doing. There'll be lookouts and patrols.'

Odo felt butterflies swarming in his stomach. This was a far cry from hunting eels and rabbits.

'What do you think we should do?' he asked her.

'When the sun goes down, let's crawl our way to the palisade. I'll go first. I can climb the corner there, and once I'm up I can help you up. Or you could wait for me to get in and I'll go and find a rope or something.'

'I'm not letting you go in there alone,' Odo said. 'Besides, I can climb too, you know!'

'I maintain that a frontal assault would be simplest,' said Biter. 'Once the first few are slain, the others will flee.'

'I don't think killing unsuspecting people is very knightly either,' protested Odo.

Eleanor nodded. 'Besides, Toland said there were dozens of smiths and apprentices. With hammers, not to mention whatever they make in there, like swords. They may not be knights, but those smiths are grown men and women and probably well armed and armoured.'

Odo nodded, agreeing, but her words had given him a thought. A thought that, the more he pondered it, quickly formed into something very much like a plan.

'I think Biter's wrong and right at the same time,' he said.

'What?' asked Eleanor.

'Simplest might be best,' he said. 'Why don't I just go up and say I want to buy some armour?'

'But what if Toland's talked to Master Fyrennian?'

'You know, I don't think Master Fyrennian would listen much to an apprentice,' Odo surmised. 'And would he see Toland straightaway? I doubt it. Like this, I can go in and have a look around. Maybe I'll get lucky and find the firestarter right away. You stay here for now. I'll report back as soon as I can.'

He stood up before he could think too hard about what he was doing, and stepped out of the treeline.

'Wait! Odo, get back here!'

Odo ignored Eleanor's urgent entreaties and strolled towards the main gate of Anfyltarn, attempting to look calm. His hand pressed firmly down on Biter's pommel as the sword tried to launch out of the scabbard.

'Stay in there until I tell you,' hissed Odo. 'Don't you dare make a move or say anything or we're both dead. I bet Fyrennian's forge could melt you too, you know.'

'Ah,' said Biter. He paused, then added in a softer voice, 'I hope you know what you are doing, Sir Odo.'

'Shhh.' Sir Odo really hoped he did too. He hadn't felt this nervous since . . . actually he couldn't remember *ever* feeling this nervous before.

The gate opened as Odo approached, and a burly man in

dirty leather armour and a blackened steel helmet stepped out of the entranceway. He carried a large double-bladed axe over his shoulder and looked strong enough to use it. Big enough to be a smith, he had a long beard plaited in two strands, too long for him to be an actual smith as his hair would soon catch fire if he worked a forge. A guard then, not someone who did any skilled work.

'What's your business?' the guard asked suspiciously. He looked Odo up and down, taking in his peasant clothing, so at odds with the great sword on his hip.

'Well met,' said Odo in as firm a voice as he could muster, imagining his great-grandfather standing tall in his shoes. Not knowing if the miller knight actually was tall, let alone his name or how long he had survived his knighthood, meant it didn't help much. 'I'm . . . I am here to buy armour.'

This was where his plan would either stand or fall. It all depended on whether Toland had talked to Fyrennian, or if Fyrennian had listened. Odo tensed, ready to turn and run. Biter, under his hand, shifted slightly, and Odo knew that the sword really wanted to snap out and take this guard in the throat before he could swing his axe.

The guard looked past Odo, over to the trees. For a moment the boy thought Eleanor had been spotted, and his heartbeat accelerated. He almost bolted away before the guard spoke again.

'Where's your boss?' the guard asked.

'What do you mean?'

'Your boss,' the guard said, looking down his nose. 'I mean, you can't be buying armour for yourself.'

Too late Odo remembered he didn't look like a knight. He looked like a muddy miller's boy of unusual size. 'No, uh, for my knight, Sir . . . Eldwyn. He sent me ahead. I'm his squire.'

'You don't look much like a squire to me.'

'I fell in the river . . . My good clothes are being laundered by our servant.'

The guard frowned. Though clearly not the smartest of fellows, he was still not convinced. Odo suppressed a rising desire to flee back home, where people didn't often hurt him for getting something wrong.

Sudden inspiration struck him.

'Sir Eldwyn's been teaching me swordplay.' He stepped back several paces so as not to alarm the guard. 'Watch this.'

Hoping that Biter would follow his lead, Odo drew the sword and mock-parried and mock-duelled back and forth in front of the guard, doing his best to remember what he had learned. Biter stayed silent and subtly added flourishes that made Odo look much better than he was.

'Stop that. Wait here,' the guard said. The gate closed behind him with the rattle of an enormous bolt.

The moment he was gone, Odo let out a gust of air in relief. So far, so good. Peering behind him, he made out the patch of cover Eleanor was hiding behind, and gave it a surreptitious thumbs-up.

A leaf twitched in reply. He took that as a good sign.

Five minutes later, the bolt rattled again, and the gate opened.

'All right,' said the guard. 'You can come in.'

Odo went through, the guard drawing the gate closed behind him. His plan had worked. All he had to do now was see what there was to be seen . . .

. . . *and* get out again.

CHAPTER
TEN

Eleanor bit her thumbnail as Odo stepped through the door. As easy as that! It seemed like cheating, but she had to admit that his impromptu plan was inspired. Only now they were separated, and she had no way of knowing what was going on. And he expected her to stay hidden until he came out again, if he ever did!

Except . . . the guard was momentarily distracted by the new arrival, and soon everyone else would be too. If she moved quickly . . .

Eleanor swept her gaze along the palisade. There were no sentries visible and no one at all on the walkway behind the wall. Slipping the paring knife into her boot, Eleanor broke cover and ran to the northwest corner, the most shielded from view. Hunkering down on the mound below the palisade, she pressed herself against the wooden poles and listened.

She half expected every beat of her racing heart to be answered by a cry of alarm or perhaps the clarion call of a sentry's horn. But there was nothing. The sound of hammering and bellows went on as steadily as before.

Eleanor waited until her heart was steady and her breath came easily again. Then she shimmied up the palisade, sticking hands and toes in the gaps between the poles — which had been badly caulked with mud, she noted, and the poles were not as tightly placed together as her mother's books would recommend. The palisade was intended to give more the look of a strong defence than the reality. This was mildly comforting.

Over the palisade, she dropped flat on the walkway and looked and listened once more. Under cover of the working noises coming out of the open windows of the big stone building, Eleanor rose to move but then instantly dropped down again as a woman came out of the central smithy and crossed to a washing line spread between two of the wattle-and-daub huts.

As soon as the woman was behind a flapping sheet, Eleanor moved again. Crouching low, she sprinted to the closest hut, looked about again, then sprinted once more to the side of the smithy, near one corner. There, she stood flat against the shadowed gap between the corner buttress and the wall, feeling the warmth of the stones against her back.

To the west, the sun was setting. Through the stink of iron and sulphur, Eleanor could smell fresh bread and some kind of stew. Dinner was likely not far away. That would further increase her chances of not being seen.

Turning to face the wall, she began to climb, using the angle between the buttress and the wall to her advantage as her fingers and toes found gaps in the loose mortar between the stones. No one saw as she climbed as swiftly and silently as a sucker-footed lizard up onto the slate roof.

The roof was low-pitched and the slate tiles inexpertly laid, so there were gaps between them as wide as her finger, many of them issuing smoke that had failed to find its way up and out of one of the many chimneys. Eleanor crawled across the roof, pausing to press her ear to the cool slate so she could hear what was going on below.

'Pass me the swage, lad.'

'Quick, dowse it!'

'If you don't sweep out that clinker by sun's set there'll be no gruel for you.'

It seemed to be just smiths talking to their apprentices. There was no sign of Odo, so Eleanor scampered lightly across the roof to another section of the smithy. Here the slate was much warmer, and the nearest chimney was billowing black smoke, indicating there was a furnace below.

'Huff!' someone called, in the age-old cry to keep the bellows working, forcing air into the forge fire. 'Puff!'

Still no Odo. Skirting a patch of the roof that was too hot to touch, she finally came to a section where men spoke as equals, or at least more so, and there at last she found her friend.

'We have, I mean, my master Sir Eldwyn has heard of your work here,' he was saying to someone, possibly Fyrennian himself. 'He has his heart set on some of your famous armour, which is much talked about by all the knights of the land.'

'Don't overdo it,' Eleanor whispered. 'This place is just upriver from us and *we* never heard of it.'

But Fyrennian, if it was he, seemed only pleased by the praise.

'My boy, you have come to the right place.' The voice was rich, deep and warm, and sounded like it belonged to a man of considerable stature. Eleanor pictured him receiving Odo in a palatial room bedecked with rich tapestries. Sir Halfdan had a tapestry in the hall of his manor, but it was only the size of a blanket, and quite threadbare. 'Step forward and let me take the measure of you.'

Eleanor wished she could see what was happening, but she wasn't going to dangle upside down from a gutter in order to peer through a window, no matter how dark it was getting. However, wriggling along the roof, she found two loose slates that *almost* gave her a view of the room below. With extreme care, afraid of sending dust raining down that would alert the smiths to her presence, she slipped the point of the paring knife into the chink and levered the two tiles further apart.

Pressing her eye to the gap she had made, she could at last see the room below.

There were no opulent tapestries, but there was a selection of sturdy leather chairs with cast-iron legs on flagstones worn from what looked a thousand years of passing feet. A fireplace burning scented wood occupied almost the whole of one wall. Odo stood before it, being examined by a man who talked tall but was hardly a giant.

Fyrennian came barely to Odo's waist. He was dressed in boots and a black calf-length smock under a thick leather apron that didn't hide the fact that he was nearly as broad around as he was tall. He had no hair at all. The fire gleamed off his polished scalp and from a gold hoop hanging from his left earlobe. Eleanor couldn't see his face properly, but she could see his hands perfectly well. They were huge and covered in a mess of thick, old scars. He didn't look half as scary as Eleanor had imagined, based on Toland's description. Apart from those hands.

Odo submitted himself to the dwarf's examination with nervous discomfort, swivelling from side to side.

'Master, don't you think –' someone started to say, a man standing just out of Eleanor's line of sight.

'It's not your job to think,' snapped Fyrennian. He turned to Odo. 'You're in luck, boy. If your knight is indeed much the same size as you, then we have a full hauberk of the finest mail available with a minimum of adjustment necessary. A customer didn't pay the full amount, so their down payment is forfeit. That is your good luck.'

'What is the fee?' Odo asked, and Fyrennian quoted a figure that made Eleanor's head spin: a hundred gold nobles. She'd never even seen *one* gold noble. A hundred was enough to buy the whole of Sir Halfdan's manor. All that for a mail coat?

'Haggle,' she whispered. 'Don't make it too easy.'

Odo knew about haggling; he was good at it, and often negotiated with villagers at the mill when his father didn't have the patience. He came back with half Fyrennian's asking price, pointing out the timing was good for both of them. They set to bargaining, and eventually arrived at the marginally less astronomical sum of seventy-two gold nobles.

'When will your master grace us with his presence?' Fyrennian asked.

'Tomorrow,' said Odo. 'In the evening, I expect. Sir Eldwyn has something he must attend to at . . . um . . . Ablerhyll, and he sent me ahead. Would it be too much to request board for the night?'

Fyrennian waved away the possibility of inconvenience, and no wonder, Eleanor thought, for such a sum. 'We would be honoured. Ramm here will show you to your quarters, where a meal will be brought to you. Unless perhaps you would like a tour of the smithy first?'

Ramm stepped into view. He was the guard from the gate, the big one with the axe.

'Say no,' Eleanor whispered. 'Don't seem too keen to stick your nose in.'

'Thank you, but I am weary from travel,' Odo said. He gave an awkward bow, which Eleanor recognised as being copied from Sir Halfdan. Since Sir Halfdan only had one foot, it looked a bit strange when Odo did it. However, it was more than a miller would do, so she supposed that it was good enough for cementing his appearance as a squire. 'Tomorrow, when my master arrives, I'm sure he'd like to take a look around.'

'Of course, of course. Until then.' Fyrennian nodded to Ramm, who indicated that Odo should follow him.

Just before they moved out of sight, Fyrennian held up a hand.

'One moment.'

Odo halted in the doorway.

'Your sword caught my eye,' Fyrennian said. 'May I look at it?'

'Of course.'

After a barely perceptible hesitation, Odo drew Biter from the scabbard and held him out hilt-first for Fyrennian to inspect.

Eleanor suppressed a groan, although there was nothing else Odo could have said or done. To deny the request would arouse suspicion. She crossed her fingers and hoped that Biter wouldn't talk, or move of his own accord, or reveal his enchanted nature in some other way.

'Interesting,' said Fyrennian, taking Biter and holding him

gently across his palms, then turning him to catch the light. 'A gift from your master, I presume? If so, his generosity is only exceeded by his taste. This is a very old sword, with highly . . . unusual properties.'

Eleanor hardly dared breathe. She was confident that Biter could look after himself, if it came to that, but what about Odo? He was standing too close to the beefy Ramm and his axe. If Biter was stupid enough to do his frontal assault thing, Odo was sure to be killed!

'Unusual properties?' asked Odo, but not before swallowing once.

'Yes, see here.' Fyrennian leaned closer, holding the sword up for Odo's inspection. 'The ricasso is asymmetrical, and so are the terminals. The steel seems very fine, very fine indeed, but there is a nick right here, halfway along the blade. I am surprised to find that in a sword of this apparent quality. Maybe that is why it is in your service, and not Sir Eldwyn's. The steel looks to be the best, but it cannot be, for such a notch would have been impossible. It is flawed.'

With a superior smile, as though he had solved a mystery to his satisfaction and delivered a slight insult in the bargain, the master smith returned the sword to Odo's waiting hand and waved him away.

Eleanor allowed herself to resume breathing, even though she had immediately lost sight of Odo again. Noting the direction they went through the house, she made an intelligent guess as to where he might have ended up. There was a long, relatively narrow wing that had a dormitory look to it. When she clambered onto its roof, there were none of the hot spots she had found before, and the single chimney wafted only white smoke in a thin column.

Moving from place to place, she listened for any sign of Odo or Biter. The smell of dinner became distinctly stronger. Her stomach rumbled and she reached into a pocket for a piece of bread she had put there after lunch, very glad now that she had. If she couldn't find Odo she might be stuck on the roof until everyone went to bed, contented and full.

'Flawed, he says? Nonsense! The man's a fraud!'

Eleanor smiled. She'd know that outraged voice anywhere, even when it was trying to be quiet.

ELEVEN

'Shhh! They'll hear!'

Odo tried to force Biter back into the scabbard but the sword would not be contained. Biter darted out of his reach and flashed back and forth across the narrow room they had been given for the night. There was barely enough space for the meagre cot and a single wooden chest. There was definitely not enough space for an indignant flying sword.

'They'll hear all right,' Biter grumbled in slightly softer tones. 'They'll hear a lecture on the finer points of swordsmithing before I'm done with them.'

Odo wiped away a fleck of grit that had fallen into his eye. 'Remember what we're here for. To find the firestarter, get some armour and help the apprentices. Don't upset everything by taking it personally.'

'How can I not take it personally? Fyrennian said I was flawed. He said there's a nick!'

'Actually, there is,' said a voice from above. 'I noticed it while I was cleaning you yesterday.'

Odo looked up in surprise. By the light of the room's candle he could see Eleanor's green eye peering back down at him.

'What are you doing up there? I was going to come out on the wall and signal to you.'

'That'd be useful, you waving about on their wall. Besides, you need me close to make sure you don't get into trouble,' she said. 'Did you miss me? Have you seen Toland? What about the firestarter? Have they brought you any food?'

Odo lay back to look at her without craning his neck, and told her everything he had seen inside the smithy so far.

Ramm had led him through two busy workshops to get to his audience with Fyrennian. Toland had been one of ten apprentices working the giant bellows. Their eyes had met, but Toland had immediately looked away. It looked like he hadn't had the chance to reveal who Odo was, and didn't seem likely to. Either he could be trusted, or he was too frightened to talk.

Of the firestarter, however, or of dinner, or of the deposed Master Thrytin, there were no signs. So he had decided on the spur of the moment to ask about staying the night, intending to snoop around while everyone was asleep.

Biter slowly settled to a resentful mutter, only occasionally stabbing or slashing at the air to make a point.

At a firm knock on the door, he dropped to Odo's side on the bed and Eleanor covered the chink in the tiles with her hand.

'Come in!' Odo called.

The door opened to reveal Toland, holding a wooden platter of soup and a round wholewheat crust. Odo sat up in surprise and went to speak, but Toland shook his head. The boy put the platter on the chest, then went back to the door and peered outside, looking both ways along the hallway. He came back once he was sure the coast was clear.

'What are you doing here?' he asked. 'Can't you leave well enough alone?'

'What?' Odo replied. 'We're trying to help you!'

'It's my problem, not yours. You'll only get me into more trouble.'

'It's Fyrennian's problem,' said Eleanor, making Toland jump. Her eye reappeared in the ceiling. 'Stealing from a dragon is bad news.'

'Dragon? What dragon?' Toland's eyes went wide as goose eggs. 'You don't mean Quenwulf, do you?'

'I don't think so . . . but I don't know,' said Odo. He wondered for a moment if live dragons vomited up firestarters, or if they could only be got out of dead ones or their ancient remains. Not for the first time, he regretted knowing almost nothing about dragons – and also not for the first time, wished he was back at home in the mill, covered in flour dust and not having to think about anything more dangerous than a mousetrap.

'The source of Fyrennian's fire came from a dragon,' said

Eleanor from above, repeating what Biter had told them, without adding the part about destroying the firestarter. 'Do you know where he keeps it?'

'I told you I never saw it!'

'That's not what she asked,' said Odo gently. 'Do you know where he keeps it?'

Toland stood mute, shaking.

'You have to tell us,' said Eleanor in an urgent whisper. 'He's hurting people with it. And what happens if a dragon comes looking for it?'

Toland looked even more terrified.

Odo followed Eleanor's lead. 'If you tell us where he keeps it, we'll make sure he can't hurt anyone, now or ever again.'

'But my apprenticeship –'

'Once we have the firestarter,' said Eleanor, 'Master Thrytin can take over again. You said he was much nicer to everyone.'

'Yes . . . but the special buyers won't be happy. There's a delegation due any time.'

'They'll see reason.' Odo put one hand on Toland's shoulder. 'We're here to help you but we need your help to do it.'

The boy warred within himself for a moment, then nodded.

'Master Fyrennian keeps the firestarter somewhere in his private chambers. He brings it out once a day to stoke the furnaces or to work particular pieces. He carries it under a cloak.'

'What does it look like?' asked Biter.

'I told you, I've never seen it,' said Toland. He shivered, then slowly added, 'I did see the shadow of it once. He held something twisted, like a crooked branch, about as long as your sword. I think the fire came out one end.'

'So he carries it to and from his chambers?' asked Odo. 'Did it look heavy?'

'Not for Master Fyrennian,' said Toland. 'But he's very strong.'

'So am I,' said Odo. That was one thing he wasn't shy about claiming. He might not be much of a knight, but he *was* incredibly muscular, as had been proven in many a midsummer fair contest. No local boy would ever compete against him in the stone-lifting, and he had even beaten many of the men. In fact he grew stronger all the time, and it was generally accepted in the village that he would be a veritable man-mountain when he grew up.

'Where are his chambers?' he asked.

'In the northwest wing. I've never been inside. He has a dog there, a little one, as a guard, I suppose. You can hear it yapping. He never lets it out.'

'And where is Master Thrytin imprisoned?'

'He's allowed to work in the day, but gets locked up in the cellar at night.'

Somewhere deep in the smithy a bell rang.

'I have to go,' Toland said. He seemed even more nervous than usual. 'I have duties.'

'Wait!' called Eleanor. 'Let me see your hands.'

The boy held them out, palms up. They were still red and peeling, but the larger blisters looked likely to scab over and heal well.

'Try to keep them clean,' she advised. 'Just go to bed as normal. We'll have everything sorted out by morning.'

Toland nodded. He looked at his hands again, and then at Odo, a tangled expression on his face, as if he wanted to say something but couldn't get it out. Then he gave a great sigh and went out the door, closing but not locking it behind him.

Odo pushed the chest in front of the door and sat on it, in case anyone else unexpectedly came to visit.

'What do you think?' he asked Eleanor and Biter.

'I think,' said Eleanor, 'that if you dip some of that bread in the stew and stick it on the end of Biter, he can fly up here and give it to me.'

'I am not a fork, squire –'

'Hurry up and do it, will you? I'm hungry.'

Odo obeyed her instructions while she busied herself widening the hole so her arm could slip through. Biter reluctantly presented his sharp tip for the bread and ascended to a point where Eleanor could just reach it.

Odo forced himself to eat, even though his stomach was already full of worries.

'What I meant was –'

'I know what you meant,' said Eleanor once her meagre

mouthful was swallowed. 'I'm sure I can find Fyrennian's room from up here. That way we'll know more or less where to go. Then it's just a matter of waiting until everything's quiet, and the deed is practically done.'

'It would be easier if we could send Biter to have a snoop around,' Odo observed.

'Impossible,' said the sword. 'I must remain at my knight's side at all times.'

'Are you just being huffy or is that really true?' asked Eleanor.

'Of course it is! A true sword, like a true knight, never lies.'

Odo thought of all the times he had dodged, obscured, or plain broken the truth in his lifetime. It was impossible to avoid in a big family. Would mentioning those instances finally disqualify him from knighthood?

Mind you, he thought, Eleanor is no better. She sometimes 'bent the truth' to avoid jobs or lessons she considered too boring. But he didn't want to disqualify her either. It was better to keep silent.

Around him he could hear smiths going about their evening business. They didn't stay up much past sunset. Candles were expensive, flaming torches dirty, smoky and dangerous, and in any case work would begin again at dawn. Odo heard people moving back and forth in the corridor outside, wishing each other goodnight and fair sleep. Odo and Biter kept conversation to a minimum for fear of being overheard. Eleanor said nothing. It was even more important that she not be discovered.

Eventually the voices in the corridor ceased and Odo heard other noises, this time through the walls – the sound of snoring, full-throated, protracted, hard-earned snores that had the slate tiles vibrating in sympathy.

Satisfied that there was little chance of discovery now, Eleanor set off across the rooftops in search of Fyrennian's chambers. The northwest wing was some distance from the other sleeping quarters, which meant quite a crawl. Maybe Fyrennian didn't like sleeping near the ordinary smiths. He probably didn't trust them.

She pressed her ear against several tiles until she heard the sound that Toland had described – the persistent yapping of a dog, and Fyrennian's voice saying, 'Quiet, Ferox!'

By strategically lifting tiles, she could trace the path of internal walls and thereby map the corridors through the smithy. It took her some time as it grew darker, but there were still remnants of light from the forges and the few lanterns hung in case of a midnight emergency, and eventually she had the path memorised. When she had that, she returned to her peephole over Odo's room.

He was either practising or being made to practice. It was hard to tell the difference, because both sword and boy were silent.

Eleanor clicked her fingers once to get their attention, and then again several times before Odo raised his sweaty face and looked up.

'Don't wear yourself out, you two,' whispered Eleanor. 'It's time to go steal a firestarter!'

TWELVE

Odo caught Eleanor as she dropped. Moving three tiles had created a hole big enough for her to slip through, and if he stood on the box he could just about reach her feet. She didn't weigh much more than Toland, all told.

She gulped down some more of the bread and stew he had saved for her, describing the way to Fyrennian's room between mouthfuls. When she was finished, Odo eased open the door of the room and peered cautiously outside.

The corridor was empty and all was quiet, save for the snores.

'It's very dark,' whispered Odo.

'For you, maybe,' said Eleanor. She'd noticed before that she could see better at nighttime than Odo. 'Follow me.'

Eleanor took the lead. It seemed Odo really couldn't see, because he held tight to the back of her tunic with his non-sword hand. It was strange seeing the corridors from ground level, because she had the map burned into her mind from above. Accompanied by the snoring of the smiths, and keeping at least one eye ever-peeled for Ramm, she tiptoed slowly down the corridor and turned right at the end.

Odo followed very cautiously as they took another right turn, then a left, going up three steps that he would have stumbled over without Eleanor's guidance.

Eleanor slowed and tapped Odo's shoulder three times – a warning. He narrowed his eyes, trying to see ahead. Gradually he recognised a large chamber he'd been through earlier. There was a dim red glow in one corner, a banked-down forge, and across from that . . . a whole lot of shadowy lumps on the floor.

One lump moved.

Odo almost jumped in fright, but got a grip on himself as he realised the lumps were merely apprentices sleeping on the floor.

Eleanor moved stealthily across the floor. Odo felt like a great ox behind her, his every footstep, no matter how careful, twice as loud as hers. Then he nudged a swage block with his toe, causing a scraping sound that seemed terribly loud.

He froze, waiting for a cry of alarm to go up from the sleeping apprentices, but apart from a sluggish murmur or two, they didn't stir. *Too tired*, Odo thought, *and perhaps used to the sound of the cooling forge.*

They resumed their stealthy creep, Odo trusting that Eleanor knew where she was going. He tried not to think of pits, or traps, or simply running into someone who had got up to go to the latrines outside.

Left. Right. One final left turn and, Eleanor knew, they would be in the northwest wing.

Here, surely, she thought, there would be guards to protect the precious firestarter.

But when they turned the corner . . . there were none. A lantern swung from a hook in the ceiling above the intricately carved door to Fyrennian's chambers, but that was all. Master Fyrennian didn't even trust Ramm with his secret.

Maybe Fyrennian placed great faith in his own ability as a swordsman. Or Ferox the dog was much bigger than it sounded, unlike its master. Eleanor felt for the stew-soaked crust she had slipped into her pocket before leaving Odo's room. That would distract the dog, she hoped. Belatedly she thought of the sleeping draught her father had packed for her, and wished she'd soaked the bread in that instead.

Eleanor motioned Odo forward and pointed at the nearest door, silently mouthing the word *Fyrennian*.

At that moment, many of Odo's unspoken fears fell away. Now that he had come this far, there was no point worrying about what might happen, because it was happening to him already. And so far, given that there were no sharp things being pointed in their direction, it was going quite well.

He drew Biter and edged closer to the door, grateful for the light of the lantern. Eleanor crouched next to the door on the other side, and both held their ears against the carved wood.

They heard snoring. One snore was deep and rhythmical, the other higher and less human.

Fyrennian and his dog. Asleep.

Eleanor examined the handle of the rope that would lift the bar on the other side of the door. She pulled it very gently, testing to see if it was pegged on the other side so it could not be moved.

It wasn't.

Eleanor slowly dragged the rope handle back. The bar scraped upwards on the inside. It sounded ridiculously loud.

With the bar raised, Eleanor paused to listen again. The snoring continued, so she pushed the door open. Not slowly, because that might make it creak, but in one smooth motion, exactly as she had done for years when sneaking out of her own house late at night.

Odo went in first, Biter at the ready. The emerald in the sword's pommel caught and reflected the faint embers of a dying fire, casting a green glow across Odo's hand. There was enough light to see fine tapestries draped upon the walls, just as Eleanor had imagined earlier.

A huge, four-poster bed dominated the room. Right in the middle of it was a dwarf-sized lump under a great many blankets. Fyrennian, still snoring. Next to the bed was a basket with another small lump under a tartan rug: the sleeping Ferox, utterly failing in his guard-dog duties.

There was no sign of anything that might be the firestarter.

Not that Eleanor had expected it to be so straightforward. After all, who would sleep with such a dangerous magical item next to their bed?

But on the far side of the room there was a sturdy iron door, made with heavy, plate-sized rivets that just screamed out *Treasure Room!* Eleanor nudged Odo and pointed.

Together, they edged around the bed. Odo flinched at his every footfall, because the floor creaked under his weight as it didn't with Eleanor. Surely either Fyrennian or the dog would wake up?

But they didn't. As they reached the door, Odo noticed a faint glow coming through a half-inch gap between it and the floor. There was a fire or perhaps a lantern on the other side.

He hesitated for a moment and looked back at the bed. The lump hadn't moved. The sound of snoring was relentless. How did the dog sleep? He looked at Eleanor, who made a 'hurry up' gesture.

Odo examined the door's hinges. It was designed to open inwards, and he saw no lock or pull-rope for a bar. He hesitated for a moment, then pushed against the cold, heavy iron.

The door squeaked softly – and then suddenly flew open. Odo stumbled forward into a furnace heat, blinking from the unexpected brightness. The room was lit with fire from three tall, golden braziers. Wall, floor, and ceiling were solid stone. There was a plinth in the centre of the room, and on it squatted a black, twisted, rootlike staff that had to be the firestarter. Next to the plinth Odo saw –

Fyrennian.

And Ramm, armed with a giant cudgel.

And, with all four legs splayed, just beginning to growl, a small, wiry bundle of white fur and snapping teeth that had to be Ferox.

'Do you think me a fool?' Fyrennian began.

But Biter was already moving. Stabbing forward with the speed of lightning, the sword angled to Odo's right, taking Odo with him, and then lunged in a direct line for Ramm's throat. The big man responded too slowly to defend himself. The cudgel was heavy and Biter too fast. Odo had a momentary premonition of the future, which contained lurid images of gouts of blood. He just managed to pull back on the sword at the last moment, deflecting the sword from a killing thrust.

Biter's tip pierced Ramm's right shoulder and sent him backwards with a howl. He instantly dropped his cudgel and pressed his hand against the wound, his once-ferocious eyes now filled with pain and fear.

Ferox, not wanting to be left out of the fight, charged forward, narrowly avoiding being cut in two by Biter before going straight for Eleanor. For a moment she froze, held captive by the firelight gleaming on his sharp teeth. Ferox was small but ferocious, fuelled by the righteous fury of an animal defending its master. She raised the paring knife, wishing she had a sword herself, eyes on those teeth . . .

Then she remembered the food in her other hand.

'Here, boy!' she cried, flinging the stew-soaked crust at the dog. Ferox growled, but couldn't help pausing to swallow the crust, which gave Eleanor a few vital seconds to reach one of the braziers. Gripping it by its slender base, she lifted it with a grunt and tipped it forward, scattering hot coals in an arc that trapped Ferox in the corner.

The dog whined and retreated, and smoke filled the air.

Ramm was down. Ferox was subdued. Odo turned his attention to Fyrennian and froze.

The smith had the firestarter in his hands and was pointing it at them.

'Back!' Fyrennian cried. 'Put the sword on the floor. I know it can't kill me without you holding it. I recognised it as an enchanted sword the moment you walked in. I know the rules. Put it down.'

Odo gripped the sword tighter. 'No,' he said.

'Do it, or I'll burn you and your friend to ashes.'

Fyrennian jabbed the firestarter at them. Eleanor and Odo retreated, circling around the plinth with their backs against the wall. Fyrennian was forcing them into a corner, away from the door.

Eleanor considered throwing the knife, but what if the smith could burn them before the blade struck? What if she missed?

'The sword, on the ground,' said Fyrennian. 'This is your last chance.'

'What's to stop you burning us anyway?' Eleanor asked him.

'I give you my word.'

'And what's that worth?' said Odo.

'I am not a monster. I am a smith. My word is my bond, or my customers would never deal with me.'

'You are no true smith,' said Biter. 'You use a dragon's fire for your own ends. That is forbidden.'

'Ah, at last it deigns to speak!' Fyrennian jabbed with the firestarter again, and they retreated a step further. Fyrennian was now in the doorway with a lightly singed Ferox at his side, blocking their only exit. The smith's eyes were bright with desire. 'Come to me, sword, or I will melt you as well.'

Understanding suddenly dawned on Eleanor. If Fyrennian had known that Odo was lying all along, why the charade? Why lay a trap for them to walk into? Why fake Fyrennian in the bed, fake Ferox beside it, fake snoring to complete the illusion . . . ?

Because, she now knew, he wanted Biter for himself. He wanted a magic sword.

'You won't blast us,' she said. 'Biter is too valuable.'

'Clever girl,' Fyrennian said. 'So clever you're stupid. I don't know where you came from, but you've given me an excellent idea. Step away from your friend. If he doesn't let go of the sword, I'll blast you first, and maybe then he'll see reason.'

Eleanor's knees felt weak, but she didn't move. Odo gripped the sword tighter, furiously thinking. There had to be a way out. There had to be!

A pale figure rose up behind Fyrennian, holding a triangular shape high above its head. Ferox barked a warning too late as Toland brought the bellows down hard upon Fyrennian's head.

The smith toppled forward like a stone.

As he fell, one end of the firestarter was caught by the edge of the plinth, the other by Fyrennian's heavy stomach. As his weight bore down, the strange, misshapen staff bent and bent, but didn't break.

Not until Biter leaped forward, almost out of Odo's hand. There was a crack like the closest thunder, and the firestarter was sundered in two, the halves shooting across the room like arrows, one nearly hitting Odo.

Fyrennian crashed to the ground, and was still.

THIRTEEN

'I was under the bed,' Toland said, staring down in shock. 'Pumping the bellows . . . faking the snoring . . . hating myself for . . . for betraying you . . . and then I knew it was now or never . . . but what have I done?'

'Exactly the right thing,' Eleanor assured him. She rushed over to check Fyrennian. Seeing he was still alive and his dog now completely cowed, she turned the smith onto his side, allowing the whimpering Ferox, tail down, to begin pathetically licking his face.

'It's what you do in the end that matters,' Odo said. 'You saved our lives! *And* helped break the firestarter. It won't work now, will it, Biter?'

'Assuredly not,' said the sword, to Odo's relief. This was one magical thing that hadn't been difficult to destroy. 'Fyrennian's reign of terror is over.'

Toland didn't look triumphant. He looked scared and worried. Even with Fyrennian unconscious and the firestarter broken.

'But there's still the –'

Ramm groaned, cutting off whatever protest Toland was about to make. Odo swung around to point Biter at the fallen bodyguard. The bloodstained tip of a fiendishly sharp blade one inch from his nose was enough to convince him to stay down.

'His wound needs seeing to,' Odo told Toland. 'You'd better get Master Thrytin out of the cellar.'

'Yes, but what about the –'

'And Fyrennian needs to be locked up before he wakes up,' Eleanor added. She went over to Ramm, lifted his hand where it was pressed against the wound and said with the certainty of an apothecary's daughter, 'It's not serious. Keep pressing against it. Toland, get a sheet from Fyrennian's bed to tear up for a bandage.'

'Yes, but –'

Outside the smithy, a horn sounded a long, questioning fanfare that was answered a moment later by a more distant and more abrasive blast.

'Someone comes,' said Biter.

'Who is it?' asked Odo.

'That's what I've been trying to tell you!' Toland yelled. 'Even before I talked, Fyrennian knew you were a fake because he only works for a particular . . . a peculiar kind of buyer. Buyers he was expecting. And now they're here!'

'What, at night?' Eleanor asked.

Odo's stomach dropped. He thought he might know the kind of buyer who would only come at night.

The distant horn sounded again, much closer than before.

Footsteps ran up the hallway and into the bedchamber. A nervous apprentice peered past Toland.

'They're here, Master Fyrennian. Master Fyrennian? What in the –?'

'Fyrennian is no longer master here,' said Odo. He raised Biter and tried to sound as knightly as he could. 'Justice has been done. Master Thrytin will soon be freed and will once more take charge. In fact, go and release him from the cellar and bring him here at once.'

'Yes, sir!' said the apprentice, hurrying away.

'Now what do we do?' asked Odo.

The horn sounded again, much closer. Clearly inside the palisade.

'What kind of particular or peculiar buyers are they?' Eleanor asked, mystified. 'How did Fyrennian know we weren't one of them?'

'He knew because we're *human*,' said Odo.

There was the sound of many footsteps upon the floor outside. Strange footfalls, clicking noises, not the thud of boots.

'They're coming in!' said Toland. He edged behind Odo.

'*Who's* coming in?' asked Eleanor urgently.

A harsh, sharp odour suddenly filled the room.

'Smells like a tannery,' said Eleanor, her forehead knit in complete puzzlement. 'But what –'

'Urthkin,' whispered Odo.

The outer door to Fyrennian's chamber banged open at the same time as Eleanor's shocked mouth. They heard another apprentice gabbling out apologies, and those strange footfalls, getting closer and closer . . .

'Angry urthkin, I fear they'll be,' squeaked Toland. 'The firestarter belonged to them!'

'What?' This was possibly the worst thing Odo had ever heard.

'They found it underground but can't use it because it's too hot and bright,' babbled Toland. He was right behind Odo now, hardly daring to look around the bigger boy's back at the doorway. 'They lent it to Fyrennian, but he has to make whatever they want – Oh!'

A dozen incredibly pale-skinned, reed-slender demihumans no taller than Eleanor burst into the room. Their skin was so translucent Odo could see the tracery of blood vessels in their necks and temples. Their hair was like spun green glass, and their eyes were as black as the smith's coal. Those eyes were half-closed now, even against the relatively low light in the room. They wore smocks and tunics of dark-coloured fabric pinned and adorned with finely carved stone. They had hoops of malachite in their ears, rings of onyx on their fingers and combs of ebony in their hair.

Every one of the dozen who crowded into the room had the same style of knife on their hip, which added up to a lot of knives.

Knives made by the smiths of Anfyltarn, Odo suddenly realised. None of the small but needle-sharp blades were out, but he didn't doubt they could be drawn in a moment.

The urthkin who wore the most adornments stepped out of the horde and approached the waiting humans. Eleanor realised that the clicking sound came from the fact that the urthkin did not have human feet, nor did they wear shoes. They had paws like a mole's, with digging claws. Their hands, however, were more humanlike, with longer fingers and curved nails that were almost talons.

'Where is Master Fyrennian?' the leader asked, the tips of her pointed teeth shining in the firelight.

'He's . . . he's not in charge here any more,' said Odo.

The urthkin leader did not show any surprise. Keeping her face averted from the light of the fire, she simply said, 'Who is your new scortwisa?'

'What does that mean?' Odo whispered to Toland.

'That's what they called Fyrennian,' he whispered back. 'It means *leader*, I suppose.'

Odo looked around to see if anyone else was going to volunteer to take charge. He *wanted* someone else to take charge.

But no — they were all looking at him.

'I speak for Anfyltarn,' said Odo. 'For now.'

'No,' said the urthkin. 'That cannot be. Do you try to trick us?'

'Um, no . . .' said Odo uncertainly. 'Why . . . er . . . why can't it be me?'

'Wisdom comes from closer to the ground,' said the urthkin.

Odo stared at her. If that were true, potatoes would be the smartest things around. He didn't understand what the strange visitor was saying.

Luckily, Eleanor did.

'I am not the scortwisa,' she said, coming forward. She was careful to slouch, so she was no taller than the urthkin. 'But I speak for the scortwisa.'

The urthkin bowed very low to the ground. Eleanor copied her, and again was careful not to stand too tall when they both straightened up.

Odo was barely able to suppress a sudden gasp of realisation. The urthkin must not trust tall people, or thought they were less intelligent or something. It was no wonder they'd given the firestarter to Fyrennian. He was the shortest man Odo had ever met.

The urthkin leader addressed Eleanor, ignoring everyone else. 'We bring ore that you will fashion into knives.'

'Um, you should know something first,' said Eleanor. She looked over at Odo, hoping he would be ready if the urthkin suddenly drew their knives and attacked. 'The firestarter is broken.'

The urthkin all looked to the ground as one, and then slowly back up to stare at Eleanor. It was rather unnerving, all those incredibly dark eyes and strange, vein-laced faces directed at her.

'Our gift is despoiled?' asked the leader quietly. 'Who despoiled it?'

'Uh, I broke it,' Odo said.

'Who is the breaker of our gift?'

'Um . . . me?'

The urthkin were still all looking at Eleanor. The girl felt the tension rise in the room. Toland was just about ready to bolt. And Odo's hand was on Biter's hilt.

'Sir Odo of Lenburh is the despoiler!' Eleanor proclaimed.

Odo shot her a look.

The urthkin did not look particularly impressed. 'You must make amends,' she said. Her voice did not change, but the air of menace in the words was unmistakable.

Eleanor said, 'We'll do everything we can –'

'I'll do it,' Odo interrupted. 'We didn't know it was yours. The firestarter, I mean. But Fyrennian should not have had it.'

Again, the urthkin paid Odo no attention. But when she spoke to Eleanor, it seemed to be in answer to this.

'Why do you say Fyrennian should not have had the firestarter?'

Odo blurted out what Biter had said to them before: 'What is a dragon's must remain a dragon's!'

This time, the urthkin all turned to look at Odo – or at least at Odo's stomach, since they would not look up. Then they turned to look at one another. There was a susurration of very low voices, so low that Eleanor couldn't make out any words, only feel the vibration of what must be the urthkin's own language. This went on for several long minutes, before the leader turned back to Eleanor again.

'We must consider,' the leader said. 'You raise doubts of procedure, responsibility and consequence. Some of us think we should kill you all and destroy this place, as you have destroyed the firestarter. Some believe that it is our greed for steel knives that has led to this, and so you are not to blame. And the earth has not spoken, to tell us which is the truer way. In short, we do not know whether to slay you all or not.'

Eleanor drew in a sharp breath. 'You don't really mean that. You wouldn't kill us, would you?'

The knives came out. And so did all the teeth.

'We mean every word.'

CHAPTER

FOURTEEN

Odo felt sick. *I should never have tried to be a knight*, he thought miserably. *All we've managed to achieve is to bring a whole village to the brink of being killed by urthkin. Not to mention getting killed myself, and Eleanor too. Her poor father . . . and my own parents . . .*

But there seemed no alternative. Odo gripped Biter so hard his knuckles showed white. If he and Biter could hold the urthkin back even for a few minutes, Eleanor and Toland might be able to climb up to the ceiling beams and out onto the roof . . .

'We cannot choose the right . . . I do not know your word . . . *tunnel*?' the urthkin leader continued unexpectedly. 'So we must let the earth decide.'

Odo relaxed his death grip on Biter just a fraction. His palms were sweating. Eleanor glanced at him, and spoke quickly to the urthkin.

'How would we do that?' she asked.

'You would call it a trial by combat, I think,' said the

113

urthkin leader. She pointed at Odo. 'The breaker of the firestarter against a champion of our people. If you win, then the earth thinks you are blameless. If we win, then you will owe blood to the earth, which we will take.'

Odo swallowed a lump the size of an apple that appeared to be stuck in his throat. Trial by combat? He wasn't ready for that. Maybe with more training . . . much more training . . . but not now!

Biter was twitching eagerly from side to side. Odo thought desperately for an alternative to pitting himself against an urthkin who would certainly be a seasoned warrior, but came up with none. His only hope was Biter himself, the magic sword who had got them into this situation in the first place. If only they hadn't destroyed the firestarter . . .

He straightened, consoling his doubts and fears with the certainty that breaking Fyrennian's tyrannical rule had been the right thing to do.

'So be it,' he said.

'Are you sure?' hissed Eleanor.

'Yes,' he said. 'Only the idle do no good, Ma says.'

'Then I guess we accept,' she told the urthkin.

'You must fight on the bare earth,' said the leader. 'Come.'

Everyone trooped outside. The halls were crowded with many more urthkin, but also all the woken smiths and apprentices, many of whom were armed and looking about nervously, expecting trouble. Outside there were even more urthkin, as well as the villagers who didn't work directly in the smithy. They had pitchforks and knives.

Eleanor looked around with worry in her heart. If Odo lost, the urthkin would probably win the subsequent battle, but there would be many killed on both sides.

She could only hope that Odo would win.

The urthkin leader walked almost to the gate in the palisade, but stopped short. Extending her arms, she indicated a circle. Her followers moved into position, standing shoulder to shoulder in a circle some fifty paces across.

Odo walked into the middle of this circle, his boots scuffing the earth. He felt very alone, with only the weight of Biter in his hand as small comfort. It was not as dark out here as he had expected, with the stars bright above and the moon half-full. Some of the humans carried torches and lanterns too, casting light from a safe distance. Everyone was staring at him with human or urthkin-black eyes. It was very difficult because he really just wanted to curl up in a ball and hope everything would go away, but somehow he forced himself to stand tall. Although he wasn't a man-mountain yet, he knew putting on a show of it couldn't hurt. It might even make his opponent nervous.

The urthkin talked among themselves again, in their low, felt-but-not-heard voices. Odo stood waiting, his heart pounding. Eleanor tried to grin at him, to show confidence, but she couldn't make herself smile. The thought that Odo might lose was like a knife twisting in her side. Helplessly, she wished she was going into battle with him, or instead of him. She knew Odo just didn't have the same instincts for battle that Eleanor was sure she possessed herself. They had got themselves into this situation together. It didn't seem fair that he had to finish it on his own.

One of the urthkin left the circle and strode in towards Odo. She was slighter than the leader, but perhaps a little taller. As she faced him, Odo saw with surprise that the visible blood vessels under her incredibly pallid skin shone in the moonlight, as if quicksilver moved through her veins.

She was unarmoured but carried a larger, curved version of the knives all of the urthkin wore. It was a much lighter and thinner weapon than Biter and looked like it might snap at a single blow. But Odo reminded himself that it had likely been forged by Fyrennian in dragon's fire, and told himself not to take anything for granted. She might well be an expert warrior, and even with Biter's help Odo knew he was far from being that.

'I am Euphe,' the urthkin said, bowing so low she touched the earth with her hands. 'Greetings.'

Odo bowed in return, hoping it hid the flutter of nerves in his chest. He too touched the earth.

The urthkin backed off five paces and raised her slender blade. A hush fell upon the crowd, and all Odo could hear was the thudding of his own heart.

'To the death,' said Euphe.

Odo *knew* a trial by combat was often to the death, but hearing the words said was almost like a blow in itself. So it wouldn't be a token drop of blood he'd have to give to the earth if he lost. It would be his life. He shifted his feet further apart and loosened his knees and elbows, trying to stand as Biter had taught him.

He was still doing this when Euphe struck with a loose-limbed grace, rushing forward to one side while swinging her sword-knife in a long arc as she passed. Biter flung himself around almost without Odo's help, parrying the blow that would have cut Odo's hamstrings and toppled him to the ground, crippled for life.

The blades rang with the impact, and the urthkin's did not shatter. She disengaged at once and stepped back. So did Odo, even as Biter tried to move forward, resulting in a clumsy shuffle that Euphe took advantage of at once, lunging with a savage cleaving blow at Odo's knees.

Biter only just parried it, the enchanted sword driven back to touch Odo's leg, so that for a moment he thought he'd been hit. He jumped back, and Biter moved to block yet another blow. Some impressed memory from training took over and Odo managed to half complete one of the Five Lethal Forms, Parting the Angry Waters, rolling Biter under the urthkin's blade and striking up towards Euphe's left hip.

She twisted aside, bent almost double, and riposted very low. Again only Biter's inhumanly fast reflexes and movement saved Odo's life, the tip of his enemy's blade sweeping the air an inch in front of his ankles.

Eleanor, watching anxiously from the human side of the ring that had formed around the combatants, bit her knuckles and gasped. Euphe was clearly a very skilled swordmistress and even Biter might not be enough to save Odo.

Eleanor held her breath through another sudden flurry of quick slashes, parries and thrusts, only exhaling when the combatants moved apart again and warily circled each other.

Each had landed a blow, though both were only minor. Odo was cut on the calf, a thin line of dark blood showing through his sliced breeches. Euphe had been cut too, on the back of her right hand. Her blood was indeed silvery and seemed to shine of its own accord as it dripped down her fingers, not just reflecting the moonlight.

Odo felt the sting of his wound, and noted the blood on Euphe's hand. That would make her grip slippery, he knew. He had a better chance of winning now.

He didn't want to kill the urthkin. Or even hurt her more than he already had. But he had to win or else everyone would be killed.

The small part of Odo's mind that wasn't completely caught up in swordfighting wrestled with this conundrum.

Euphe attacked again, once more going low, stabbing at Odo's knee. Biter moved, as fast as ever, trapping the urthkin's blade against the ground.

In that moment, Odo found a solution. Even as Euphe slid her sword out from under Biter, Odo let go of his weapon. Biter, as surprised as anyone, continued to hold Euphe's sword-knife down as Odo wrapped his great arms around the urthkin and hoisted her above his head.

The sudden move and the slippery blood on her palm worked together. Euphe let go of her sword and cried out in surprise as Odo lifted her high, spun her about twice in his favourite wrestling move – the waterwheel, he called it – and threw her down at the far end of the circle, where she skidded across the bare earth, sending dust flying.

Odo put his foot on Euphe's blade and picked up Biter, hoping no one noticed that the sword had continued to press down on his enemy's weapon after he'd let go.

Euphe slowly sat up, holding her head, silver blood from her hand now staining her translucent hair.

The urthkin made their deep, rumbling noises.

Odo stood panting, and tried to work out how he could tell the urthkin he wasn't going to kill Euphe, that even though this was a trial by combat it shouldn't have to end in death. But before he could speak, the urthkin leader began.

'You are the victor,' she said. 'We declare this fight over, with honour to both sides.'

'You mean we don't . . . I don't have to kill . . . ?' sputtered Odo.

'The earth has spoken. The *matter* is dead. Did you think I meant the death of our champion?'

'What? It was to *my* death, but not your –'

'No, that's not what we thought,' interrupted Eleanor, hoping the urthkin couldn't read the disbelieving expression on her face. 'Not remotely, I promise.'

Relief flooded Odo in a powerful wave. He bowed low to Euphe, who picked herself up and returned the bow, once more low enough to touch the ground. Odo picked up her sword and handed it to her, hilt-first.

'The grievance of the broken firestarter is settled,' said the urthkin leader. 'But even with the firestarter lost, we have other business, orders to place and knives to collect and pay for. May we attend to this now, scortwisa?'

'Oh, right, yes,' said Eleanor. 'Of course. But I've decided to stand down as the . . . mouthpiece of the scortwisa.'

She pulled Toland forward. 'Here's the new speaker for the scortwisa. He speaks for the smiths, in fact. All right?'

The urthkin leader bowed to Toland.

'But . . . wait!' protested Toland. 'I'm not . . . I'm not sure I'm allowed –'

'Cease your drate-poking,' Eleanor hissed in his ear. 'You're the right height, and this all started with you, remember? Just listen to Master Thrytin and you'll be fine. And if you could spare us some light armour in thanks, that would be uncommonly kind of you.'

'Of course . . . I think . . . Wait, are you going somewhere?'

'This has been fun, but we're on a quest. Isn't that right, Sir Odo?'

Odo was dabbing the hem of his tunic against the cut on his leg and only slowly recovering his wind and some sense of calm.

'Yes,' he said. 'I suppose we have done what we set out to do here. We must go on.'

'You'll wait for sunrise, at least?' asked Toland.

'Our business?' reminded the urthkin leader.

'Yes!' replied Toland. 'I must just consult my . . . ah . . .'

He was looking over the crowd towards a minor commotion where a large man in a dirty smock was shaking hands with many of the other smiths as he walked towards Odo, Eleanor and Toland.

'Master Thrytin!' called out Toland in relief. 'Over here!'

The master smith shook a few more hands, slid between two urthkin, and looked Odo and Eleanor up and down.

'Well,' he said, with a knowing smile, 'I didn't expect a . . . a knight . . . with such a sword . . . and a squire to come to my aid, but I am very grateful that you did. How are you, young Toland?'

'I'm fine, thank you, Master,' said Toland. 'But I've become the speaker for the scortwisa to the urthkin. It wasn't my idea.'

'It seems a good one,' said Thrytin. He bowed low to the urthkin leader and Eleanor noticed that when he straightened up, it was not to his full height. 'You're a smart lad, if not the best smith, but perhaps you will make the best trader, in time.'

'What will you do with Fyrennian and Ramm?' asked Eleanor.

'I'll let them cool their heels for a few days in the cellar,' said Thrytin. 'Then send them on their way. Fyrennian was a travelling smith before he came upon the firestarter and used it to challenge me. He can wander again. But I will also spread the word about his practices to prevent him making trouble elsewhere. Unless you want to pronounce some other judgment, Sir Odo?'

'No, no,' said Odo, waving his hand. 'Right now I just want to go to bed and sleep.'

'After I've cleaned that cut,' said Eleanor.

'You won't go without saying goodbye?' asked Toland.

'No, we won't,' said Eleanor. She paused and added a bit awkwardly, 'That armour I mentioned . . . and maybe a sword?'

Toland looked at Thrytin. The master smith smiled.

'I am sure we can equip you as befits your station,' he said gravely. 'After sun-up, when our other guests have departed.'

'Thank you,' said Eleanor. She suddenly felt very tired herself, even though she hadn't been the one fighting. All that adventuring in the middle of the night, she told herself. Nothing to do with being frightened that Odo would be killed, and herself, and all the inhabitants of Anfyltarn. Nothing to do with that at all.

'Goodnight,' Odo said to the urthkin leader. 'I'm happy we didn't all have to fight.'

'You have the beginnings of wisdom,' said the urthkin. 'May the earth speak to you, Sir Odo.'

She bowed once again. Odo staggered as he bowed back, suddenly so weary he could barely stand. Eleanor helped the exhausted boy stumble back towards the smithy and the waiting bed within.

'Our first trial,' Eleanor said as they stepped inside. 'A triumph! The firestarter destroyed, Master Fyrennian deposed, the urthkin threat turned aside, armour obtained, or will be soon. You really are becoming a knight, Odo!'

Odo nodded slowly because she wanted him to agree. How many knights were forced into battle by the actions of their swords, unwilling and unprepared as he had been?

Not many, he thought, but he was definitely too tired to argue.

CHAPTER

FIFTEEN

Next morning, weary after only a few hours' sleep and still unsettled by how everything had almost gone hideously and terminally wrong, Eleanor, Odo and Biter left Anfyltarn and descended the hill to retrieve their packs.

They wore armour now, Odo in the full hauberk he had bartered with Fyrennian to buy, a coat made of hundreds of interwoven steel rings that stretched down to his knees, and had full sleeves and a plate gorget to protect his neck. It was very heavy and hot, particularly with the thick felted undergarment he had to wear as well so as not to be chafed.

He had a conical steel helmet too, but he wasn't wearing that because it was also very heavy and sweaty, and it made it hard to see. Biter told him knights usually didn't put their helmets on unless there was a risk of ambush, or battle was clearly imminent. So he'd tied the helmet to his belt for now, where it was annoying him as they walked downhill.

Eleanor had a similar helmet tied to her belt, and wore a short-sleeved mail shirt that extended to mid-thigh. It was made from lighter rings, and was neither as well made nor as heavy-duty as Odo's hauberk. But she could move more easily.

She was much more captivated by another weight at her side, as she kept her hand on the hilt of her new weapon. It wasn't precisely a sword, as the smiths had not had one of a suitable size for her, but to her mind it was almost as good: a long, curved sword-knife identical to the one the urthkin Euphe had used in the duel, with a belt and scabbard to match. Deep down she had hoped for a true sword of her own, even though it wouldn't have been magical, but all she had to do, she told herself, was bide her time until Odo retired . . .

The packs remained where they had left them, tucked up in the crook of an alder near the gorse bushes where they'd had their hasty conference the previous day. Eleanor and Odo checked them over, and tied their helmets to the tops.

'We could change back to our normal clothes,' said Odo before he swung the pack on his back. Overbalanced by the unaccustomed weight on his shoulders and hips, he missed entirely, very nearly flinging the pack into what remained of the river.

Eleanor chuckled, fetching the pack for him. In the process she tangled the sword-knife in her mail shirt so she almost fell face-forward into the mud.

'Normal clothes, definitely,' she said, accepting Odo's help to stand upright.

'You must grow accustomed to armour!' protested Biter, shooting several inches out of his scabbard. 'A knight in full mail with shield must be able to vault a low wall, mount a charger without difficulty and march in mud for a full day before fighting at twilight.'

'I guess we leave the armour on then,' said Eleanor with a roll of her eyes.

Odo sighed and nodded. It wasn't just the weight of the armour, as he could carry far more once he grew used to it. It was the discomfort. The weather was warm for autumn, and they had a long way to walk. He knew he would be very sweaty, and with the river so low there was no prospect of a cooling swim ahead.

But more than the discomfort, the armour constricted his every move. He couldn't swing his arms normally, or bend down, or even breathe in as easily as he was used to. Everything just felt too tight, like he'd been tied up with rope. Every movement took more effort, and then half the time he overdid it and ended up tripping, or lurching, or almost straining a muscle.

But Biter did say he would grow accustomed to it, and Odo still remembered how he had found the big sacks in the mill almost impossible to lug about when he'd first started, and now he could pick up two at once. So he supposed he would get used to the armour as well, in time.

And, he reminded himself, he looked considerably more

knightly than before, and his new appearance would surely dissuade casual bandits and the like.

Eleanor consulted the map that Master Thrytin had given them with the armour that morning. The next village along the river road, called Scomhylt, was several leagues away. The map was rather more vague beyond that, and after the half dozen or so closer villages along the river, the rest of it was simply marked as *The Upper Valleys*. This was where the river rose, and where Quenwulf was reported to be.

'Let me check those cuts and grazes before we go,' said Eleanor as she fished around among her father's salves. It would be terrible if Odo survived his first fight only to succumb to infection.

First sword fight. First tyrant deposed. First encounter with the urthkin. First injuries.

None of it seemed entirely real to Odo, who was as weighed down by the memories as he was by the armour. He hadn't killed anyone, but he might have, and he too could have died. Victory was supposed to be sweet, but he didn't feel it. All he felt was relief, and a kind of creeping dread that he would have to do something similar again.

'Are you going to mope all day?' Eleanor asked him.

Odo forced himself out of his thoughts.

'No. I'm sure Biter won't let me anyway.'

'Indeed, Sir Odo,' said the sword. 'We have new forms to learn and many old ones to practice!'

Odo nodded. He was coming to accept that this was his lot, at least for the immediate future – and besides, the exercises had definitely come in handy during the fight with Euphe. He had no doubt they would come in handy against a dragon.

With packs much heavier than before, stomachs full of a hearty smithy breakfast, and a clearer sense of where they were going, Eleanor and Odo set off again. Both paused when they saw the river, but did not speak, simply sharing a concerned look. It was lower than ever. The trickle in the middle was no wider than Odo's hand.

As they marched, Biter called out moves and made Odo practise. He was soon sweating indeed, as he had to take three or four steps to every one of Eleanor's, going on and off the path as Biter dragged him this way and that to perform various actions.

After a league of this, Odo had to call a halt. Unlacing his hauberk, he leaned against a willow, red-faced and panting. He was used to hot, hard work in the mill, but this went far beyond that.

'Biter, don't you ever get tired?' asked Eleanor. She'd been following along, watching everything, practising in her mind.

'I will not flag until Sir Odo is in peak condition –'

'That's not what I mean. Do you ever become too weary to continue? Do you ever . . . stop?'

Biter made Odo's arm fling about, executing one of the Nine Deadly Strikes, and then came to rest on the boy's shoulder.

'One day I will die, like all things, if that is what you are asking, squire.'

'No. I want to know if you could keep doing this all day, if Odo would let you.'

Odo shot her a 'what are you doing to me?' look. He was still panting for air, and felt as though he could drink what remained of the river in one gulp. Was she trying to kill him?

'I have never had a knight whose endurance exceeded my own,' said the sword, after some consideration.

'All right then.' Eleanor felt she was getting somewhere, finally. 'What do you do when your knights sleep?'

'I watch over them, as you have observed me doing.'

'So you yourself don't sleep?'

'No.'

'But you did in the river,' said Odo.

'I am . . . unsure what I was doing in the river,' said Biter. The only time he ever sounded puzzled was when he talked about those times, and the times immediately before. 'I was ensorcelled. My mind was not my own.'

Eleanor shrugged. She knew that Biter fell back on sorcery rather than admit to any fault of his own.

'So will you die one day?' she asked. 'I mean, of old age?'

'I do not know. I would once have said that I was impervious to any minor injury or decay . . .'

'But there's that nick,' said Eleanor.

Biter said nothing.

While the smiths had been outfitting Odo and Eleanor, they had also attended to their enchanted sword. Biter had been thoroughly cleaned and polished, and with great care and tact the matter of the nick had been raised. Only when Biter was shown his reflection in a silver mirror would he even admit to the flaw. And as to repairing it . . . Master Thrytin had laughed when Odo suggested it.

'We have nothing that could grind or burnish the steel of this sword,' he'd said. 'I cannot imagine what made that nick, save another sword of the same temper, or perhaps a dragon's tooth. Something of magic, for certain, not of any mortal make.'

'Perhaps that is why you were in the river,' Odo said now, thoughtfully.

'Sir Merian would never have thrown me away simply because of a little nick,' Biter said, his protest sounding just a little bit forlorn. 'He was strong of heart –'

'– and mighty of arm, we know,' Odo finished for him. 'I didn't say you were thrown away. But maybe something happened, you got that nick, and ended up in the river. I don't know.'

He was beginning to feel more than a little sorry for the ancient sword. Biter might have magic powers, but he wasn't perfect, and no one liked having their nose rubbed in their imperfections. The number of times Eleanor made jokes about Odo being too slow, for instance, when he was just being sensibly cautious . . .

'Indeed, Sir Odo,' said Biter stiffly. 'You do not know. Now, we must continue. What Deadly Strike were we up to? Ah, yes. The sixth, Reach for the Crimson Sun. Three to go! Place your right foot forward and plant it firmly in the earth, inasmuch as that is possible while you are walking . . .'

Odo sighed again, pushed himself away from the tree and submitted to the sword's instructions.

Eleanor followed along behind, watching them like a cat intent upon a mouse, anticipating and memorising every move of foot and hand and body, and every line of the sword's actions.

CHAPTER SIXTEEN

An hour after midday they reached Scomhylt, a tidy hamlet tucked into the side of a low cliff, where they were entreated to join the search for a lost child called Young Jeffrey. The villagers seemed inclined to think a knight would succeed where they had failed, or make them happier with their failure if he failed too.

They did find him quite quickly, as it turned out. Young Jeffrey was hiding up a tree, eating autumn apples. Eleanor spotted him first, but assumed he couldn't be who they were looking for because of his thick beard and bald head. Odo thought it worth asking if he was the object of their quest, and so it proved. No one had told them that the 'child' was actually a full-grown man with a mind that wandered as often as his feet.

Odo was quite pleased by this small task. Secretly, he wished that all his knightly duties would be so easy, particularly when they were rewarded with a fine noon meal accompanied by excellent cider.

They reached Brygward, the next village, shortly before dusk. A farmer kindly let them share a byre overnight with three good-natured cows. Eleanor and Odo were grateful for the shelter, because it rained heavily for several hours in the middle of the night. As soon as the first drops fell, they heard the villagers rushing out with bowls and other containers to catch the water. They did the same with their helmets.

In the morning, the river was no higher, and the only sign of the rain was some puddles next to the tiny stream.

They journeyed on, becoming used to the weight of their armour and the constant instruction of Biter. Eleanor took to copying whatever Odo did with her own sword-knife, slowing their travel even more as both knight and squire stepped forward and back and sideways, and circled and jumped and lunged forward and then quickly retreated, all to Biter's stern orders.

On the fifth day of their journey they reached Eage, a much larger village than Lenburh. It even had a proper inn, and there, as they bought bread, hard cheese and more cider with some of their precious pennies, they heard tales of refugees coming from the north, fleeing terrifyingly vast clouds of smoke and steam high in the mountains, without doubt caused by a dragon. Odo and Eleanor didn't actually see any of these refugees who might have seen the dragon, but the stories about them were being shared by everyone in the inn and repeated for new arrivals.

They applied some of Symon's ointment to the blisters of an old man at Eage, who claimed to have seen the smoke himself. But as always, all he could say was that it was further along the river, in the Upper Valleys. Odo and Eleanor couldn't see any valleys ahead, but they were on the map.

That night, at a tiny hamlet called Horadle, Odo was called upon as a knight to settle a dispute over a flock of chickens that might or might not have been partially or completely stolen from someone who claimed to be a blood relative of the person who thought they owned the birds.

Thankfully Odo didn't need to fight anyone to resolve this conflict. He just needed to look impressive. The armour helped with this. And when he suggested the obvious – that they should divide the flock in two or at least agree to share the eggs between them – the combatants agreed readily enough . . . at first. Then they proceeded to argue over who should provide the knight and his squire with a meal in payment for the lawgiving.

This was only prevented from turning into an all-in family brawl when Odo, at Eleanor's prodding, slapped the flat of Biter's blade on the table and roared, 'Enough! We've food of our own! GO TO BED!'

The villagers fled, leaving Odo and Eleanor in possession of the barn and another supper of stale bread, cheese, dried plums and water. The cider they got never seemed to last very long.

Eleanor didn't care. She was so tired she fell into a haystack as soon as she'd eaten, and went instantly to sleep.

They woke the next morning to the sound of renewed arguing and the squawking of alarmed poultry.

'Do we have to go through all that again?' asked Odo, reaching for his hauberk with a groan.

'Please tell me it's not a knight's duty to save people from their own stupidity,' Eleanor groaned.

'𝕿here is no shame in retreat from a tussle that will only reduce our dignity.'

Under cover of raised voices, the three made a stealthy escape through the back of the barn and ran for the hills.

'What's the next village?' Odo asked Eleanor, who had the map.

'Spedigan. I think it's very small. Look, the mapmaker draws one house symbol for a hamlet, two for a small village, three for a bigger village.'

'What about a town?' asked Odo idly.

'No towns on this map,' said Eleanor. She frowned. 'I guess Eldburgh downriver from home must be the nearest town. I think Father said that's sixty leagues. He goes there every few years.'

Odo looked at the map. He hadn't noticed before, but they were reaching the edge of the detailed part, where villages were named and indicated. Ahead was the mostly blank space labelled *The Upper Valleys*.

'Let's not stop in Spedigan,' Odo said. 'I quite like sleeping in the open.'

Eleanor did too. It reminded her of summer nights when their parents would let them camp by the river, listening to night birds, frogs and crickets. She knew too that Biter bristled at hiding his true nature from people who would be alarmed by the reality of a talking sword. They had developed a system of one twitch for yes and two twitches for no so he could still communicate.

'The only problem is,' she said, 'we're going to need water.'

Odo sighed. That was true. Their canteens were almost empty and the river was now too muddy to drink. He sniffed at his armpit. A good wash wouldn't go astray either.

'I hope they've got a well,' he said.

'We'll have to boil it anyway,' said Eleanor. Her father was very strict about boiling water that wasn't from a fast-flowing river. In fact, at home they hardly drank water, instead sticking to the very weak ale that Symon brewed himself. It was much less likely to sicken the drinker.

Spedigan would have been a charming place to visit under any other circumstances, but it was presently full of refugees. There was no food to be bought, save at ludicrous prices, and there was a long line of people waiting for the village well.

Eleanor and Odo joined the line, refusing offers for the young knight to come ahead. Unintentionally, this gave them the chance to overhear several conversations that hinted at what lay before them.

'She's absolutely terrifying,' said one man to another, 'but also magnificent. Golden and long-limbed, with flashing eyes.'

Odo's ears pricked up.

'I heard she killed three men with one blow,' said the next man in line, 'and stands no less than nine feet tall!'

'Well, that last part is an exaggeration,' said the first man. 'She couldn't be more than seven feet tall – but she is easily three broad.'

'Men!' scoffed the women with them. 'She's little taller than either of you.'

Odo glanced at Eleanor with the beginnings of relief. Could it be true? That sounded very small for a dragon.

'Don't meet her eyes, whatever you do,' said the first man, with a wistful look. 'She's broken more hearts than she's stopped in combat!'

Eleanor frowned. And before she could stop herself, she asked the man, 'You're in love with Quenwulf?'

The man recoiled as though the dragon herself had appeared in front of him.

'What? No! I'm talking about Sir Saskia!'

'Who?' asked Odo.

'Haven't you heard? She's a knight from far-off lands who's come to slay the dragon. She and her coterie are camped at Hryding, gathering supplies for the march north. That's where we saw her. Oh, she's magnificent –'

'When?' Eleanor cut him off before he could begin another long description of the knight's finer points.

'Just yesterday, lass. Why do you ask?'

'Knights' business,' said Eleanor, effectively silencing any further questions.

Odo knew what she was thinking, because he was thinking it too: Hryding was the next village along the river, one marked with three houses on the map. If they hurried, they could meet Sir Saskia there and join forces with her!

Judging by the way Biter was twitching, the sword was thinking this too.

As the line moved slowly forward, Odo found himself daydreaming about Sir Saskia. If everything they heard about her was true, maybe she would kill the dragon. Then they could go safely home and no one would meet a horrible end.

He tried not to listen to one of the refugees up ahead who was quite gleefully telling a story about corpses drifting down the river, the bodies of people cooked to death in boiling water. No one asked him how a body, or indeed anything larger than a twig, could float down the muddy trickle that was all that was left of the Silverrun. 'The work of dragon's fire,' the refugee said. 'People who had thought themselves safe.'

Instead of focusing on the refugees' tales, Eleanor was trying to see the state of the water they were being given. If it was really bad, they'd have to strain it through her scarf first and then boil it – and that would take a lot of time.

When they finally got to the well, Eleanor was relieved to see the water was clear and cool. It would still need to be boiled, but not strained. She and Odo filled their bottles and the goatskin water bag and set off once more. They were the only people going north. Everyone else was headed in the opposite direction.

The sun began to set as they left the village, painting the clouds a bright pink. They passed more people hurrying south on the road but didn't stop to talk. Neither did Biter insist that Odo practise. They continued in silence, each deep in private contemplation.

A young knight, thought Eleanor, a knight on a heroic quest and, best of all, a lady knight. Sir Halfdan was none of those things, and Sir Saskia was all of them. She was everything Eleanor dreamed of being.

'If she's a real knight,' she asked Biter when the road was empty, 'does that mean she'll have a sword like you?'

'Unlikely,' he said. 'We are exceedingly rare.'

'But she might have one . . .'

Eleanor's mind wandered off along ever more fabulous possibilities while Odo thought about Eleanor's question. From his own experience, knights didn't have enchanted swords. It seemed to him that it was more the other way around.

He told himself not to complain. He was acutely conscious of Eleanor's jealousy. But every village they'd passed through had reminded him of home in one way or another, and also reminded him that he was only a miller's boy. He did not feel like a real knight, and he knew they'd only succeeded – and survived – at Anfyltarn with some very good luck. It could easily have ended otherwise.

Going up against a dragon would be far more dangerous.

Odo stumbled, not really looking where he was going.

'𝔚hat is the matter, 𝔖ir 𝔒do?' asked Biter.

'Nothing,' Odo replied.

But he was thinking, I really hope this Sir Saskia deals with the dragon so I can go home.

CHAPTER
SEVENTEEN

They heard Hryding long before they saw it.

'Is that . . . singing?' asked Eleanor.

Odo said, 'Sounds like a feast.'

They picked up their pace, neither feeling the fatigue that had previously dogged them. Soon they could smell cooking. Ahead in Hryding there was bread toasting and meat being roasted. Their mouths watered.

When they reached the crest of the next low hill they stopped in amazement at the scene in the valley below.

Hryding wasn't a large village, but it sported an enormous red pavilion in the middle of its green, a tent big enough to hold thirty people. Outside the tent, a large fire pit was in use to roast several whole pigs on spits, and two barrels of ale had been broached. It looked as if everyone who lived in the village, men and women, young and old, was gathered around the tent. They were laughing and toasting as one.

All around the tent, at intervals of three or four paces, there were six men and eight women in leather armour, all wearing sashes the same colour as the pavilion.

'Sir Saskia's entourage, I guess,' said Eleanor. 'Quite a few of them. And that tent – it must take a wagon and four oxen to move that!'

The members of Sir Saskia's entourage were not as resplendent as Eleanor had anticipated. She hadn't seen many fighters over the years, as Lenburh was so peaceful. These looked like the irregular types who wandered through and were rapidly encouraged to leave again by Sir Halfdan. They were weathered and slightly dirty, and though they drank and ate with the villagers, they didn't move from their positions, nor talk to those who brought them food and ale.

They reminded Odo a little of how dogs behaved with sheep. They'd work with them, but were always separate, always aloof and watchful.

'I don't see Sir Saskia,' said Odo. 'Do you?'

'She must be inside the tent,' said Eleanor, feeling suddenly shy and awkward, an ordinary girl from an ordinary village. What would Sir Saskia possibly think of her?

Odo said, 'We should straighten up our armour. Scrape the mud off at least.'

Eleanor smiled in gratitude. 'Good idea.'

They retreated back over the hill to tidy themselves up. There wasn't a lot they could do, but their boots were better for being cleaned, and Odo's hauberk and Eleanor's mail shirt each had a turn in the sand bag to give them a shine. They took extra care putting them back on again, tightening all the laces and making sure everything sat straight. Finally Eleanor buffed up both their helmets, which, while they didn't shine, at least looked well maintained.

'What do you think, Biter?' Odo asked. 'Will Sir Saskia be impressed?'

'There is more to a knight than the manner of his dress.'

That sounded less cheerful than Odo had expected, even sullen.

'What's the matter? Are you jealous that she might get to kill the dragon before we get a chance?'

'It is useless to speculate how anyone will feel about a deed until it is done.' The sword fidgeted in his scabbard. 'Let us meet this Sir Saskia and test her resolve.'

They stepped back onto the road and marched in time towards the village. If anything, the merriment of Hryding's inhabitants had increased. There were fewer children now, and more mugs of ale. Several songs competed for dominance, creating a rowdy but good-natured hubbub. Odo made out a verse of 'Speed the Spring' clashing with 'Of Victory Sing We', and perhaps even the chorus of 'A Young Cousin Have I', a song his father only sang when very deep in his cups. Odo had never heard it properly because his mother always put her hands over his ears.

Eleanor and Odo were noticed as soon as they entered the green. A cheer went up and mugs were pressed into their hands. Perhaps, Eleanor thought, they had been mistaken for members of Sir Saskia's entourage. Her initial attempt to explain who they were to a man wearing his hat backwards went unheard, thanks to an outbreak of spontaneous cheering that nearly deafened her.

'What are you celebrating?' she asked when the echoes died down.

'Sir Saskia's defeat of the brigands of course. Hurrah!'

'What brigands?' asked Odo.

'Churls and malcontents,' said the backwards-hat man, placing one hand on Odo's shoulder for emphasis, or perhaps to keep his balance. 'These are terrible times. The river is practically bone-dry and our livelihoods are threatened. We can't sleep at night for the whining of our children and the rumbling of our own bellies. And there are those who would steal what little we have purely for their own benefit. Brigands, the lot of them!'

'The lot of them!' agreed the small audience that had gathered around him.

'But she sent them away, she did. Packed them off smartly with their scabbards tangling between their knees. They'll not forget the lesson they learned in Hryding, will they? Sir Saskia showed them. Sir Saskia the strong . . . and beautiful . . .'

The rapturous conclusion to the backwards-hat man's tale was ruined by his eyes suddenly rolling back into his head and his falling backwards, unconscious. Fortunately the arms of his friends were ready to catch him, and another man stepped eagerly forward to pick up the soliloquy where he had left off.

'Her broadsword shining in the starlight, her thews mightier than a man's, the good sir knight tracked them for days, awaiting the right moment to strike. And strike she did, fortunately just moments after they attacked us! The brigands escaped, cunning curs as they are, and she will leave tomorrow to round them up. When that is done she will go north to slay the terrible dragon, and then we will all sleep safe in our beds again.'

'Hurrah!' chorused the crowd. Someone started singing 'The Ballad of Brave Sir Leax', with 'Saskia' in place of 'Leax', but without much success.

'Is she in the pavilion?' asked Eleanor over the racket. 'How do we get to talk to her?'

'You'll have to talk to Mannix, her squire,' said a boy who was probably Odo's age, though only three-quarters his size.

'Which one's Mannix?'

The boy pointed out a tall, wiry young man with snake tattoos curling across his shaved scalp. He was standing in front of a partially closed flap in the pavilion – clearly the entrance. He had a proud nose and forbidding expression, and wore matching quillon daggers at his waist. At that moment he was wagging a long finger in the face of a red-cheeked man with a nose the shape of a turnip.

Focusing, Eleanor could hear Mannix's deep voice over the noise of the crowd.

'. . . food, drink, everyday repairs, and let's not forget the good sir knight's time. If you truly want to express the gratitude of your village, Master Reeve . . .'

'We have to talk to him,' Eleanor whispered to Odo.

He nodded and followed her as she slid through the crowd. The revellers barely noticed, with their cheering and singing and swallowing of great draughts of ale. Being saved from brigands was well worth celebrating. They would worry about the river and the dragon tomorrow.

'. . . more than anticipated,' the village reeve was saying to Mannix as Odo and Eleanor approached, 'but in thanks for the good sir knight's kind intervention, we will find a way.'

'Thank you, Master Reeve.' Mannix bowed to him, not very low. 'We will expect delivery by midday tomorrow.'

'Sir, a moment –' said Eleanor.

'Midday?' The reeve looked alarmed. 'We can't possibly . . . That is, with more time –'

'Sunset, then. Sir Saskia has other villages to save, you know. The dragon.'

'Of course, of course.' The reeve looked pained, but bowed again deeply to Mannix. 'We understand. Thank you, thank you . . .'

'Sir?' Eleanor tried again.

Both men turned to face her.

'Yes?' said Mannix. His expression was forbidding.

'We desire an audience with Sir Saskia.'

'My knight is resting,' said Mannix. 'Go away.'

'We have matters to discuss,' said Eleanor. 'We won't trouble her.'

'You *won't* trouble her, because I won't let you. You've troubled her enough already for one day, you poxy villagers.'

'We are not villagers,' said Odo. He tried to pitch his voice low and sound authoritative, but it came out more as a squeak. 'We heard of Sir Saskia in Spedigan and we –'

'So you have ears,' interrupted Mannix. 'Use them and listen as I say, "Go away, trouble me no more."'

'We wish to help her slay the dragon,' said Odo.

Mannix snorted in amusement. 'You?'

'Yes,' said Eleanor. 'At least, Sir Odo will, and as his squire, I will assist him.'

'You're squires?' asked Mannix, with new interest. 'There's another knight? Here?'

'Before you,' said Eleanor. She bowed and made a gesture she hoped was courtly towards Odo. 'Allow me to present Sir Odo of Lenburh. I am Squire Eleanor.'

Odo could feel himself blushing, but he did his best to stand tall.

Mannix looked at him properly for the first time.

'Oh, this is going to be fun,' he said, waving them into the tent.

CHAPTER
EIGHTEEN

The sounds of merriment outside fell into the background. Inside the tent, the air was warm and close, smelling of rose water and sweat. Fires burned in braziers spaced evenly around four solid wooden benches with a low table between them. On the table, next to a helmet and a pair of gauntlets, were bowls of meat and fruit and jugs of water and wine. From behind a broadcloth screen came the sound of movement. Metal on metal. The clearing of a throat.

Suddenly she appeared, a splendid figure in once-gilded mail, the gold wash now uneven across the steel. She had a broad face, bold features and eyes as keen as the edge of a killing dagger. Her thick yellow hair was tied back in braids.

Sir Saskia was drying her hands on a towel – which, when she was done with it, she tossed casually aside. Her cheeks were pink from where she had just finished washing her face.

'The most puissant knight, Sir Odo of Lenburh,' announced Mannix in an exaggerated fashion. 'And his brave squire, Eleanor.'

'Thank you, Mannix. Welcome, welcome.' She waved them forward, into the light of the braziers. 'Let me see you.'

Odo felt the knight's grey gaze sweep over him, taking in every detail. Her eyes narrowed as she caught sight of Biter at his side.

'You bear a fine sword, Sir Odo,' she said. 'Of some antiquity, if I judge aright. Have you words to match your steel?'

Odo felt very young and clumsy, but somehow he managed to stutter out, 'I am but a young knight, newly . . . um . . . come to my . . . er . . .'

'Estate,' whispered Eleanor, who was standing close behind him.'

'Estate,' said Odo. 'Words are not . . . that is, my actions speak for me, I trust.'

Sir Saskia grinned, exposing a row of bright white teeth. One of them was capped in a shining black metal, something neither Odo nor Eleanor had seen before, though there was a famous peddler who came through Lenburh from time to time who had a silver tooth.

'Hail and well met. This is an auspicious day. Please, sit. Take your fill of food, drink . . .'

She gestured expansively at the table, but at that moment neither Odo nor Eleanor had any appetite. They were too awed to do more than stare. Sir Saskia seemed to be everything a knight should be, a sun that put their own small presence in the shade.

'You mention an estate,' said Sir Saskia. 'From where do you hail, Sir Odo? And your family?'

Odo hesitated. He wanted to blurt out the truth, but there was a coldness in Sir Saskia's eyes that warned him off. Knights were better than ordinary people, although sometimes ordinary people could become knights. If he was to join her in defeating the dragon, it would be best if she didn't suspect his common origins.

'From the south,' he said. 'I am but newly knighted, though I follow in the footsteps of my ancestors.'

The great-grandfather I never even knew about, he thought, until my mother mentioned him when I was leaving.

'I can see that.' Sir Saskia clapped Odo on one shoulder, a mighty buffet that made him rock on his heels. 'Barely weaned by the look of you. But no matter. We all have to start somewhere!'

She put one foot on the nearest bench and let it take her weight. The wood creaked. Eleanor closely studied every detail of the knight, noting the many scuffs and scratches on her mail hauberk, her sword's large wheel pommel, the scars from many sword-cuts on the back of her hands . . .

For once, Odo was finding it easier to talk than Eleanor.

'It is a very good thing you have done for the villagers here, Sir Saskia,' he went on. 'Driving off the brigands.'

Sir Saskia waved the compliment away.

'Why else is one a knight if not to help the weak, eh? That's why we're going after that wretched dragon next. Can't have people shaking in their boots all day, afraid of being eaten. How are they supposed to farm or knit or whatever? Protecting the little people, that's what a knight is supposed to do. It's a simple life really. If it doesn't kill you.'

She grinned, and Odo had to admit that, yes, Sir Saskia was beautiful. He found himself blushing again.

'But tell me more about you two,' she said. 'Have you travelled far? What is your destination? Your purpose? I'm all ears. Well, apart from this one.' She pointed at her right ear. 'If you look closely, you'll see where a bilewolf once took a snap at me. That was the last thing it ever did.'

Both children admired the notch before remembering the question.

'We are searching for whatever blocks the river,' said Odo. 'We wish to free the waters –'

'Byfightingandkillingthedragon!' The words burst from Eleanor's mouth. It was her turn to flush pink when she realised how she must sound. 'That is, Sir Saskia . . . I mean, we didn't know *you* had already taken on this quest.'

The knight tipped back her head and laughed, not in mockery or scorn, it seemed, but delight. The peals physically shook her, making her armour jangle.

'In all my thirty years,' she said, wiping her eyes, 'I have never witnessed such spirit from mere striplings! Sir Odo, you shame me. I salute you, and I thank you for reminding me of a knight's true strength. No dragon can prevail against us!'

Her grin was broad and infectious. Odo and Eleanor found themselves grinning back at her, filled with joy that was as profound as it was confused. Were they fighting the dragon with Sir Saskia or not? Neither of them had actually raised that point yet . . .

Sir Saskia stood and her hand fell to the hilt of her sword.

'But first, you and I, we must fight,' she declared.

Odo's mouth fell open. Biter twitched emphatically in his scabbard. 'What?'

'Fight, I said. Not now, of course. It is late and I am weary. But tomorrow, before breakfast. Nothing like single combat to work up an appetite!'

'But . . . but why?' asked Eleanor.

'Because we must,' Sir Saskia told her. 'Two knights come to the same field . . . if we were ahorse, we would joust, but there is little fodder for horses here and I have left mine elsewhere. But if you have two chargers, why then –'

'No,' Odo interrupted. 'I am afoot also. Uh, why must we fight?'

'Why?' asked Sir Saskia. 'I have said. We must test each other. Not to the death of course. A wound, a broken limb – that is enough.'

Odo didn't know what to say. He stood there, gaping.

'Unless you are a coward, a caitiff who wishes to declare himself no true knight.'

Before Odo could reply, Biter shot out of the scabbard, slapped himself into Odo's hand, pulled the boy's arm forward and stuck his point almost into Saskia's face, the emerald in his pommel flashing in the firelight.

'Sir Odo of Lenburh accepts your challenge!' cried Biter.

'To arms!' shouted Sir Saskia. She drew her own sword with astonishing speed, interposing it between her and Biter and stepping back.

Eleanor turned, hand on her own sword-knife, as Mannix rushed into the room, his daggers out. A dozen more of Saskia's scarlet-sashed followers entered from all corners, their weapons ready. Suddenly the room was full of armed men and women, all waiting for the order to kill.

'Wait!' Eleanor raised her hands to show that her knife was still in its sheath. 'We're not attacking anyone!'

'It's my sword,' said Odo, struggling to return Biter to his scabbard. This was the situation with the urthkin all over again! 'He gets excited sometimes. He doesn't mean anything by it.'

Sir Saskia's expression, which had been grim, almost frightening, suddenly softened, then broke into a smile. Finally she laughed and her sword came down. There was a sudden relaxation of tension in the room.

The prospect of imminent death receded.

'I see now,' said the knight, staring in astonishment at Biter, who was bucking about in Odo's hand. 'I see it clearly. Did you inherit this magnificent sword, Sir Odo, or have it delivered to you in a mysterious package by persons unknown, perhaps as a sign that you are destined for greatness? Or . . . ahem . . . chance to pick it up from someone else?'

'𝕳ow dare you impugn my knight's honour!' roared Biter.

'That's enough!' snapped Odo. Exerting all his strength, he forced the sword back into the scabbard, where his complaints were muffled into inaudibility.

'No, I didn't inherit the sword or receive it mysteriously or steal it, as you seem to suggest,' said Odo, not wanting to say that Biter had been living in mud for hundreds of years or lay claim to any specialness he didn't feel. 'We, um, met a while ago and Biter knighted me. Now we're questing together. Him, me, and Eleanor.'

'Off to kill the dragon!' Sir Saskia trilled. 'A story for the ages! Truly we were destined to meet. May I speak to the sword?'

Somewhat reluctantly, Odo eased off on holding Biter down. The sword sprang out of his scabbard and, perhaps embarrassed by his previous outburst, allowed Odo to hold him angled across one shoulder.

'What is your name, good sword?' asked Sir Saskia. Unlike others who had suddenly met Biter before, she did not seem at all alarmed by the enchanted blade.

'Hildebrand Shining Foebiter,' said Biter. 'Dragonslayer and Scourge of . . . well, enough of that.'

Sir Saskia blinked and inclined her head.

'I am honoured to greet you, Hildebrand Shining Foebiter, Dragonslayer and Scourge. My own sword, though it bears no enchantment, is also an ancient and mighty weapon. It is called Ædroth.'

She drew her sword and showed them its blade flat-on, so they could admire it. Eleanor made out a faint rose-window pattern on the steel, polished almost to nothingness.

'That is a fine blade,' said Odo quietly. He was looking at Sir Saskia, a real knight – a real knight he was going to have to fight . . .

'In the morning, Sir Odo, our swords will clash. Then we will see who prevails: the enchanted or the experienced.'

She winked at them, then turned to Mannix. 'Ensure our friends are comfortably billeted for the night. It is time to retire. Tell the revellers outside to be quiet.'

Sir Saskia inclined her head and went back behind the screen. Her soldiers slipped away. Mannix guided Odo and Eleanor through the front flap and told them to wait next to the tent while he went in search of the village reeve, pausing to speak some quiet words to the closer villagers as he went.

Within minutes the party began to quieten.

'So what do you think of Sir Saskia?' Odo asked Eleanor.

'I think she's everything a knight should be.' Eleanor

indicated the villagers who were staggering off to their beds. 'She doesn't just save people. She makes them happy too!'

'I'm not happy,' said Odo. 'A single combat tomorrow . . . and we never talked about us helping to fight the dragon.'

'She'll go easy on you,' said Eleanor with confidence. 'It's probably just something knights do for show.'

'𝔖𝔦𝔯 𝔖𝔞𝔰𝔨𝔦𝔞 𝔥𝔞𝔰 𝔱𝔥𝔢 𝔢𝔶𝔢𝔰 𝔬𝔣 𝔞 𝔠𝔬𝔩𝔡 𝔨𝔦𝔩𝔩𝔢𝔯,' said Biter, pitching his voice low.

Eleanor sniffed. 'Says the sword who wanted to slay a shepherd and his sheep. She is a true knight! You're probably just jealous of Ædroth.'

Biter did not reply. Mannix returned at that moment with a villager who offered them fresh straw to sleep on in her cow byre, with the cow to be turned out.

Eleanor and Odo thanked Mannix and followed the woman. Odo's thoughts were all about the single combat to come, Eleanor's of the marvel of Sir Saskia. She bet the knight wasn't going to sleep on straw in a cow byre. No, she'd have a feather bed in that pavilion for certain.

Sir Saskia was what Eleanor wanted to be. A real knight. Not a worrywart like Odo.

NINETEEN

The morning of the single combat dawned blue and bright, with a thin mist that hugged the ground in diaphanous wisps. The village was quiet apart from the occasional groan as people stirred. When a fanfare went up to announce the combat, it was answered by a chorus of complaints.

Sir Saskia was having none of that. Her entourage spread out through all of Hryding, banging on doors and reminding the villagers that the festivities weren't over yet. They were brigand-free and host to not one knight but two, who would fight spectacularly the moment a respectable audience assembled. How often did they expect to see such a wonder? What would they tell their grandchildren if they missed it?

The other knight had been up for an hour and was practising in a muddy field, watched by a pair of imperturbable pigs. Biter did his best to cram several years' worth of lessons into one morning, the sword also instructing Odo on the protocols and manners expected in any knightly encounter. There would be no punching, pinching or biting, not even wrestling moves like the waterwheel that he had successfully employed against the urthkin.

'Be courteous,' said Biter, for the fifth time, 'and you will receive courtesy. Ill manners might result in your death.'

'But Sir Saskia said this would only be until one of us was wounded,' panted Odo.

'Accidents can happen. Even in a contest of skill and honour between knights.'

'But not on purpose,' said Eleanor. 'Not Sir Saskia.'

'Hmmph,' said Biter. 'In any case, we must fight well, Sir Odo. Forward!'

By the time Mannix came for them, Odo had worked up a sweat and felt as ready as he was ever going to be, if he ignored the nervous churning of his guts, which had sent him to the privy twice that morning, although that could equally have been the well water that Eleanor was always warning him about. Sheathing Biter, he followed the two squires to the green, where Sir Saskia's giant tent had already been dismantled in order to make space. As Eleanor had predicted, it was transported on a wagon, though it was drawn by only two oxen, not four.

It seemed that everyone for leagues around had been woken and 'encouraged' to come to witness the combat. There were at least a hundred people gathered on three sides of the green. Even children and babies were there, the prospect of blood notwithstanding.

A cheer rose up as Sir Odo walked onto the green.

He waved back, wondering if he should say something. But anything he might have said was drowned out by Sir Saskia's appearance, which prompted a roar like nothing he had heard since Lenburh had beaten the rival village of Gelton in the greased-pig-chasing contest.

If the combat was to be judged by popularity, he had already lost.

Eleanor noted, though, that Sir Saskia's people were vigorously encouraging the cheering. She frowned as she saw one of the soldiers slap a young man hard on the back. He hadn't been cheering. Now he was.

'Good morning, people of Hryding!' Sir Saskia cried, waving gauntleted hands that caught the sunlight, sending golden flashes into the eyes of her admirers. 'This is a rare and wonderful day. I am delighted to introduce to you Sir Odo of Lenburh and his enchanted sword, Hildebrand Shining Foebiter!'

Odo took an awkward bow, then drew Biter and waved him above his head. He tried to reflect the light the way Sir Saskia had, but that only made people squint and look annoyed.

Eleanor stood to one side with Mannix, trying to imitate his impassive stance, although she was barely half his size. Mannix looked as though nothing ever bothered him. Maybe a squire was all he'd ever dreamed of being. He seemed happy enough standing on the sidelines while someone else got all the glory.

Eleanor wondered if she should grow her hair long and plait it like Sir Saskia's.

'Your boy looks nervous,' Mannix said to her out the side of his mouth. 'Ten to one says he gets trounced.'

'Not if Biter has anything to say about it.'

'Ah, yes, the sword.' Mannix smirked. 'All talk and no teeth, I bet. What else have you got?'

Eleanor rose to the defence of her friend. 'His armour was forged in a dragon's fire. Beat that.'

He looked down at her, perhaps wondering if she was making it up. 'This place you come from . . . Lenburh, was it? I must pay it a visit one day.'

A third cheer dragged their attention back to the field of combat. Sir Saskia was bowing to Sir Odo and beaming encouragement. He bowed too, their heads almost touching.

'Don't worry, lad,' she whispered to him. 'I'll go easy on you.'

Odo nodded in gratitude. Then his stomach lurched inside him again as their swords came up and the blades touched in salute.

The rules of the contest were simple. They would fight until one of them yielded, or was unable to go on due to wounds, unconsciousness or death.

'Have at you, Sir Odo!'

Eleanor held her breath as Odo fell into the opening stance he had been practising for days now. With the sun shining on his new armour, he cut a pretty figure, and Biter of course knew how to look good.

Odo and Sir Saskia moved at the same time. Odo flowed into his favourite of the Five Lethal Forms, White Eagle Threads the Needle, and Biter moved smoothly in his hand, weight shifting subtly to guide his stroke towards Sir Saskia's exposed forward leg.

But Odo pulled Biter's blow, not wanting to sever Sir Saskia's limb, not realising until it happened that the knight wasn't going to be hit anyway. She was extremely fast, bending to one side so quickly that Odo barely registered how she did it. One moment she was where he had aimed, the next she was not, and then she was striking at him!

Biter managed to parry the blow, but the force of it was so great that Odo was pushed backwards and down, almost to his knees.

Sir Saskia struck again, and Odo only just managed to avoid it, throwing himself to one side and clumsily managing to get upright and back away.

The crowd roared. They were cheering for Sir Saskia. Eleanor found herself cheering too, then forced herself to stop.

Sir Saskia allowed Odo no respite. She attacked again and again, with fast, heavy blows that only a combination of Biter's speed and anticipation allowed Odo to parry or dodge. Every time he had to back away as well.

Soon he was almost at the edge of the green, and the crowd had to part to give the combatants room. Odo tried to get past Sir Saskia with several attacks of his own, but she parried and blocked and counterattacked, giving no ground.

'She's so quick,' Odo whispered to Biter.

'*I know.*' The sword's admiring tone didn't help Odo's confidence in the slightest. '*But together we will defeat her!*'

Odo nodded and launched into another of the Five Lethal Forms, Twisting the Tiger's Tail. He thought he had started it pretty well, but Biter moved in his grip, throwing his weight off. Odo knew what Biter was doing – he was trying to fight better than Odo could alone – but the blow didn't stand a chance with both of them trying different things at once.

Sir Saskia easily dodged them and brought her sword around to strike in return. Odo went to block, but again Biter took him by surprise, moving in a way that counteracted what he was trying to do. The flat of Sir Saskia's sword struck him on the right shoulder, his hauberk ringing with the sound of metal on metal. But he kept his footing and retaliated with a desperate sweep at her midriff. She danced backwards. Biter's tip missed her middle by barely an inch, but she didn't seem fazed. With a triumphant 'Hah!' she came close while Biter was still moving, pushed with one fist against Odo's chest, and tipped him off balance.

He went down in a tangle of feet, arms and sword. Eleanor

was amazed he didn't impale himself in the process.

Odo closed his eyes for an instant, panting. The combat was barely two minutes old and he was already out of breath. Sweat trickled down his face. He felt boiled alive inside his hauberk. The crowd called a mixture of mockery and encouragement, Eleanor's voice loudest in the latter camp.

With a grunt, he stood up.

'You're game, Sir Odo, I'll give you that,' said Sir Saskia with a grin, shifting eagerly from foot to foot.

'Maybe we should yield,' Odo said to Biter, daunted by Sir Saskia's enthusiasm.

'𝔑ever!'

And then the sword was moving, dragging him along behind. The ferocity of the blow took Odo by surprise. It was all he could do to hang on, a dead weight dragging Biter's tip upwards, causing it to miss his target. Sir Saskia responded with a backwards step and another blow to Odo's shoulder, exactly where she had hit it before. He cried out as she struck. The mail held, and his collarbone beneath, but he would be severely bruised.

Biter struck again, and again Sir Saskia easily parried the blow, a sweeping movement that brought her great blade once to the left, and then again to the right, her mouth set in a serious line.

She wasn't playing now. Odo's right arm wasn't working properly – his shoulder felt like it was swelling up inside the armour. He had to hold Biter with both hands, but he no longer had the strength to help the sword fight, or even to adequately follow his movements.

Sir Saskia got another blow through Biter's frenzied defence – on his shoulder again, jarring it so he lost feeling all the way down his arm. His fingers could no longer hold the sword, and the grip of his left hand was too weak.

Biter fell from his grasp and went point-first into the green, quivering in place.

Sir Saskia drew her sword-arm back, the blade level with Odo's eyes, ready to punch it forward and kill him instantly.

'I yield!' Odo gasped.

Instantly Sir Saskia withdrew. Her good-natured grin returned.

'Excellent!' she said, raising and sheathing her sword with one easy movement. 'A fine combat, and now it is over. Here, let me help you with this.'

She extended her hand to Biter, going to pick him up. But Biter suddenly darted away, sliding across the grass and trimming a swathe of it as he went.

'Ha! The blade still has fight in it. Come here, you.'

Sir Saskia went after the sword. But Biter flew across the green like a scared hare, far too fast for the knight to catch him. The audience gasped at the sight of a sword moving on its own.

'I am not trying to take you,' Sir Saskia said. 'I wish only to return you to . . . Oh, you have your fun with me, eh? So be it!'

Biter flew like an arrow between Sir Saskia's legs and leaped into Odo's hand. Odo grimaced with the shock of it, but managed to hold on, leaning the blade against his good shoulder.

'Are you all right?' Eleanor called out anxiously as she wove through the crowd to Odo's side.

'Bruised shoulder,' said Odo, with some difficulty. 'Nothing broken, but my arm . . . hard to use it.'

'I've got an ointment,' said Eleanor. 'And bandages. I'll fix it up. Let's get you away.'

Odo kept his eyes down, feeling humiliated and beaten. He had never wanted to fight anyone, least of all a proper knight. Even in a friendly contest, it hurt to lose.

As Eleanor helped Odo away, Sir Saskia approached and inclined her head to him in something well short of a proper bow.

'A fine knightly combat,' she said. 'And lucky for you, my boy, it was a chivalrous contest. I'd think hard on that if I were you. That magical antique of yours won't save you in a serious fight. It belongs on the wall of some great noble's hall, not on a battlefield. And you – you're a child. You should go home before you get seriously hurt.'

Odo nodded, unable to meet her eye.

'But we can still help you, can't we?' protested Eleanor.

'If you let us join your party we can start off small, help fight bandits, and –'

'Hush, child.'

Sir Saskia's eyes were kind and sad at the same time, or so they seemed to Eleanor.

'I know you mean well, and believe me, I am flattered by your offer. But the truth is, you have no idea of the dangers that await you on this quest. Yes, I know you are not afraid, but you should be, and it worries me that you are not. I fear that your recklessness will see you hurt, perhaps seriously, and . . . I do not have time to worry about your well-being. I am a knight. My mission is to slay a dragon, not nurse children. Do you understand?'

Odo felt tears pricking at the corners of his eyes. 'I understand.'

'Good lad. Maybe when you are older, come look for me. Or if I'm ever passing Lenburh . . .'

Her smile was like the sun, but Eleanor was not soothed.

'Couldn't we just travel with you at least?' she asked.

Sir Saskia leaned in close, her lips brushing Eleanor's ear to whisper six words that only she could hear.

'You would get in the way.'

Before Eleanor could think of a reply, Sir Saskia turned to face the crowd. As she did so, Mannix started a chant, instantly picked up by the other soldiers, and then by the crowd.

'Sir Saskia! Sir Saskia!'

The knight walked into their midst to accept their praise, with awed children throwing rose petals provided by her entourage, admiring adults falling to their knees as she passed, as if she was a queen, and young men and women offering their daggers hilt-first, begging to become part of her retinue.

Red-faced Eleanor walked away, Odo stumbling at her side.

TWENTY

'Sir Saskia is right,' said Odo, grimacing as Eleanor finished applying her father's bruise ointment. 'I'm not a real knight, you're not a real squire, and if we go on, we will die. And what good will that do anyone?'

'You get better all the time,' said Eleanor. Sir Saskia's words still burned inside her, but she had overcome the humiliation. Now she burned to show the knight just how wrong she was. 'It's no shame to be beaten by a knight with so much more experience. How can we go back home and tell my father and your parents that we simply gave up?'

'Better than never going home at all.' Odo moved his arm and winced. But at least he could move it now. He sighed and began to fold his hauberk, ready to pack it away. There was no point continuing to wear the armour of a knight. 'Think of your father, waiting for his daughter who never came home, getting word of your death –'

'My father knows who and what I am,' interrupted Eleanor

hotly. 'What about you, Biter? Surely you think we should all keep going, right?'

The sword came only half an inch out of his scabbard and spoke in a sulky voice.

'An antique, she said. I belong on a wall, she said.'

'You don't believe that –'

'Sir Saskia is a great knight. Why shouldn't I believe what she says? She bested us in single combat. Sir Odo was no match for her, and I was no match for an ordinary sword. Even with a novice knight I should have triumphed. I am nicked, and old, and I slept too long. My time is past.'

'I want to go on,' said Eleanor, her voice and her heart firm. 'We have a duty.'

'Sir Saskia will slay the dragon and restore the river,' said Odo dully. He laced up his pack and gingerly lifted it onto his left shoulder, leaving the right-hand strap hanging. 'We're going home.'

Eleanor couldn't speak, she was so furious. She picked up her own pack and took three very deep breaths.

Was the adventure really over? Were they really going home?

A very small voice inside her, breaking through the anger and the foiled ambition, said that perhaps this was the only sensible course. Maybe she had always wanted too much, had dared to hope for too much. And now . . .

She couldn't go on without Odo, and neither could she defeat Quenwulf without a sword.

She would never be a knight.

Odo started off, heading south. Back the way they had come, towards Spedigan, first of the many villages on the way back to Lenburh.

Her face set, no obvious alternative open to her but marching on to a pointless death, Eleanor followed.

Neither of them spoke on the long walk back to the outskirts of Spedigan. This time they didn't enter the village. Instead they found a ruined cottage with only half a roof and many holes in its wattle-and-daub walls. But it was better than facing up to the villagers who had last seen them as brave adventurers going to face a dragon.

It was strange to be making camp without sword practice. Biter didn't demand it and Odo didn't suggest it. But the boy didn't feel as relieved as he thought he might. He and Eleanor went through their evening routine without speaking, kindling a small fire, eating sparingly and then settling down for the night.

As per usual, Odo unsheathed Biter and set the sword near the hole in the wall that had once been a doorway, where he would keep watch. Then he rolled himself in his cloak, wriggling about until he found a spot where his shoulder hurt least, and went to sleep.

Eleanor stayed awake, staring at the embers of their small fire. She had felt hopeless when leaving Hryding, but now the anger inside her was hotter than ever, burning more fiercely than even the dragon-started forge of Master Fyrennian.

Before she gave up and went home, she wanted to show Sir Saskia that she and Odo were not foolish villagers without a hope of defeating the dragon. They were beginners, true, but learning very fast. And even the greatest knights in the world had to start somewhere.

Eleanor did not want to give up. There had to be something she could do . . . but there was Odo. He had totally lost heart, which was unsurprising given he had never wanted to be a knight in the first place.

But Eleanor did. She still wanted to be a knight. It was the centre of her being, her single ambition for all her life. Was she supposed to give it up now because her best friend wanted to go home?

Eleanor lay there for another five minutes, wrestling with what she had almost decided to do. Then she sighed and sat up.

'Biter, did you hear that? Out the front?'

'I heard nothing.'

'Well, I did. I don't want to wake Odo – he needs his sleep to heal. Can you have a look?'

'You look,' said Biter grumpily.

'Please,' said Eleanor. She let a little quaver enter her voice. 'I'm afraid.'

'hmmph!' exclaimed Biter. But he rose into the air and slid out through the doorway.

As soon as he'd gone, Eleanor lifted up her pack and went out through what had once been a window, into the darkness. She didn't look back.

She thought Sir Saskia was probably still camped somewhere near Hryding. Eleanor could catch up with her and do her best to earn her way into the knight's good graces. Surely determination was a knightly quality? And being true to oneself? If Eleanor simply refused to go away, Sir Saskia would have to take her in eventually.

It was better than playing second fiddle to a miller's son and a sword content to rust away to naught.

On the road, Eleanor made good time under the stars and moon. She felt bad about leaving Odo behind without any explanation, but she thought he would understand. He wouldn't want to make her unhappy by forcing her to go home. That was what he wanted, not her. He would be happy there, particularly as Eleanor was sure Sir Saskia would defeat the dragon and the river would come back. The big waterwheel would turn again, Odo would be formally apprenticed and all would be well.

She would send messages to Odo and her father once she was taken on as Sir Saskia's second squire. No doubt she would return to Lenburh one day, having earned her knighthood her own way, without anyone else's help. They would laugh about old times, a young giant of a miller and an already famous, slightly scarred young knight with her own pavilion – probably blue rather than red – and an entourage of her own soldiers. *All women*, Eleanor thought. That would be best.

The road was empty, though she had a slight scare shortly before the dawn, coming upon a small band of urthkin going in the opposite direction. Eleanor briefly thought she was in for a fight and drew her sword, ready to charge through them and run for it. But when the urthkin saw her blade they withdrew to one side and gave her the low bows, right down to the earth. She replied in kind and walked on, her heart hammering at what felt like five hundred beats a minute.

The encounter made her even more determined. She bore an urthkin blade, wore good armour and had taken in much of Biter's training. Sir Saskia probably hadn't wanted her because of Odo, who was already a knight and would cause problems. But a squire alone, a very promising squire, Sir Saskia would take her on at once . . .

These daydreams evolved into the pleasant fantasy that it might be Eleanor herself who slew the dragon. Then Sir Saskia would undoubtedly knight her on the spot. Eleanor could see it: she would be kneeling by the dragon's severed head, a little blackened and perhaps with a cut above her eye, and Sir Saskia would have her sword upon her shoulder.

'I dub thee Sir Eleanor. Sir Eleanor the Dragonslayer!'

The sky was growing light by the time Eleanor found Sir

Saskia's encampment. She was surprised to find the knight's company on the *southern* side of Hryding, only three leagues from that village, when she had expected they would be going north towards the dragon. The pavilion was pitched in a field bordered on three sides by low hedges, with soldiers sleeping all around the tent, out under the sky.

There was only one sentry, leaning against her spear. She was upright, but looked to be asleep.

There were a lot more soldiers in the field than Eleanor had seen with Sir Saskia before, a good score more. These fighters were not as well kept as the others, their armour dirtier and more ragged and they did not wear the red sashes. They looked more like bandits than soldiers.

The sight of them made Eleanor pause. She'd thought to simply announce herself and ask to speak to Sir Saskia. But now that she was here, she hesitated. All these extra soldiers unnerved her. It was likely if she stepped out of the hedge now, they might spring up and attack her. At the very least they would turn her away.

No, she needed to get closer to Sir Saskia. This would prove something too – that Eleanor was clever enough to infiltrate the camp. If she could reach the pavilion through all those warriors, Eleanor would surprise the knight. In a good way.

Eleanor slipped through a gap in the hedge and crawled on her hands and knees past the first group of sleeping soldiers. One grunted and half-raised his head as she drew near. Eleanor froze as he spoke without opening his eyes.

'What goes?'

No one answered. Eleanor lowered herself to the ground, as if she too was just another sleeping soldier.

'Not my watch,' grumbled the man. He opened one eye and gazed up at the sky, which had just begun to fill with the pre-dawn light.

'Ugh,' said the man, and settled down again.

Eleanor waited a full minute before rising up to crawl again towards the pavilion. Every now and then she glanced at the sentry, but the woman still leaned on her spear. It seemed that she was not afeared of any attack by bandits or the like.

As Eleanor reached the side of the pavilion, a light flared inside. A lantern, just lit. She could see its glow through the cloth as it was raised up and hooked onto one of the tent poles.

A moment later Eleanor heard Sir Saskia herself.

'We'll have a share-out after the troops break their fast,' said the knight. 'What did we take?'

'A helmet full of copper, twenty-seven silver pence, one gold noble,' said Mannix.

'A noble?' asked Sir Saskia. 'Who had that?'

'The reeve,' chuckled Mannix. 'He was loath to give it over, but I helped him see reason.'

They both laughed.

'What else?'

'Eighteen chickens, a goat, two sheep, a wheel of cheese — all for the commissary of course.'

'Go on.'

Eleanor listened, puzzled. They were discussing supplies, but what was the talk of a share-out?

'Four dozen eggs. Two barrels of ale, so that's good. A pig and a pig's head.'

'We'll eat all right, but surely there was more to share? Jewellery, raw metal, something?'

'None of value.'

'You should've squeezed them harder,' said Sir Saskia. Dishes clattered, as though she had thrown something. 'Those onion-eyed misers . . . all they needed was a good reminding of what we did for them!'

'I pushed as hard I could,' Mannix protested. 'They're beginning to starve around here. The pickings get leaner with every village. Maybe it's time for all of us to be simple bandits, instead of playing at driving them off.'

'That would attract too much attention,' Sir Saskia said, 'even in this sleepy corner of the world. There are real knights not much further to the south, maybe even King's Wardens and the like. No, we'll just have the bandits kill a few people in the next village. An old goodwife or someone like that. They'll give us anything then, their children even.'

'Like those two brats who wanted to join us?' Mannix

crowed. 'What was it? "Sir" Oddkin and the would-be squire girl. You know, we could've used them to dig latrines and hump loot.'

'Not with that sword. I've seen one before. They're more dangerous than a yearling dragon. If I killed the boy, it would find a way to get to me. No, better to send them back with their little tails down. Think of them helping *me* kill Quenwulf!'

'The *mighty* Quenwulf at that,' said Mannix. There was something sly about the way he said that.

'Even a glimpse of the beast would scare the britches off those two,' replied Sir Saskia. 'In all my forty years, I don't think I've seen anything more pathetic.'

They laughed and laughed.

Eleanor wanted to bury herself into the ground like a mole and never emerge again.

TWENTY-ONE

She had been so wrong.

No, she told herself firmly. It was Sir Saskia, not her, who was in the wrong. Sir Saskia was a liar and a thief and . . . and maybe she wasn't even a real knight at all! If she was, she wasn't a very good one. Exploiting the threat of the dragon to extract tribute from starving people, sending her own 'bandits' to terrorise them first, was about the most monstrous thing Eleanor could imagine. It was as bad as Fyrennian. No, worse, because people looked up to knights. They were supposed to serve as good examples. If they couldn't be trusted, everything would fall apart.

Everything Eleanor believed in, anyway.

'What's that sound?' asked Mannix.

Eleanor stifled her sobs. It was the sound of her heart breaking, but Sir Saskia could never know that.

There was silence from within the tent. Eleanor's hand went to her urthkin sword-knife. If she was discovered, she would take someone with her, she thought fiercely. Maybe even the false Sir Saskia –

'Bah! One of our sluggards waking,' said Sir Saskia. 'Warm me another pot of ale and then rouse the camp. I want to make what's-it's-name . . . Spedgap . . . Spayedban –'

'Spedigan,' said Mannix. He was deeper inside the tent now, his voice less clear.

'Spedigan, then. I want the bandit party to hit them an hour before dusk tonight, then we'll come in at sunset and make a brave show.'

'As you will, Sir Saskia,' answered Mannix.

Eleanor had heard enough. She turned around and crawled back the way she had come. But even in the scarce few minutes she'd been listening, the sky had grown lighter. More of the soldiers were stirring. None had got up, but the sentry was no longer leaning on her spear. She was walking backwards and forwards along the hedge, as if she'd been doing it all night.

The fifty yards back to the hedge was a nightmare for Eleanor. While the sentry was looking the other way, the girl scurried forward, dropping flat as the sentry turned. Every time, Eleanor felt sure she would be discovered. There were noises all around her, soldiers beginning to wake, close enough to trip over her.

Somehow she made it to the hedge and slid through a gap, even then expecting the alarm to be raised. But there were no unusual sounds until Eleanor was well out of sight, down near the river. Then she heard the sudden blast of a trumpet and, distantly, Mannix's voice, his words carried by the wind.

'Up! Wake and ready yourselves! Wake!'

It wasn't an alarm. Just the usual morning call.

Eleanor hurried down the road away from the camp, her head hanging low, her mind spiralling. She'd put her faith in Sir Saskia, so much misplaced faith, she now knew, and betrayed Odo in the bargain. What could her path be now?

'Halt!'

Eleanor's gaze snapped up and her hand reached for her urthkin blade. She was alone on a road frequented by thieves and starving refugees and hadn't been paying attention –

But it wasn't a person who spoke.

It was a sword.

A sword with a flashing green emerald on his pommel and a tiny nick out of the blade, held in the unswerving hand of a young knight who did not look at all like the friendly companion Eleanor knew. He was even wearing his armour again.

'Biter! What are you doing here?'

'You abandoned your duty!' roared Biter, while Odo himself was grimly silent. 'You deserted your knight! What kind of squire do you call yourself?'

'My knight gave up!' shouted Eleanor. 'I didn't have a knight to follow any more!'

'So you went looking for one,' said Odo in a deathly calm voice. 'Did she refuse you again?'

'No,' muttered Eleanor. 'It's a lot worse than that. Sir Saskia's a fake. Those bandits are her own soldiers; she pretends to defeat them to get tribute from the villages. She's not going to take on Quenwulf or do anything for the river. Nothing at all.'

Odo nodded slowly, his expression unreadable.

'So,' said Eleanor, '*we* have to do it, right?'

Odo still didn't say anything.

'Odo?'

'You ran off without me. I imagined terrible things happening to you. Death, slavery . . .'

Eleanor hung her head.

'I did run off,' she admitted in a very small voice. 'I thought . . . I thought if there was any chance left to be a knight, I had to take it.'

Odo sighed. 'You *are* meant to be a knight. It's in your nature more than mine. Me? I don't know what I'm supposed to be.'

'Whatever you're supposed to be,' said Eleanor, 'you *are* a knight. A good one. Unlike the false Sir Saskia.'

The faintest hint of ease flitted across Odo's face. Very slowly, he nodded. Eleanor moved close and gave him a quick hug.

'Eww!' she said. 'You smell!'

'I did run half the night to get here,' said Odo. 'And I put my armour on, just in case . . . well, just in case you needed rescuing.'

'I'm glad you didn't leave it behind . . . and I'm grateful,' said Eleanor. She hesitated, then asked, 'Will you take me back as your squire? I presume you are going to go on against the dragon now, aren't you?'

'I don't know,' said Odo. 'All I've been thinking about was rescuing you. There wasn't room to think about anything else.'

'Well, do it now,' said Eleanor.

'Could it be my destiny to take on the dragon?' he said. 'I thought I'd avoided it when we met Sir Saskia, but now . . . she's something to be dealt with as well. Somehow. Like I'm being reminded of what I know I should do. And I think I do know, now.'

Biter flew into his hand with a cry of, 'Indeed, Sir Odo. We must vanquish the false knight once and for all!'

'As for a squire,' said Odo, 'are you sure you want to be mine?'

Eleanor smiled, then bowed like the urthkin did. Odo gravely responded in kind.

'So what now?' he said once the bow was over. 'I'm asking my squire for advice.'

'We'll have to leave Sir Saskia for the moment,' Eleanor replied. 'She has more than two score soldiers. There's no way we could sneak up on them, not you anyway, believe me. At least with the dragon there's a chance we could do it.'

'I suppose so. The unknown enemy is better than the enemy we know is too powerful?'

'Something like that.' Eleanor hesitated, then added, 'The dragon is our true goal. I mean, we started out to find and fix the problem with the river. But we will still need to do something about Sir Saskia. I suggest we send messages. Warn the villages downstream. Sir Halfdan too.'

Odo nodded. 'Yes. We can send runners from Hryding, though it will take a good part of our coin. And we will go on, against the dragon. Come what may.'

'Come what may,' echoed Eleanor. She smiled and raised her fist. 'That's a very knightly thing to say.'

Odo looked embarrassed.

'It's nothing to do with being a knight. It's just doing what's right.'

'Accomplish this and no one will ever doubt our valour again,' said Biter. 'Or our mettle.'

'Our metal?' asked Odo.

'M-e-t-t-l-e,' spelled Biter. 'But come to think of it, it is much the same thing. For a sword.'

'Onward!' said Eleanor.

She'd always wanted to say that.

CHAPTER
TWENTY-TWO

They hid in a ditch near the road as Sir Saskia's party went by in the opposite direction, heading to Spedigan with a clank and a rattle, a long, sprawling train of ill-disciplined soldiers. Odo watched the men and women of Sir Saskia's band of brigands with his jaw tightly clenched, telling himself firmly that their time would come. Biter twitched at his side, imagining, no doubt, how it would feel to enact a more immediate revenge. Neither of them relaxed until Sir Saskia was long out of sight.

'When Biter woke me up and told me that you were gone,' Odo said to Eleanor as they headed off again, 'I felt so awful, because I knew exactly what you'd done. I should've seen it coming, but I was too wrapped up in myself and my own problems. Promise me that that won't happen again. I'll listen to you and you won't give up on me. All right?'

'I should have talked to you first as well,' said Eleanor. 'I'm sorry.'

'Let's just agree that neither of us will head off alone,' said Odo.

Eleanor nodded. Odo smiled in relief, and they walked on in companionable silence. After they'd gone a league or more, Eleanor suddenly spoke.

'If we can . . . I mean, *when* we kill Quenwulf, are you still going to give up being a knight? And give up Biter?'

Odo frowned. The most likely future he could think of was one where he was killed by the dragon, but he didn't want to say that to Eleanor.

'I'm not sure,' he answered instead. 'I think so. I'd like to not think about it for now. Just take each day in its turn.'

'All right,' said Eleanor. And that was a relief too. His decision was entirely out of her hands. Worrying about it would only distract her from what needed to be done now.

In Hryding they found the reeve bemoaning how much the village had had to pay in order to be saved from the bandits. When they told him about Sir Saskia, he jumped up and almost threw himself in the town well before he could be restrained. On calming down, he happily agreed to send word to all the southern villages, and to the far-off town of Eldburgh, in the hope that there might be King's Wardens there.

'Don't you have your own knight?' asked Eleanor curiously.

'Not for decades,' said the reeve. 'She died in my grand-father's time, and we got on fine without one. We've never had any trouble here, until the river began to dry up. Then these bandits . . .' He stopped, grinding his teeth too hard to talk.

'Make sure your messengers stay away from Sir Saskia's people . . . and also Spedigan,' Odo advised. It was too late for Spedigan. The 'bandits' would strike there before any messengers could warn them. Odo felt very bad about that, even though he knew there was nothing he could do.

'Can you also make sure these letters get to Symon the healer and Sir Halfdan, both of Lenburh?' asked Eleanor, handing over two rolled-up scrolls of parchment. She'd been writing busily for the last half-hour. Her hand was much neater and more precise than Odo's, and she supposed that it was more of a squire's business anyway. 'What do we owe you?'

'Nothing!' spat the reeve. 'We thank you for the warning about the false knight. To think we were so taken in!'

'We were taken in too,' said Odo.

'Yes,' said Eleanor, feeling herself turn red. 'Good speed to your messengers, Sir Reeve. And luck to your village.'

'Luck to you, good squire,' said the reeve. 'And you, Sir Odo, in your venture.'

With Hryding behind them, and heading north once more, Odo and Biter resumed their practice with furious intensity, Eleanor mimicking their every move. It was harder for her, lacking an enchanted sword. She had to use her own muscles and wits to learn each pattern.

It was exhausting.

When they halted, Eleanor checked the map to see what was coming up next. There were some familiar names: Nægleborg, where Firman, the first person they had met on their journey, had come from; Sheppy, home of the refugee sheep they had scared (along with their shepherd). The Upper Valleys were still some distance away, but the foothills were close. In fact, if the map was to be believed, the landscape ahead was about to undergo some dramatic changes.

'There's a fork in the road coming up,' Eleanor told Odo. 'One way keeps following the river. The other goes into the Old Forest. It looks to be the quicker way to the Upper Valleys and . . . the dragon.'

'Through the forest? That'd be slower, surely?'

'No, really. Look, if we take the Old Forest road, it actually gets us to the mountains in fewer miles. See? The river bends right out west, and we'd bend with it if we took that road, going the wrong way. The Old Forest road cuts right across, saving us leagues. We'd meet the river again here, in Welmder Vale.'

Her finger traced out the two routes, demonstrating the considerable difference between them.

Odo had to admit that her suggestion looked a lot shorter.

'The Old Forest,' he mused. 'The road is probably much worse than the one next to the river.'

'Maybe for carts,' said Eleanor. 'But for us, afoot? Even a

track would be all right. And people live there. They must go back and forth.'

'How do you know people live in there?' Odo asked.

She pointed again. There were three named villages along the Old Forest road: Carcastel, Hertech and Fangholt. Their locations were marked exactly the same way as the other villages they had passed.

Odo had heard stories about the Old Forest. Stories about packs of bilewolves hunting anything that moved and giant moths that smothered travellers in their sleep. Hunting was forbidden there, and some ancient monarchs had enacted terrible punishments on those who broke these laws.

'What about the bilewolves and the giant moths and all that?' he asked uneasily.

Eleanor laughed.

'Those are just stories, my father always said. There haven't been any bilewolves for centuries – and as for the giant moths, they never existed.'

'Oh yes they did,' protested Biter. 'Long ago. Almost before my time, even. Though I fought bilewolves often enough. You say they are no more?'

'Well, according to my dad,' said Eleanor, with rather less conviction.

'If they're not around any more, we would save a lot of time,' said Odo, studying the map. 'It looks to be half the distance at most.'

Eleanor watched him, clearly waiting for him to decide.

That's what knights do, he told himself. *Among other things.*

'All right,' Odo said. 'The Old Forest road.'

'We take the right fork then.' Eleanor briskly folded up the map and looked at the sky. 'At least we'll stay drier under trees. Look at those clouds. Can you smell rain in the air?'

Odo could. Thick black clouds were rolling in from the west, accompanied by a steady rumble of thunder. The rain carried with it a fresh, heady scent that soon had them picking up their heels in the hope of reaching cover before being drenched.

The first drops struck them when they reached the fork in the road. It was here Eleanor had her first twinge of doubt. There was no sign saying *Do Not Enter On Pain Of Death* or anything, but the right-hand road was definitely less travelled, as Odo had suggested it might be, and barely a hundred paces ahead the trees closed right over it, forming a thick roof.

'Uh, maybe the forest road isn't the best way,' she said.

But for once Odo didn't hesitate. He strode off along the Old Forest road, picking up speed as the rain began to fall more heavily. 'Come on! We've got a dragon to slay, remember?'

Eleanor shrugged and ran after him. Lightning flashed and thunder boomed and the storm began in earnest. By the time the trees closed their branches overhead, Eleanor was soaked through and the day had turned to something very much like night.

Eleanor slowed to ordinary walking speed as she came abreast of Odo. Water dripped around them, but by and large the undergrowth was dry. The air was still and heavy with a very different smell than that of rain. There was damp to it, and the kinds of things that liked to live in the damp, such as mushrooms and moss, but there was also an ageless, woody smell of bark and cracking branches, and pine needles underfoot.

Odo liked the smell. He didn't, however, like the way the forest seemed to close in around them, as though the branches were grasping hands pulling them towards some terrible fate. Their footsteps didn't echo, and it seemed to him as though they had fallen into a dream.

Eleanor studied the shadows for any sign of boars or bilewolves, or anything else that might mean them harm. She neither saw nor heard anything. If there were monsters living among the trees, they watched silently and let the children pass.

Slowly drying from their brief drenching, Eleanor and Odo followed the road deeper into the Old Forest. It snaked from side to side, so they could see only a short distance ahead and behind them. In places the road was boggy or almost entirely overgrown, little more than a track. The ancient ditches that defined its edges were sometimes very difficult to make out, and both of them took great pains not to get lost.

At one point, they climbed over the corpse of a giant tree

that had fallen across the path so long ago that the leafy canopy above had closed up over it, erasing the wound of its passage. Its trunk was taller than the roof of Eleanor's home, and had been adopted by a vast colony of lizards, spiders, and fat-bodied ants. The lizards ate the spiders, the spiders ate the ants, and the ants feasted on the lizards when they died. This delicate balance was thrown into chaos as Odo and Eleanor crashed through, but returned to normal soon after.

They walked all day without rest. Since they had chosen this route for its swiftness, it made sense not to stop for lunch, nor even to consider it aloud. That way neither had to admit to being nervous, which was the truth.

Odo practised for a while, but the noise of it covered the sound of anything that might be creeping up on them, so in the end he stopped. But he didn't sheathe Biter, instead walking on with the sword drawn and held before him, ready for anything, although he tried not to think about what 'anything' might be. Eleanor did likewise, drawing her own blade.

Sometimes branches fell to the forest floor far off in the distance. Sometimes a bird flew by without calling, ruffling the leaves to send a brief rain shower down on them. Every time, both Eleanor and Odo jumped in fright. Every time, Eleanor found it harder to relax afterwards.

Towards nightfall they came to Hertech, the first village on the map. Only it turned out there was no village there, just some overgrown patches where houses might have been, and a barrow, a steep-sided mossy mound no less than thirty yards long and eight across.

A grave mound.

'I don't like this,' said Eleanor, at last giving voice to both their misgivings.

'Nor I,' whispered Odo. 'Let's find the road on the other side.'

Together they skirted the barrow, both flinching as a massive flight of delicate blue-winged butterflies suddenly burst out of the bushes ahead and to either side of them. Eleanor opened her mouth in delight, and Odo blinked back sudden tears. The butterflies swept up in a spiral, widdershins, flying up towards a gap in the forest canopy before slowly descending to settle on the barrow, rendering it blue from end to end. When the last one folded its wings, the scene was still again.

Odo had the peculiar sense that they had disturbed someone, who was now quiet again, like a person rolling over in their sleep and finding a more comfortable position.

'Who do you think's buried there?' Eleanor whispered, gesturing back at the barrow.

'I don't know,' said Odo. 'And I don't want to find out.'

A few minutes later they found the road again. Eleanor hurried onto it, but Odo glanced behind him and saw an unnerving thing:

The barrow had been disturbed.

Exposed earth lay in clumps around a hole in the far end of the mound, upon which no butterflies rested. The hole led into the heart of the barrow, but the light was too dim for him to see far inside. His first thought was that someone had dug there in search of treasure, but there was something about the way the dirt was scattered that suggested a very different explanation.

Something had dug its way *out*.

The small of his back itching, Odo turned his eyes forward and hurried to join Eleanor.

He didn't mention what he'd seen.

Before night fell and they lost what little light remained, Eleanor and Odo made camp among the roots of the biggest oak they had ever seen. They didn't light a fire, eating stale bread and dry, cracked cheese rather than foraging along the path or hunting, although they heard rabbits and other night creatures stirring as dusk deepened. Neither wanted to draw unwelcome attention to their makeshift camp. As scary as the darkness was, they were more scared by the thought of what the light of a fire might lure out of it.

Biter placed himself at the entrance of a triangular space formed by two wall-like roots, each taller than Odo's head. The children lay awake for some time, marvelling at the butterflies and wondering if the other two locations on the map, Carcastel and Fangholt, were also abandoned. The Old Forest had put the humiliations of Sir Saskia far from their minds, but had provided new fears and uncertainties. Eleanor slept fitfully, reminded of the stories of smothering moths, but dreamed of nothing to cause her fear.

Odo, on the other hand, had a nightmare of being chased by a lizard so wizened and gnarled that it looked more like a tree. It came out of the hole in the end of the Hertech barrow, and when it opened its mouth, bats flew out of its gullet in a shrieking rush.

He woke with a gasp to sunlight filtering through the canopy. It was morning, and Eleanor was already setting out more bread and cheese. After their meal they made off once more, both footsore and hungry but pleased to be making such progress. There were no rotten knights or unfortunate refugees to impede their progress now. They were alone, on a road that wound slowly upwards through the heavily wooded foothills.

On the crest of a stony ridge after a long ascent, they paused for breath and to sip from their water skins, which they had filled that morning from a spring. The forest had thinned here, large trees finding it hard to take root in the stony soil, and the air seemed fresher, less stifling than it had deeper in the forest. They even glimpsed patches of blue through the canopy, and heard birds calling to each other from perches high above. The map suggested that they were near Carcastel, and as Odo stretched his aching legs he looked about him for any sign of habitation.

All he saw were thin-trunked trees and several granite outcrops that looked like a lot like trees themselves, or the prows of ancient ships that had been buried underground.

He idly traced their forms with his eyes, noting their unusual regularity in both spacing and height, and slowly came to the understanding that what he was seeing wasn't natural.

Eleanor had seen it too.

'Is this a stone circle?' she asked, walking towards it. 'Look, it is! We were sitting right inside it!'

Odo stared around him in amazement. It was true. The road went right through the middle of the ring of stones, but they hadn't noticed because trees obscured the pattern. If he and Eleanor hadn't stopped to rest in that very spot, they might never have noticed it.

'I wonder who carried the stones up here, and how,' he said, looking back down the steep path.

'It's like a crown,' said Eleanor, moving from stone to stone and touching each of them. The columns were age-worn but surprisingly free of moss and lichen. 'Or a cage,' she added, shivering at the thought. What kind of creature required heavy bars of stone to keep it contained?

One of the stones lay askew, and part of her wanted to stand it up again, just in case it was important. But the stone would need at least a dozen Odos and ropes and tackle to lift. It had to stay where it had fallen.

As at the barrow, they didn't linger. Fangholt was some hours' distance away and the edge of the forest was almost a full day beyond that. If they stopped anywhere too long, they would be forced to spend a third night in the forest, and neither of them wanted to do that.

But either the map was wrong or Eleanor had misjudged the distance, because the sun set long before they found any sign of Fangholt, and they were forced to call an unhappy halt in the middle of a broad valley densely populated by vastly tall redwoods. They had run out of bread and cheese, so Odo and Biter went off to look for game while Eleanor lit a fire to cook it, striking sparks from her flint and steel over a small pyramid of bone-dry kindling shaved from the inside of a fallen log.

As the flame caught, she heard a harsh cry echo through the redwoods. It wasn't an owl or a wolf – it sounded like a human shrieking, but much louder, lasting much longer than any ordinary throat could sustain. Piercing echoes filled the night, so it was impossible to exactly pinpoint its origin. Eleanor quickly added a handful of twigs to the fire, and then some larger ones, willing it to burn high.

A crashing sound came from behind her. She dropped the log she was about to add and spun around, drawing her urthkin blade.

'Just me,' cried Odo, hurrying out of the darkness to join her in the flickering circle of light cast by the fire. He held a dead rabbit in one hand, bloodstained Biter in the other. The cry had raised all the hairs down the back of his neck. He didn't want to be alone in the forest for one second longer than he had to be.

'What was that?'

'I don't know,' said Odo. 'Build up the fire. Biter, do you recognise that scream?'

'No,' said the sword. 'A faint memory nags at me . . . but no . . .'

They piled the wood Eleanor had scavenged on the flames, taking care not to stifle them in the process. Slowly the fire licked along the wood, taking hold and growing brighter. Odo kicked over a dead tree and dragged it on as well.

When the fire was burning as high as Odo's head, they both stood with their backs to it, peering out in different directions, wondering what could make such a terrifying noise.

Then the cry came again, ending with a drawn-out rasp that made Eleanor wince.

'Was that closer?' whispered Odo. 'It sounds closer.'

'Yes,' croaked Eleanor. Her throat was dry, but her hand gripping her sword-knife was wet with sweat.

The creature, whatever it was, shrieked a third time. It was definitely closing in.

'What do we do?' called Odo over the noise.

'We must adopt a defensive position and prepare for battle,' said Biter.

'I'll make us some torches,' said Eleanor, prodding the ends of two solid branches deeper into the fire. When they caught, she gave one to Odo and kept one for herself. Wielding the flaming sticks in their left hands, weapons in their right, they stood ready for whatever was to come.

The creature shrieked a fourth time, so loud Eleanor's ears rang with the sound of it.

Something thudded into the leaf litter just outside the circle of light cast by the fire. Odo and Eleanor spun to face it.

But it was only a branch.

With a crash, another branch fell nearby, torn from its tree and flung at them by forces unknown.

Or not flung at all, thought Eleanor. *Dropped.*

'It's above us!' she cried, as a shrieking, black-winged shape crashed into the fire, lighting up the night with an explosion of sparks.

The creature reared up over them, opening wrinkled leathery wings to reveal a coal-black hide, pockmarked and scarred. Odo's mind momentarily froze in shock: It was the monster from his dream, the giant lizard that spewed bats instead of fire! But how was that remotely possible?

Eleanor stabbed upwards with both torch and sword-knife. The creature opened its mouth, which was full of row after row of obsidian teeth, and snapped the torch in two. The weapon skittered off its hide with the sound of metal scraping stone.

The beast sucked in air through two dinner-plate-sized nostrils and exhaled from its mouth. Eleanor staggered back, enveloped in a hot, sooty wind that smelled like death.

'Back!' Odo cried.

Brandishing Biter, he put himself between the creature and his best friend, stabbing up at its exposed belly. It shrieked and flapped at him with its wings, knocking him sideways.

He rolled and came up with both feet firmly planted in the perfect defensive pose.

'Eleanor, get away from it!'

'Squire, behind us!'

Eleanor retreated, even as the thing struck. It bit into the earth where she'd stood, sending up a great gout of dirt. She gasped and backed away again, and it lunged further forward, only to be intercepted by Odo swinging Biter at its snout.

The blade scored a vivid line in the blackened hide, exposing softer bone-white flesh beneath. The beast hissed and reared back, trying the wing trick again, but this time Odo was ready. Holding Biter with two hands and bracing himself, he stabbed forward and pierced one wing right up to the cross-guard.

Biter was snatched away from him as the creature's wing whipped back from the unexpected sting, but the sword returned an instant later, blackened but not otherwise worse for the unexpected detour.

'Excellent stroke, Sir Odo,' Biter exclaimed. 'Once more!'

The creature hunched low like a cat, its spine arching high above the level of its head. As its mouth opened, Odo braced himself for battle.

Without taking its eyes off him, the beast took a bite out of the fire, chewed it and then drew in a deep breath.

'Watch out!' cried Eleanor. 'It's trying to burn you!'

Odo dropped beneath a rush of smoky air that scattered

dozens of hot embers over him. He rolled to put them out, got up and retreated again.

The two children crouched behind the biggest tree trunk they could find, watching as the monster ate what remained of their fire.

'𝕿𝖍𝖎𝖘 𝖎𝖘 𝖒𝖔𝖘𝖙 𝖚𝖓𝖚𝖘𝖚𝖆𝖑 𝖇𝖊𝖍𝖆𝖛𝖎𝖔𝖚𝖗,' Biter said.

'What is it?' gasped Odo.

'I think . . .' said Eleanor, staring in frightened wonder at the creature's black tail, which slithered and twitched behind it like a maddened snake, 'I think it's a dragon!'

'𝕹𝖔𝖓𝖘𝖊𝖓𝖘𝖊,' said Biter. '𝕯𝖗𝖆𝖌𝖔𝖓𝖘 𝖆𝖗𝖊 𝖈𝖔𝖓𝖘𝖎𝖉𝖊𝖗𝖆𝖇𝖑𝖞 𝖑𝖆𝖗𝖌𝖊𝖗.'

'And why is it eating our *fire*?' Odo asked.

'I don't know,' snapped Eleanor. The creature had eaten almost all the fire. The only light they had now came from scattered embers. 'Maybe it's young . . . or sick. Let's just be grateful it doesn't have any fire of its own. Watch out, here it comes again!'

'𝖂𝖎𝖙𝖍𝖉𝖗𝖆𝖜!'

They scrambled in opposite directions as the creature rose up on its hind legs and readied itself for another blast.

Before it could unleash the contents of its fiery crop, the maybe-dragon froze and cocked its head, listening.

Odo and Eleanor heard it too: an enquiring shriek from elsewhere in the forest.

'Another one?' Eleanor said, aghast.

Odo shushed her. For the moment the creature wasn't

paying them any attention. The distant shriek came again, accompanied by a flash of yellow light from far off through the trees.

Fire.

The creature tensed. Smoke leaked out of its nostrils. Suddenly it was moving, leaping up into the nearest redwood and clinging to the bark with its powerful claws. It tensed into a ball of muscle, then jumped to the next tree along, using its wings to glide. When the shriek sounded a third time, the dragon-creature was gone, the sound of its crashing through branches echoing in its wake.

Eleanor sagged back onto the ground, breathless with relief. She had expected to be eaten at any moment, and Odo with her. Somehow they had survived.

'We can't stay here,' said Odo. 'We have to move before it leads the other one here. What if it's even bigger?'

'𝔚𝔢 𝔰𝔥𝔞𝔩𝔩 𝔣𝔦𝔤𝔥𝔱 𝔞𝔫𝔡 𝔡𝔢𝔣𝔢𝔞𝔱 𝔦𝔱,' said Biter.

'Be quiet, Biter,' ordered Odo. 'Quick. Get our stuff.'

His voice was shaky, but Eleanor found she couldn't talk at all. Her legs were quivering as well. She was grateful that for once Odo was taking charge. Fighting people didn't frighten her, but monsters, it turned out, were very scary indeed. Though, Eleanor told herself, this was probably just because she hadn't fought any. With practice, she was sure she'd get used to it. Wouldn't she?

Together they rushed around the camp, gathering their

scattered belongings, proceeding by feel as well as the occasional lingering ember.

It was so dark they could barely see the road.

'Which way?' asked Eleanor doubtfully. 'I've got turned around.'

'Ah, I think . . . no . . .' muttered Odo. He looked up, trying to find the moon or some familiar stars. 'Let's just pick a direction and find a clearing –'

'Shhh!' warned Eleanor. 'Something's coming!'

There was a sly crunching sound coming through the forest towards them, the sound of careful footfalls among the debris of the forest floor. They crouched down next to a tree, weapons ready.

'I know you're there,' called a voice out of the darkness. 'But I can't see you. Come out. You're safe now.'

Odo wished he could see Eleanor's face. The voice sounded like a woman's, but dragons could talk (or so the stories said). Who was to say that this wasn't the other creature they had heard? A fully grown wily dragon.

'The bannoch is gone,' the voice continued. 'My name is Wenneth, and I assure you that I mean you no harm. There are two of you, I believe. I can smell you . . . Ah, yes.'

The source of the crunching noise, which had been coming closer, now stopped.

'Perhaps this will shed light on our situation.'

Cool toadstool light flared from the mouth of a curled brass horn held by a woman who appeared out of the darkness, standing just three yards away. She had long grey hair and wore a black robe cinched around her waist by a red cord. Her face was pinched, her skin oddly glassy-looking, and although she was facing Eleanor and Odo, she wasn't looking at them. Her eyelids were sunken hollows fused shut by scar tissue.

The woman called Wenneth was blind.

'Can you see me now?'

'Yes,' said Odo. Lying didn't seem an option.

'Are you hurt? I can smell blood, but it doesn't seem to be human.'

'We killed a rabbit, and that thing . . . whatever it was . . . I cut it, but it didn't bleed.'

'No, it wouldn't. Come with me to the chapel and I will tell you about it.'

'The chapel?' Eleanor asked.

'Yes. In Fangholt. That's where I live. I don't think the bannoch will return, but if it does we will be safe there.'

'What was it? The . . . the *bannoch*?'

'I will explain, I promise.' Wenneth beckoned to them. 'Come, come. You haven't cooked that rabbit, which means you have not eaten and will be hungry. I have food. And I promise I won't eat you, if that is why you hesitate. I am not a wicked witch from some silly story.'

With that she smiled, but the expression was stiff. Eleanor

realised then that more than her eyes were burned. Her entire face was a mask of scar tissue.

A monster in the heart of an Old Forest . . . a blind, burned woman who lived in a chapel . . . This didn't seem like the kind of story that had a happy ending.

But they didn't really have a choice.

Eleanor looked at Odo. If she had to fight another monster, she was ready. That was what knights-in-training did! As Odo was the one with the magic sword though, it was up to him to make the decision to advance or retreat.

He nodded.

They stood up and came forward one step.

'What are your names?' asked Wenneth.

'Sir Odo of Lenburh.'

'Squire Eleanor.'

'A knight-errant, eh? Who was your sponsor?'

'My sponsor?' asked Odo.

'Who knighted you? I know many knights, but the only knight of Lenburh I know of is Sir Halfdan.'

'Uh, my sword knighted me,' said Odo, sensing that in the strangeness of the night there was no point in keeping secrets. 'His name is Hildebrand Shining Foebiter. We call him Biter.'

'That sounds irregular, if not entirely without precedent,' the burned woman said. 'But why does your sword not show me the proper respect?'

'I'm sorry, good mother,' Biter replied in a surprisingly meek tone. 'I ought to have greeted you sooner.'

Odo shot Eleanor a mystified glance.

'Do you know each other?' he asked as Wenneth turned and led them through the forest, the light from the brass horn guiding their feet. Wenneth herself needed no guidance. Eleanor wondered if she could smell the way.

'I do not know your particular sword,' the woman said. 'But I know his kind and can tell when I'm in such company.'

She sniffed the night air.

'An old sword, and damaged. And yet . . . washed clean . . .'

Surprise upon surprise.

'You can tell that just by smelling him?' asked Eleanor in amazement.

'It's a skill anyone can learn.' Wenneth's voice took a solemn edge. 'If you're willing to pay the price.'

'What do you mean by "washed clean"?' asked Odo.

'Scoured, laved, baptised. When a newly forged sword is still hot, it is quenched in water. This hardens the metal. Some swords are reforged and made anew, but not, I think, in this case. This sword has a story. Do you know it?'

'No,' said Eleanor. 'But we'd like to.'

'What does the sword have to say for himself?'

'I do not remember, good mother.'

'Well, there's something odd about you, something oddly familiar . . . We shall discuss this later. Let's be quiet for a moment in case the bannoch is nearby. We are passing the decoy fire, which I lit to draw it away from you.'

The light from the horn dimmed slightly as they crossed an ashen clearing where a fire had recently raged. The air above it was still warm. If Wenneth had lit the fire deliberately to distract the creature that had attacked them, Odo speculated, then maybe she had also made the other shrieking sound – perhaps by blowing through the horn, assuming it was more than just a magical light-bringer. He was beginning to understand that this was, if not a usual occurrence, then at least an anticipated one.

A dozen paces beyond the ashy clearing they came to a series of ragged stone walls belonging to a ruined settlement, charred black by ancient fire. Wenneth led them unerringly among the ruins to the sole surviving building, a steep-roofed chapel with an empty bell tower and boarded-up windows, granting them access through a heavy iron door. When it boomed shut behind them, she hung the horn on a hook by the door and clapped her hands once.

A dozen glowing stones scattered through the chapel sprang into life, casting irregular patches of cool white light across an incredible jumble of oddments, too plentiful to catalogue in a single glance. At the same time, Eleanor felt the flagstones beneath her feet grow warm.

Wenneth crooked a finger. The children followed her through paths and tunnels formed by the leaning piles, deeper into the chapel's heart. Seeing her lightly touch things as she went by, Eleanor understood that the arrangement was designed for someone who could not see. Open spaces were lost on someone whose preference was to navigate at arm's reach.

'Here. Welcome.' Wenneth ushered them into the inner room in which she clearly spent most of her time. There was no chimney, but there was something that looked very much like a stove, and there was food to cook on it. 'Sit while I make you something hot.'

Wenneth clapped her gnarled hands again, and a scattering of stones in the stove began to glow a deep red.

Odo lowered himself into a chair, while Eleanor perched on a spindly stool.

'You really live here?' she asked, staring around her at a space filled with shelves and boxes out of which spilled everything from gold chains to rotting celery stalks. The low light gleamed off surfaces that might have been spun glass, but might equally have been something alive, once. The cavelike space reminded Eleanor of her father's apothecary, which was equally full of surprising things, although much better organised.

'Yes, I live here.' Wenneth put a kettle on the stove and cut some onions, moving swiftly and surely despite her lack of sight. 'I am a monk of the Order of Adloma. We live in the great old forests, and to us falls the care of the bannoch.

One day a year, at Addlemas, we meet to perform a census and to elect new members, if needed. Otherwise, we are alone with our charges, the bannoch.'

'What is a bannoch?' Odo asked.

'A bannoch is what is left of a dragon when it has stopped being a dragon.'

'I don't understand,' said Eleanor.

'Few do. Much has been forgotten. Some dragons don't die, you see. They may lose their firestarters and their iron hides, and their minds with them, but what remains is still very dangerous. The Order of Adloma exists to keep them contained. You saw the barrow at Hertech, yes? And the stone circle at Carcastel?'

Eleanor and Odo nodded, then answered aloud when they remembered that she couldn't see them nodding.

'Yes, yes, we saw them.'

'They are attempts by my predecessors to put bannoch to rest. A grave and a jail . . . neither worked. I let my current charge roam freely these days. There are wards around the forest, so it cannot escape completely. I am ready to intervene if anyone is so foolish as to light a fire in the Old Forest.'

She turned to face them, her scarred face very stern.

'Bannoch are drawn to fire like salmon to rivers. What you did was a very dangerous thing.'

'We, uh, didn't know.' Odo shifted uncomfortably in the falling-down chair. If the bannoch was a decrepit dragon, he hated to imagine a fighting-fit one, like Quenwulf. 'No one ever told us.'

'And there was no warning sign,' said Eleanor.

'Perhaps I should erect one.' Wenneth shrugged. 'In days past, the villagers outside the forest would warn travellers. But Time marches on forgetful feet, as they say.'

Odo wondered who said that. He had never heard the expression before. Thanks to her scars, it was hard to tell how old Wenneth was.

'And all your . . . things?' asked Eleanor, looking around at the piles of candlesticks, shoes, books, crockery, tools, and much, much more. 'Did you find it all in the ruins?'

'Some. Fangholt was once a thriving town, before the bannoch in its dragon life burned it. Some are gifts from people we have helped. The collection is passed down from monk to monk, each adding something in their turn.'

'Can I have a look around?'

'You may look as you wish, but please be careful. There are items in here that are very old, and some are dangerous.'

Eleanor took her up on the offer. Gingerly touching one of the smaller glowing stones, she found it cool to the touch, so picked it up and used it to properly illuminate what she found. There was no obvious order to the collection. One stack contained many sheets of vellum, mostly scraped clean of whatever had been written on them; the next held lots of small wooden boxes lined with velvet – all the ones Eleanor opened were empty. Then she opened a large bag and found it full of finely made but individually different silver spoons, all jumbled together.

While Eleanor indulged her curiosity, Odo asked the questions foremost in his mind.

'You said Biter seemed familiar to you. Do you know something about him?'

'Perhaps. Tell me how you found him, and we will see what we will see.'

Odo recounted the tale of Dragonfoot Hole and his unexpected knighting in the mud. He described the unusual nick in Biter's edge, and how Biter himself had no memory of how he had received it, or how he had ended up in the river. Wenneth questioned the sword on this matter too, and instead of being defensive, Biter answered all her questions respectfully, balancing on his tip on a stack of old books, emerald swivelling to follow her every movement.

'A sword at the bottom of a river,' she mused when they had finished. 'That explains why you smell so clean, Biter. But were you put there deliberately or by accident? That is the question.'

The three of them mused about this while Eleanor wandered deeper into the monk's collection. There were tin helmets in stacks, glass jars full of ivory buttons, walking sticks with knobs of crystal, maps of countries she had never heard of. She had a sense of mining deep into the past, but a past that made no sense. How long had the chapel been here? How many monks had tended it and its strange collection?

A delicious scent filled the chapel as Wenneth stirred a mixture of onions, mushrooms and potatoes in a heavy iron skillet over stones as red as coals. The smell made Odo's stomach ache, in a good way.

'There used to be a smithy here, long ago,' she said as she cooked. 'Only the wood from the oldest trees of an ancient forest such as this one can forge an enchanted sword, you see, when it is made into charcoal and ignited by a . . . lit in a certain way. When the smithy burned, this chapel was built on the ruins. If Biter was forged here, that might explain why he seems familiar to me.'

'I have never been here, good mother,' said Biter. 'My forge was in the forest of Eathrylden. I remember that clearly.'

'Well, there must be another explanation. Clearly we haven't met, if you were underwater for so long. I am old, but not that old.' She smiled forgivingly. 'There is another enchanted sword here, in the chapel. There might be a connection between them. I will find it for you later, Odo, after you have eaten. You must be famished.'

Eleanor's ears pricked up, not at the mention of food, but at the notion of another sword. So far she hadn't seen any swords during her exploration of the chapel, but that only encouraged her to look harder. She squeezed past a bookcase full of carved chalkstone animals and found herself in a section of the collection that had not been disturbed for decades, full of cobwebs and dead flies. Her glow-stone cast light into darkened corners, sending things with black legs scuttling for cover and illuminating pieces of mismatched armour in a pile, a mound of rusty axe heads next to a stand of splintered axe handles, what looked like an ancient musical instrument with numerous pipes in complicated knots and finger holes too far apart for a human hand . . . and, at the very end of the cramped space, a large, half-melted anvil.

Stuck into the anvil, so deep it had to go into the oak-heart block of wood beneath it, there was a sword.

Eleanor slipped through a gap between the musical instrument and the wall to get a better look. The sword's hilt and sharkskin grip were very similar to Biter's, but where he had a large emerald in his pommel, this sword sported an equally large ruby. There was no gleam to the gem, as it was buried under a thick layer of dust, and the blade looked dull.

It had to be the one Wenneth was talking about.

Without thinking, Eleanor reached out to take the sword by the hilt and tried to pull it from the partially melted anvil. It shifted an inch, but then stuck, so she pulled harder, and then harder still. The anvil rocked on its oaken base, making the junk around it rattle. Eleanor held her breath, praying the piles wouldn't collapse on her. Then she put a foot against the anvil for leverage and pulled one last time.

With the low, awful shriek of metal upon metal, the sword slid free of its iron prison.

Eleanor expected it to cry out, just as Biter had.

She expected her life to change immediately, to feel glory.

Instead, the sword hung heavy and silent in Eleanor's hands.

It was an ordinary sort of sword after all.

She set the point on the hole in the anvil and prepared to put it back, and at that moment the sword kicked like a rebellious cat and leaped away. Eleanor held on tightly, even as a shower of dust rained down around her.

'Why am I disturbed?' moaned the sword, sounding very much like an agonised, ancient woman. 'Who has woken me from my rest?'

'Eleanor?' called Odo. 'Is that you?'

'What are you doing back there, dear?' asked Wenneth.

'My name is Eleanor,' she told the sword. 'I want to be a knight. A true knight.'

'Then you have made a terrible mistake,' groaned the sword. 'You will never be a true knight, for I am cursed. I am death to all who hold me!'

TWENTY-FIVE

Eleanor gasped. She knew about curses. One famous knight had been cursed to break all the promises he ever made, which didn't sound so bad until his queen executed him for refusing to swear allegiance to her. Another knight thought she had escaped a curse to die on the Battlefield of Merscas, only to be murdered during an argument one year later in exactly that spot. No one even dared mention the Knight with the Cursed Name for fear they would suffer the same fate. Curses were not to be taken lightly, and cursed swords doubly so.

But when she tried to put the sword back in the anvil, the wound had healed itself. The melted iron was now smooth and unblemished. So she dropped the sword, but now instead of trying to get away from her, it sprang back into her hand.

'You have claimed me now,' said the sword menacingly. 'And I shall be your doom.'

With a rattle and a crash, Odo forced his way into the space behind her, Biter in his hand.

'What's wrong?' Odo asked. 'Who's saying such terrible things?'

'It is I, Reynfrida Sharp-point Flamecutter,' said the sword. 'And if the truth is terrible to you, so be it.'

Shedding a cloud of dust and cobwebs, the sword swung Eleanor around as though to strike at Odo.

'No!' Eleanor cried, pulling the blade back with all her strength, as she had seen Odo do many times. 'He's my friend! You can't hurt him!'

'I hurt all who know me. That is my nature. I am cursed to cause nothing but despair. You should have left me sleeping. I will be the ruin of you all!'

Odo fell back, Biter quivering in his grasp. Odo frowned – if even Biter was afraid of this cursed sword, they were doomed indeed.

But when Biter spoke, he sounded excited and amazed, not afraid.

'Runnel?'

Eleanor felt the cursed sword twitch.

'I am not Runnel. I am Reynfrida Sharp-point Flamecutter!'

Behind Odo, Wenneth pressed her way through a collection of hanging fabrics that were suspended from the ceiling on an ancient rope.

'The Sorrowful Sword!' she exclaimed. 'Child, what have you done?'

Eleanor stared from her to the sword, to Biter, to Odo,

and back again. She had been impulsive, and now she was cursed to die!

'I found a sword,' she managed to choke out. 'I just wanted to try it . . .'

'I understand,' said Odo. He knew it was far more than that, but he didn't want to say so in front of Wenneth.

'𝔦 𝔞𝔪 𝔡𝔢𝔞𝔱𝔥 𝔱𝔬 𝔪𝔶 𝔴𝔦𝔢𝔩𝔡𝔢𝔯,' muttered Eleanor's sword. She made a halfhearted stab at Odo, but was easily pulled back by Eleanor.

'Stop that!'

Biter pulled Odo's arm forward as Eleanor pulled back, and the tips of the swords met, just for a moment.

'𝔎𝔲𝔫𝔫𝔢𝔩? 𝔇𝔬𝔫'𝔱 𝔶𝔬𝔲 𝔯𝔢𝔠𝔬𝔤𝔫𝔦𝔰𝔢 𝔪𝔢?' asked Biter plaintively. '𝔦𝔱 𝔦𝔰 𝔦, 𝔥𝔦𝔩𝔡𝔢𝔟𝔯𝔞𝔫𝔡 𝔰𝔥𝔦𝔫𝔦𝔫𝔤 𝔣𝔬𝔢𝔟𝔦𝔱𝔢𝔯.'

'𝔶𝔬𝔲 𝔠𝔞𝔫𝔫𝔬𝔱 𝔟𝔢,' the sword moaned. '𝔐𝔶 𝔟𝔯𝔬𝔱𝔥𝔢𝔯 𝔦𝔰 𝔩𝔬𝔫𝔤 𝔡𝔢𝔞𝔡, 𝔞𝔫𝔡 𝔦 𝔞𝔪 𝔠𝔲𝔯𝔰𝔢𝔡. 𝔞𝔩𝔩 𝔫𝔢𝔞𝔯 𝔪𝔢 𝔰𝔥𝔞𝔩𝔩 𝔰𝔲𝔣𝔣𝔢𝔯 𝔞𝔫𝔡 𝔡𝔢𝔰𝔭𝔞𝔦𝔯.'

Odo stared at Biter in astonishment. 'You have a sister?'

'𝔦 𝔡𝔦𝔡 . . . 𝔦 𝔡𝔬,' said Biter. '𝔦𝔫 𝔢𝔞𝔱𝔥𝔯𝔶𝔩𝔡𝔢𝔫 𝔴𝔢 𝔴𝔢𝔯𝔢 𝔣𝔬𝔯𝔤𝔢𝔡 𝔣𝔯𝔬𝔪 𝔱𝔥𝔢 𝔰𝔞𝔪𝔢 𝔬𝔯𝔢 𝔞𝔫𝔡 𝔦𝔫 𝔱𝔥𝔢 𝔰𝔞𝔪𝔢 𝔣𝔦𝔯𝔢, 𝔞𝔫𝔡 𝔢𝔫𝔠𝔥𝔞𝔫𝔱𝔢𝔡 𝔟𝔶 𝔱𝔥𝔢 𝔰𝔞𝔪𝔢 𝔱𝔯𝔲𝔢 𝔰𝔪𝔦𝔱𝔥. 𝔎𝔲𝔫𝔫𝔢𝔩, 𝔞𝔰 𝔥𝔢 𝔣𝔬𝔫𝔡𝔩𝔶 𝔠𝔞𝔩𝔩𝔢𝔡 𝔥𝔢𝔯, 𝔴𝔞𝔰 𝔱𝔥𝔢 𝔣𝔦𝔯𝔰𝔱 𝔰𝔴𝔬𝔯𝔡 𝔥𝔢 𝔪𝔞𝔡𝔢, 𝔦 𝔥𝔦𝔰 𝔩𝔞𝔰𝔱. 𝔰𝔢𝔳𝔢𝔫𝔱𝔶 𝔶𝔢𝔞𝔯𝔰 𝔡𝔦𝔳𝔦𝔡𝔢 𝔲𝔰. 𝔴𝔢 𝔥𝔞𝔳𝔢 𝔫𝔬𝔱 . . . 𝔱𝔥𝔞𝔱 𝔦𝔰, 𝔦 𝔥𝔞𝔡 𝔫𝔬𝔱 𝔱𝔥𝔬𝔲𝔤𝔥𝔱 𝔱𝔬 𝔴𝔬𝔫𝔡𝔢𝔯 𝔴𝔥𝔞𝔱 𝔰𝔥𝔢 𝔪𝔞𝔡𝔢 𝔬𝔣 𝔪𝔶 𝔡𝔦𝔰𝔞𝔭𝔭𝔢𝔞𝔯𝔞𝔫𝔠𝔢 . . .'

The pain in Biter's voice was awful to hear. Odo didn't know what to say. How did one offer reassurance to a sword that was hundreds of years old and had spent half its life under a river?

'We will take the sword into the chapel proper,' said Wenneth to Eleanor. 'You will behave there, won't you, Reynfrida?'

'𝕴𝔱 𝔦𝔰 𝔞 𝔥𝔞𝔩𝔩𝔬𝔴𝔢𝔡 𝔭𝔩𝔞𝔠𝔢,' said Reynfrida. '𝕴𝔱 𝔰𝔬𝔬𝔱𝔥𝔢𝔰 𝔪𝔶 𝔠𝔲𝔯𝔰𝔢. 𝕱𝔬𝔯 𝔞 𝔱𝔦𝔪𝔢.'

Eleanor dragged the sword down and backed past the anvil and then through an arched doorway Wenneth indicated. Odo and Biter followed cautiously, with Wenneth behind.

The room beyond was not full of strange bits and bobs. It had a much higher arched ceiling, with ancient black beams that were adorned with hundreds of small bronze ornaments, designs that neither Odo nor Eleanor recognised. The floor was tiled with blue stones the colour of a summer sky, and at one end there was a rectangular pool of shallow water that glittered as if many coins or even gems lay beneath the surface.

A high window of clear glass allowed the dawn light in, diminishing the effect of the glowing stones, but already clearly illuminating the room.

It was a very restful place.

The sword in Eleanor's hand became still as she entered the chapel, and she had to hold it up. The mysteries of the glittering pool called to her, and when she went to look in she was surprised to find six small slots in its tiled edge, each deep enough to take a sword. Kneeling, she slid Runnel into one, the sword quivering as it stood upright.

Odo followed her and also knelt, setting Biter into the stone scabbard next to his sister sword.

The resemblance to Biter was even more pronounced now that they were next to each other, bathed in the swathe of light from the high window.

'She has been here for a hundred and sixty-seven years,' said Wenneth, gesturing towards Eleanor's sword. 'The anvil is much older, being all that remains of the smithy that once stood in this place. One stormy eve, the story goes, a troubled knight took shelter here, but found no peace. All night he raved, driving himself deeper and deeper into madness. When the monk at that time tried to soothe him, he struck down my forebear and killed him. In a fit of anguish, the knight then plunged his sword into the heart of the anvil, swearing never to wield it again. He rode off at dawn, and was later killed ignobly, in a tavern brawl.'

'𝔘𝔫𝔞𝔯𝔪𝔢𝔡 𝔞𝔫𝔡 𝔩𝔞𝔠𝔨𝔦𝔫𝔤 𝔞𝔩𝔩 𝔴𝔦𝔰𝔡𝔬𝔪,' said the knight's abandoned sword in as mournful a voice as any Eleanor had ever heard. '𝔍 𝔰𝔥𝔬𝔲𝔩𝔡 𝔥𝔞𝔳𝔢 𝔟𝔢𝔢𝔫 𝔞𝔱 𝔥𝔦𝔰 𝔰𝔦𝔡𝔢, 𝔟𝔲𝔱 𝔥𝔦𝔰 𝔪𝔞𝔡𝔫𝔢𝔰𝔰 𝔴𝔞𝔰 𝔲𝔭𝔬𝔫 𝔥𝔦𝔪. 𝔄𝔱 𝔱𝔥𝔢 𝔢𝔫𝔡, 𝔥𝔢 𝔟𝔩𝔞𝔪𝔢𝔡 𝔪𝔢 𝔣𝔬𝔯 . . . 𝔢𝔳𝔢𝔯𝔶𝔱𝔥𝔦𝔫𝔤, 𝔦𝔱 𝔰𝔢𝔢𝔪𝔢𝔡. 𝔍 𝔠𝔬𝔲𝔩𝔡 𝔫𝔬𝔱 𝔲𝔫𝔡𝔢𝔯𝔰𝔱𝔞𝔫𝔡. 𝔄𝔩𝔩 𝔍 𝔨𝔫𝔬𝔴 𝔦𝔰 𝔱𝔥𝔞𝔱 𝔍 𝔣𝔞𝔦𝔩𝔢𝔡 𝔥𝔦𝔪.'

'The story of the Sorrowful Sword does not end there,' Wenneth said. 'Three times has it been drawn from the anvil by knights seeking an enchanted blade. Those knights, all three of them, met unhappy ends, though none so bad a death as the first. Afterwards, each time, the sword returned to the anvil of its own accord, knowing no other course to take.'

'I'm sorry,' Eleanor said. 'I wish I had never touched it.'

'How do you know all this?' Odo asked Wenneth.

'On stormy knights, it talks in its sleep.'

'Is this true, Runnel?' asked Biter. 'You are cursed?'

'All who wield me will die,' said the sword bitterly.

'But wait,' said Odo. 'Don't knights usually die? I mean, they fight a lot, and often come up against monsters like dragons. I mean, four dead knights in a row can't be that unusual . . .'

He trailed off as the ruby flashed at him.

'Do you doubt my curse?'

'Well, yes. Couldn't you just be unlucky rather than cursed?'

'Sir Hollis told me I was cursed,' she said. 'He called me an evil blade and said I was his master, not the other way around.'

'Yes, but he was mad – Hey, you said so yourself!' he added as Runnel shivered in the floor slot, as if preparing to leap up and strike.

'Sir Odo speaks wisdom,' said Wenneth in a calming voice. 'Luck can be tested . . . and curses broken.'

Hope stirred in Eleanor's eyes at the suggestion.

'Yes! We could help you, Runnel.'

'None can help me,' moaned the sword. 'Anyone who

bears me will die because of me. Sir Treddian boiled in a volcanic lake, Sir Faline fell in the first moments of the battle for the causeway at Thradbyrn –'

'I don't believe they died because of a curse,' interrupted Eleanor, though in truth there was more than a small part of her that thought they might have. 'But even if it is true, like Wenneth said, curses can be broken.'

'Indeed,' added Biter eagerly. 'It is well known that high deeds and brave action may break any kind of ill-wishing.'

'Yes, see?' said Eleanor. 'And we can certainly offer you high deeds. We're on a quest, Sir Odo, Biter and me. Come with us and we'll prove to you that you're not cursed or unlucky or whatever.'

'Nothing may end my curse but my destruction,' said Runnel.

'You don't know that,' protested Eleanor.

'It is all I desire,' said Runnel. 'One day, a dragon will come, and my curse and I will die together in its fiery breath. You should never have woken me, Eleanor, for you merely prolong my doom and ensure your own!'

'Would you at least agree to not actively try to kill me?' asked Eleanor. 'I mean, don't do anything on purpose against me?'

'I mean you no ill will,' said Runnel. 'By choice, I would stay asleep.'

'Sleep is full of eels,' said Biter. 'I do not recommend it.'

'Will you just promise not to actively help this curse of

yours along, whether it's real or not?' said Eleanor, who had been thinking hard. 'If you do that, perhaps we can give you what you say you want.'

'What do you mean, child?' asked Runnel.

'We are travelling north,' said Eleanor. 'To slay the dragon who has boiled the river dry and is going to kill everyone who depends on it.'

'Which dragon?' Runnel asked.

'Quenwulf,' said Eleanor.

Runnel jerked out of her slot with a suddenness that made Eleanor jump.

'Quenwulf! The great dragon whose fire burns hotter than any other! You have my promise. I shall do all I can to resist, if only you take me to the dragon to end my curse forever!'

TWENTY-SIX

Wenneth insisted they eat the meal she had made for them before they could even think about leaving, and then while they ate she convinced them that resting afterwards would be wise too. Dragons could wait, she said, be they great or old. Waiting was something dragons were very good at, as all the stories told.

They slept on the warm flagstones, leaving the swords to talk to each other in the chapel. Or at least Odo hoped they were talking – he knew well that not all brothers and sisters got on. It was hard to keep track in his own family who was whose best friend or worst enemy. Sometimes they were both simultaneously.

When Eleanor and Odo woke, the sun was high. They found their packs supplemented with numerous small items culled from Wenneth's collection, such as old but still valuable coins similar to the silver pennies they knew, some ancient playing cards, two glow-stones, and, in Eleanor's case, a scabbard of just the right dimensions for Runnel. Runnel was almost exactly the same size as Biter, very large for Eleanor. She would have to wield her two-handed, unless the sword could be convinced to help.

When they were ready to go, Odo and Eleanor went to the chapel and took up their swords.

All morning Eleanor had grappled silently with her situation, sleeping only in fits and starts, her mind too active. Part of her fizzed with excitement: Now she had a proper sword at long last, and a magical one to boot. That excited part was balanced by another, full of dread, because the sword claimed to be cursed. But the excitement won out, even if only by a little, because Eleanor now thought she was finally about to get her lifelong desire.

'Three knights drew you out of the anvil before I came along,' she said to Runnel. 'Does that mean only a knight could take you from it? So shouldn't I be made a knight, like Odo?'

'Of course not!' Runnel snapped. 'You must earn that privilege. I do not go around dubbing the first person who pulls me out of a river . . . unlike some swords I could mention.'

'There was blood involved,' Biter defended himself. 'I had to. The ancient laws are quite specific –'

'You and your ancient laws, little brother!' scoffed Runnel. But at least it seemed from these words she accepted Biter as her brother, just as she had agreed to help Eleanor in order to work against her curse.

'You both have the hearts of knights,' said Wenneth, farewelling the children outside her strange abode. Her sightless face seemed no impediment to taking their measure. 'I knew it the moment I met you. Most travellers run from the bannoch, but you stood up to it. That took great courage.'

'It's not much good having the heart of a knight if you can't call yourself one,' muttered Eleanor as they waved goodbye and began to walk along the path that would lead them back to the road. It was easy to see in the daylight.

'Hmmph!' said Runnel. 'You, girl, are on a knight's quest with a knight's sword. Time will tell if you really have the heart of a knight too. If it is so, I am sure you will be knighted.'

'When we slay the beast, no one will doubt it,' said Eleanor.

'My knight and I will slay the beast,' said Biter. 'Sir Odo has the greater experience, and I am the superior sword.'

'Superior?' scoffed Runnel. 'I saw that nick in your side, little brother. And besides, rusting at the bottom of a river doesn't count as experience . . .'

Eleanor rolled her eyes. It was going to be a long trip if the swords were going to bicker the entire way.

'At least none of my knights went mad,' grumbled Biter. 'And I don't rust –'

'Enough!' snapped Odo. 'Quiet, both of you.'

The swords settled into moody silence, but only for a while. When they reached the road and the going got easier, Biter spoke again.

'I have been training Sir Odo in the proper skills and duties of knighthood. You should do the same for Eleanor. She will of course remain Sir Odo's squire, but it would be wise to prepare her for any eventuality.'

'What's the point of being trained by a sword who thinks I'm going to die?' Eleanor asked. 'Can't you train me, Biter?'

'I cannot see what anyone can accomplish while travelling,' objected Runnel. 'We need a training field, an armoury, pells to strike, a quintain to joust against –'

'Indeed we do not!' exclaimed Biter. 'Everything begins with basic principles and we work up from there.'

'A proper knight cannot be taught upon the road!'

'They most certainly can!'

'We don't need to know everything,' interrupted Odo. 'Just enough to kill a dragon.'

'So little?' asked Runnel sarcastically. 'Many a knight has faced dragons armed with all the knowledge a knight should possess, and still died.'

'At least you could tell us what not to do,' Eleanor said. 'That would help. And you promised you would help by not hurrying the curse along.'

'Yeeees,' Runnel conceded. 'Very well. You speak of principles, little brother? I suppose you have taught

227

your knight the Eight Proper Stances and the Feints of Fæstenunga?'

'We have begun,' said Biter cautiously.

Odo frowned. The sword had never even mentioned the Feints of Fæstenunga.

'I've learned them too,' said Eleanor eagerly. 'The Proper Stances anyway. I followed whatever Odo did.'

'Forget them!' instructed Runnel. 'They are foolish proscriptions unsuited to actual battle. I will teach you real fighting.'

'Bah!' said Biter. 'The principles are sound. Where else can you begin but there?'

'As eldest, I will instruct you,' said Runnel. 'Look for a suitable clearing upon the road and we will begin.'

The woods soon rang with the sound of metal on metal, accompanied by barked instructions and grunts of effort from the student duellers. Eleanor forgot her concerns and concentrated on enjoying the lessons, which were very different from Biter's. Where he was strict about traditional forms, ensuring Odo knew the proper names for every stance and movement, it soon became clear that Runnel was entirely more practical. 'Strike at the Knee with Intent to Maim' meant exactly what it said.

Practice slowed their progress through the forest somewhat, and they wore out faster than they otherwise would have, but no one suggested taking a break. It was much more enjoyable to learn swordplay against an opponent, even one much bigger in Eleanor's case, or one much quicker in Odo's. What Eleanor lacked when it came to the force of her blows she more than made up for by dodging or sneaking past Odo's guard, which alternately frustrated and delighted him. He liked seeing his friend enjoying herself again, even if it meant being the object of frequent jabs and blocks. Fighting her was very different than sparring with shadows and imaginary fiends.

Eleanor soon learned that Odo was a worthy opponent in his own right. What he lacked in speed he more than made up for in strength, and he had the added advantage of some practical experience with a sword as well. Runnel seemed pleased with her progress, and suggested that if she could curb her automatic urge to strike first and think later, fighting with the sword in one hand and her urthkin knife in the other would make her a fearsome enemy.

Biter, however, grumbled that what Runnel was teaching her was worthy of a common soldier but not a knight.

'Would you have her spit in Sir Odo's eye next, or throw dirt in his face?'

'Yes, if it would help her survive. Remember this, Eleanor, along with the other tips I taught you, in case you need them one day.'

'But a knight never seeks victory at cost to his honour,' Biter said.

'A knight seeks victory at all costs, if that's the way she can do the greatest good.' Runnel's ruby flashed. 'That is the only rule you need to remember. Now, Eleanor, again – the lunge followed by the block athwart my cross-guard. I will show you how to kick with the side of your boot to trip your opponent off balance . . .'

The training was hard, and the way ahead long, but the time passed quickly, and Eleanor and Odo were surprised when the green shade of the forest gave way to direct sunlight. Behind them was a wall of ancient trees stretching to their left and right. Ahead a steep-sided canyon lay directly across their path. They had ascended much higher than they realised, to the very top of the foothills. Beyond the canyon lay mountains, partly visible behind a thick column of blue smoke, the source of which lay just out of sight.

Despite the late afternoon sun, Odo felt a sudden chill.

The smoke had to come from a dragon's lair.

TWENTY-SEVEN

'We'll have to be more careful from here on,' said Eleanor. She too felt daunted by the sudden imminence of their destination. 'We don't know that it's Quenwolf – but it could be. If the dragon sees us coming, she could fly over and burn us in a moment.'

Odo shielded his eyes against the setting sun with his free hand and studied the canyon, the mountains beyond and the rising smoke.

'We'll have to wait here under cover of the trees till nightfall,' he said. 'Then move at night. Our only hope is to surprise Quenwulf. Even with two enchanted swords.'

'Good thinking,' said Runnel.

'Bah!' exclaimed Biter. 'The two of us can dispatch any dragon –'

'How well do you remember fighting dragons?' asked Runnel.

'Ah,' replied Biter, somewhat taken aback. 'Not very . . . not at all really . . .'

'I do,' said Runnel, very much the older sister. 'Flame from above, hot enough to melt even us, and the merest edge of it will kill a knight by sucking the air from their lungs. Close-up, they have an armoured hide with few weak spots, claws that can slice through the best mail, and jaws that can bite a warhorse in half. Both knights and swords are fortunate that so few dragons go bad.'

There was a moment of silence as Odo and Eleanor considered having the air sucked out of their lungs or being bitten in two, and Biter thought about being melted.

Then Odo spoke. 'What do you mean, so few dragons go bad? Aren't they all bad?'

'No, indeed,' said Runnel impatiently. 'Who has been filling your heads . . . ?'

She stopped. They all heard branches shifting and creaking behind them, on the fringe of the forest. They turned, swords raised and ready.

Further back, where the trees began to grow more closely together, a dark shape stealthily climbed the trunk of a vast beech, always keeping to the shade.

'The bannoch!' cried Odo.

'It's less frightening in the day,' said Eleanor. She almost believed that.

'It definitely seemed much bigger the last time we saw it,' said Odo, watching the creature slink up into the higher branches. Now that he could see it clearly, it looked more batlike than lizardlike, and was merely about three times the size of a big hunting dog, though its wings extended out at least a dozen paces on either side.

'Wenneth said it couldn't leave the forest,' whispered Eleanor.

The bannoch uttered a high-pitched keening sound, but made no move to attack.

'It just wants a fire,' said Odo. 'Maybe we should make one for it.'

'Smoke would alert Quenwulf to our presence,' said Biter. 'We must not relinquish the element of surprise.'

'And once it swallows a fire, it has fire,' said Eleanor. She waved her sword and shouted, 'Begone!'

Much to everyone's surprise, the bannoch went.

'It'll be back come nightfall, I reckon,' said Odo, looking as he did whenever one of the village dogs gave birth to puppies.

'And we won't be here,' replied Eleanor sternly. She sat down with her back against a tree and got out the map, turning it so it was oriented to the landscape. 'Look, the smoke is rising here. That must be on the river. The valley ahead is Welmder Vale. We can either follow the road along the valley to the river, or go across and up the other side and then follow this track along the ridge to the river. So which way?'

'The most direct!' said Biter.

'The high road,' said Runnel.

Odo looked at the map and out across the valley, putting

the fate of the imprisoned bannoch from his mind.

'There are tumbled rocks along the ridge,' he said slowly. 'They would hide us. If we follow the valley and the dragon flies over, there's nowhere to hide.'

'The ridge it is,' said Eleanor. 'And what then?'

'That smoke shows us where the dragon is,' said Odo. 'We creep up, spy out the lay of the land and then –'

'𝕮𝖍𝖆𝖑𝖑𝖊𝖓𝖌𝖊 𝖙𝖍𝖊 𝖋𝖔𝖚𝖑 𝖇𝖊𝖆𝖘𝖙!' declared Biter.

'Um, no,' said Odo hesitantly. 'We know it has already killed villagers and dried up the river. It hasn't fought fair, so we don't have to either. We creep up and surprise it.'

'𝖂𝖎𝖘𝖉𝖔𝖒,' said Runnel. Biter made a grumbling noise.

'What are a dragon's weak points?' asked Eleanor. 'We should decide who attacks which bit.'

'Yes.' Odo sat down too and rested his pack against a tree. It was very hard to believe that soon they would be going up against a dragon. They'd come an awful long way from Lenburh and his life at the mill. 'Runnel?'

'𝕿𝖍𝖊 𝖊𝖞𝖊𝖘; 𝖆 𝖇𝖆𝖗𝖊 𝖕𝖆𝖙𝖈𝖍 𝖚𝖓𝖉𝖊𝖗 𝖊𝖆𝖈𝖍 𝖜𝖎𝖓𝖌 𝖜𝖍𝖊𝖗𝖊 𝖎𝖙 𝖏𝖔𝖎𝖓𝖘 𝖙𝖍𝖊 𝖇𝖔𝖉𝖞; 𝖆 𝖘𝖎𝖒𝖎𝖑𝖆𝖗 𝖕𝖆𝖙𝖈𝖍 𝖇𝖊𝖑𝖔𝖜 𝖙𝖍𝖊 𝖑𝖔𝖜𝖊𝖗 𝖏𝖆𝖜 𝖜𝖍𝖊𝖗𝖊 𝖘𝖔𝖒𝖊 𝖘𝖙𝖗𝖎𝖓𝖌𝖞 𝖇𝖎𝖙𝖘 𝖔𝖋 𝖘𝖐𝖎𝖓 𝖍𝖆𝖓𝖌, 𝖈𝖆𝖑𝖑𝖊𝖉 𝖙𝖍𝖊 𝖜𝖆𝖙𝖙𝖑𝖊,' said Runnel. '𝕿𝖍𝖆𝖙'𝖘 𝖎𝖙. 𝕷𝖊𝖙 𝖒𝖊 𝖉𝖗𝖆𝖜 𝖆 𝖕𝖎𝖈𝖙𝖚𝖗𝖊 𝖎𝖓 𝖙𝖍𝖊 𝖉𝖎𝖗𝖙.'

Eleanor let the sword go. Runnel quickly traced the outline of a dragon in the dirt, placing bold *X*'s at the weak points she had mentioned.

'Maybe we sneak up either side,' said Eleanor thoughtfully.

'If she takes off, go for the underwing points. If she doesn't, stab her in the eyes.'

'I guess so,' said Odo, although blinding an oblivious enemy seemed a particularly cruel tactic. Perhaps, if the alternative was being flamed, he could do it. 'We should take a look at the lay of the land first anyway.'

With mountains to the west, the sun dipped out of sight even sooner than Odo had expected, and the twilight was short. As soon as it became fully dark, they set off down the road, leaving it when it turned to go along the vale.

It was hard work climbing the northern side of the valley, made even more difficult by the lack of light. When the moon came out, it was frequently obscured by clouds.

By the time they reached the top of the ridge, both Odo and Eleanor were very tired. They stopped to rest for a while, propped against a large boulder.

But even as weary eyes slowly closed, they were shocked open again by a sudden, deep roar that echoed along the valley. At the same time, a great column of fire rose up to the northwest, and twenty or thirty seconds later the sharp tang of sulphur came on the back of the wind.

Eleanor sneezed. Odo handed her one of the patched handkerchiefs he had found in his pack that morning.

Slowly, the fire in the west sank. Odo and Eleanor looked at the sky anxiously, staring at every misshapen cloud that might hide a dragon in the moonlight.

'We're safe up here while the dragon's down there,' said Odo, taking out another handkerchief and wiping nervous sweat from his brow. 'Right?'

'No matter how high you are,' Runnel said, 'dragons can always go higher.'

'Not if you tie rocks to their feet while they're sleeping,' said Eleanor, smiling at Odo in a way she hoped was reassuring. 'I read a story about that once.'

'The Pulverisation of Sir Arleigh,' said Runnel. 'Do you recall how that ended?'

Eleanor shook her head.

The sword continued. 'The dragon tried to fly anyway, crashed into Sir Arleigh and crushed her to death.'

Odo shot an imploring glance at Eleanor.

'Look, Runnel, I know you want to get melted,' she said, 'but you remember your promise? You won't do anything to get us killed just so you can get burned up, will you?'

'I won't have to do anything,' said Runnel grimly. 'I'm sure the curse will do it for me. It's a shame, for I must confess I have grown to like you . . . a little.'

'Just remember your promise,' said Eleanor. 'Come on, Odo.'

She got up and began to follow the track along the ridge. Odo followed some distance behind, thinking about what lay ahead. It still seemed wrong and un-knightly somehow to just creep up on someone and kill them, even if that someone was a dragon who was causing so much trouble. But then, doing it Biter's way would be stupid, and they would definitely get killed, and he definitely didn't want that.

'I do not understand her,' said Biter softly. 'She is not the sword I admired when I was newly forged.'

'What?' asked Odo, brought out of his thoughts. 'Runnel? Did you know her well?'

'Mostly we were apart, but several times we served knights who fought in the same company, and there were other times between campaigns when we enjoyed the hospitality of the King's Armourer. She told me of her adventures. What tales! I will confess to you, Sir Odo, that she was nearly my equal.'

'Only nearly?'

'One would expect one's maker to improve with practice.'

Odo hid a smile. He could see how a smith might get worse with age too, but didn't think Biter would appreciate the thought.

'Is there anything more we can do for her?' he asked. 'I mean, to lift the curse she thinks she's under?'

'You are doing it, good knight. All she needs is to aid in valiant deeds, to smite a foe or two, and she will return to her proper self.'

The track along the ridge was narrow, often unclear, and wound through great boulders, making their progress much slower than it had been in the forest. But finally, just at dawn, they found themselves yawning and bone-tired at the point where the ridge began to descend. Below them lay the river, or rather a mostly dried-up ravine of cracked mud, and on its banks was the remains of a village. It had been burned, and the remains tumbled over. Only one stone house remained amidst the mounds of blackened timber and wattle and daub. The stone house had no roof and only three walls. There were no signs of any people, living or dead.

'This would be Hellmere, or what's left of it,' said Eleanor.

Odo looked down at the ruins and thought how similar the village must have been to his own Lenburh. First the river had dried up, and then the dragon had come. He must never allow that to happen to his home.

'We must be close to Quenwulf's lair now,' said Eleanor. She was looking along the river's course, where it slanted off to the northeast, entering a gorge between two hills. 'I reckon that column of fire came from somewhere in there.'

'In the gorge?' asked Odo. It was completely shadowed, the sun blocked by the high rock walls on either side, and they were at the wrong angle to see inside anyway. 'I suppose we could walk in up the dry river —'

'No,' said Runnel. 'The high road again. Think. If you're spotted, the dragon has you trapped in the gorge and unable to flee. We must be above it, and thus come down on the dragon.'

'Those hills are high,' said Odo. 'It'll be very difficult.'

'An enemy never guards the difficult ways as closely as they do the easy ones,' said Runnel.

'I guess we'll have to go at night as well,' said Eleanor.

'Yes,' confirmed Runnel.

'There's a hollow under that big boulder with the lichen,' said Odo, pointing. 'We'll be out of sight there. Let's have some breakfast, and sleep.'

'Sleep,' agreed Eleanor, with another long yawn.

'Beware the eels,' said Biter darkly. 'I will keep watch.'

'Soon, my dragon,' whispered Runnel, so quietly that none of the others heard her.

TWENTY-EIGHT

When the sun went down, they set out again. The night was eerily quiet, except for the roars the dragon they assumed was Quenwulf occasionally let out. When they were part of the way up the hill that bordered the gorge, the column of fire rose again, lighting up the landscape as if there was another, brighter moon. It lasted easily a full minute, an enormous gout of flame, and the smoke formed a vast, black cloud overhead.

As they got closer to the top, they moved into this smoke, though the column of fire had subsided. The air was almost too foul to breathe. Eleanor and Odo slowed as they came to the top of the hill, and the edge of the gorge lay only twenty or thirty paces further on.

'Crawl,' whispered Runnel.

Eleanor and Odo got down and made their uncomfortable way to the very edge of the gorge, where they looked down into the smoke-shrouded darkness.

'Is that . . . is that her?' whispered Odo, squinting. The

gorge was deep, and though the sky was clearing as the smoke dissipated, it was still very hard to make out details. There was something below them, a great dark shape crouched in the riverbed, completely blocking the gorge. He could see the sandy bed of the river in front of it, but behind it was something shimmering . . .

'Is she lying in the gorge?' Odo asked. 'That's water behind . . . um . . . her . . . isn't it?'

'I'm not sure,' said Eleanor. She was as confused as he was. 'Is she sitting on some kind of wall?'

The swords slipped out of their sheaths and came to peer with them.

'Sitting on a wall across a river?' asked Runnel. 'That makes no sense, even for a dragon.'

'That looks like a lake behind the wall,' observed Biter. 'But where there is a lake, there should be no lack of water for the river.'

The truth of what they were seeing came to Eleanor and Odo at exactly the same moment.

'That's not a wall,' he said.

'It's a *dam*,' whispered Eleanor. 'Not a dragon at –'

Even as she spoke, a deafening whoosh came from below, and the column of flame rose again, almost directly in front of them, rising higher than the walls of the gorge. They could feel its intense heat, and the choking black smoke once more spread across the sky.

In the sudden light, they could also see very clearly into the gorge.

The column of fire did not come from a dragon's mouth. It spewed out of a tall chimney from a building in the middle of the dam, a wooden dam backed with earth and rubble.

'The dragon is a fake!' cried Biter.

'Alas,' said Runnel quietly.

'Who would do such a thing?' asked Eleanor. It was this dam – not a dragon – that was blocking up the river and ruining life for all of the towns downstream.

'We'll have to take a look,' said Odo. He was studying the side of the gorge beneath them. 'I think there's a narrow path down – See there?'

Eleanor looked, shielding her face with her hands against the heat of the fiery column.

'That's *very* narrow,' she said doubtfully. 'And a long way to fall.'

'Can you see any guards on the dam?'

'No,' said Eleanor. 'But there must be someone in that hut in the middle. What if they come out and see us while we're climbing down?'

'We'll wait for the fire to stop,' said Odo. 'It'll be dark.'

'Besides, people rarely look up,' said Runnel. 'Even sentries.'

'They will if they hear me falling off and screaming,' said Eleanor, looking once again at the narrow path. 'Or you, more likely, Odo. You really think you can balance on there? It has to be less than a single pace wide.'

'We'll leave our packs here,' said Odo.

'And armour?' asked Eleanor.

Odo shook his head. 'We'll probably need to fight. Anyway, I'm used to my hauberk now. I'm sure I can make it down that path.'

He had steeled himself to creep up on a dragon, but it had been a cold feeling, an effort of will. Now that he could see that it was a dam holding the river back, a dam made by people, he felt a hot anger that any human could hatch such a plan. And he had a budding suspicion he knew why they had done it, and who was responsible.

Eleanor was feeling the same suspicion. Whoever was behind the fake dragon fire, the dam and the drying up of the river, she swore that she and the swords would make them pay.

As before, the column of fire began to shrink. This time, they were close enough to hear a strange clanking sound as it did so, a rhythmic noise rather like the ironbound wheel of an oxcart rolling over cobbles.

Eleanor started up as soon as the fire was completely gone, but Runnel stopped her with a few words.

'𝔚𝔞𝔦𝔱! 𝔏𝔢𝔱 𝔶𝔬𝔲𝔯 𝔢𝔶𝔢𝔰 𝔞𝔡𝔧𝔲𝔰𝔱 𝔟𝔞𝔠𝔨 𝔱𝔬 𝔱𝔥𝔢 𝔫𝔦𝔤𝔥𝔱.'

They waited a dozen breaths, and slowly details crept back into the landscape, the moon and the stars breaking through the straggling smoke. Soon her eyes were able to make out the path, though it looked even narrower than before, hugging the side of the gorge.

Again, Eleanor started towards it. This time it was Odo who held her back.

'Let me go first,' he said quietly.

'But I'm the better climber!' Eleanor argued.

'Yes,' said Odo. 'Therefore I'm more likely to fall, and I don't want to fall on you.'

Eleanor opened her mouth to protest, but she swallowed her words on seeing his determined face. He was right.

Odo started down the path, taking it very slow, his body half-turned into the side of the gorge as his feet probed ahead, his fingers moving from handhold to handhold. Biter was silent at his side, perhaps thinking that if they fell, both would end up in a watery grave, deep in the dammed-up lake below.

There would be eels there no doubt.

Eleanor followed, for once just as cautiously as Odo. She too thought about the deep water of the lake. It was hard to imagine what someone innocent would want with all that water. Why build the dam here, where it was barely accessible? And the fire — how did they do that? Her mother's books on siegecraft spoke a little of such things, tubes that could spout liquid flame against attackers. But the books gave no details of how it was made, or how it could be sent forth, or what use it would be here.

Ahead of and below her, Odo's foot slipped completely off the path.

Eleanor choked back a cry as he slid down, feet scrabbling violently, small stones falling in a shower into the water below, making a sound like hail.

For several seconds Odo hung against the rock face, his knuckles white as he held on. Then he found a foothold, and another, and clung to the side of the gorge, panting.

'Are you all right?' whispered Eleanor. She desperately hoped so, for he was far too heavy for her to pull back up.

Odo nodded, unable to speak. He had come so close to falling. And in saving himself, he might have alerted whoever was down below in that strange hut upon the dam.

They stayed where they were, pressed against the rock, both watching the dam below. Waiting for enemies to emerge and look up. Enemies with bows, or even spears. They would be picked off without the slightest chance to defend themselves.

But there was no movement below. The night remained quiet and calm. After a silent eternity that might have been no more than a minute, Odo let out the smallest sigh and continued down, handhold to handhold, foothold to foothold, regretting with every single chancy movement that he had said he could take the path.

Finally, the hard way, he reached the dam, and Eleanor slithered down the last leg of the path to join him. It was darker there, a good two hundred feet below the top of the gorge, but Odo could see that a much wider and better path ran down and along to the entrance of the gorge, probably to the destroyed village. It would have been much easier to take that road, now they knew the dragon was a fake.

Odo and Eleanor drew their swords and advanced along the dam wall towards the hut in the middle. Unlike the dam itself, this was made of crudely dressed stone. Close-up, they saw that the chimney in the middle was a tube of hammered bronze, flared at the top like a tulip. It was easily four times Odo's height, and he would have had trouble stretching his arms around its girth.

There was a door in the side of the hut. A simple wooden door, no different than the one to the mill at home, with a rope-pull for the latch inside. Odo and Eleanor moved up to it and listened.

They could hear a voice inside.

'Turn the wheel, Old Ryce, turn the wheel. One hundred and one, one hundred and two, one hundred and three –'

Odo pulled the rope, lifting the latch, and eased the door open.

Soft lantern light spilled outwards across the dam. Odo and Eleanor entered together, ready to fight, only to stop suddenly and stare.

The hut was only the topmost part of a tower that extended some way down into the body of the dam. Odo and Eleanor stood on a small platform that protruded over the space below. A series of ladders extended down from there, while another ladder led up to a trapdoor in the ceiling.

The inside of the tower was almost completely filled with an enormous cylindrical container made of hundreds of bronze plates riveted together. Black pitch oozed out around many of the rivets, and the whole thing stank of sulphurous fire.

At the base of the cylinder, some thirty feet below, was a thick tangle of huge pipes connected to a huge wheel, also of bronze, which was being turned by an old but muscular man dressed only in a loincloth and a leather apron that extended from his neck to his ankles. His arms were wiry and hairless in patches, where they had obviously been burned. His feet were bare. On his head he wore a tattered acorn hat that leaked strands of flyaway white hair.

'Turn the wheel, Old Ryce, turn the wheel,' he sang to himself, oblivious to his visitors above. 'One hundred and six, one hundred and seven, two thousand turns for the dragon to roar . . . one hundred and nine!'

'Stop doing that!' ordered Odo.

'One hundred and –'

'Stop!' roared Odo.

The old man froze with his hands on the wheel and looked up.

'Who are you?' Odo asked.

The old man blinked and said in a hesitant voice, 'Old Ryce, Your Honour.'

'What are you doing?' asked Eleanor.

'Turning the wheel, turning the wheel,' answered Old Ryce. 'Got to do it two thousand times. It's a pump, you see, a most ingenious device, if I do say so myself . . . but Old Ryce is not supposed to talk to you. How did you get past the guards?'

'Guards?' asked Odo, looking behind him but seeing no one.

'Are they down there with you?' Eleanor asked.

'Gone to get dinner! Only Old Ryce here. Those others is afraid of the device. The first one I made, it burst, I admit, but none were killed. And Cobb got a new name – One-Eye, a perfectly good name –'

'You made this device?' asked Odo. 'This engine that flings fire to the sky?'

'Oh yes,' said Old Ryce with pride. 'I'm a master smith, and an artificer besides. I followed the old book, true, but I made it, and the two little ones before. Just as the Captain ordered, Old Ryce.'

'Who is the Captain?' asked Odo.

Old Ryce looked up and down and sideways and did not immediately answer.

'Come up here and talk to us, you mangy cumberwold,' ordered Eleanor, getting tired of shouting.

Old Ryce raised his leg with the jangle of steel links. His

right ankle was manacled to a chain that was set into a staple in the floor.

'The Captain's not very trusting, no, she isn't,' he said sadly. 'Let Old Ryce get back to turning. They'll be watching for the dragon fire. No bread and water for Old Ryce if he don't turn the wheel. She doesn't like shirkers, oh no.'

'She?' asked Eleanor and Odo, both at the same time, their expressions almost identical.

'What's the Captain's name?' asked Odo.

'The Captain? Oh, the Captain . . .' Old Ryce gripped the wheel tighter than ever, though he didn't try to turn it. 'The Captain will be back soon, Old Ryce, and if the Captain finds them the Captain will kill them and then kill Old Ryce too. She doesn't need another device; she doesn't need Old Ryce no more if he won't turn the wheel. She said so –'

'Tell us the Captain's name,' Eleanor insisted.

'Vile,' said Old Ryce. His lower lip quivered.

'I know she's vile, but what's her name!'

'Vile,' repeated Old Ryce. 'Vile . . . heart. The Captain. Captain Vileheart, and never was there a truer name.'

'Vileheart?'

Eleanor looked at Odo in puzzlement. 'I thought it was going to be . . .'

'It is,' said Odo. 'It has to be.'

He leaned over the railing and shouted down at Old Ryce.

'Does Captain Vileheart have other names?'

Old Ryce nodded and quivered.

'Many, many names,' he said. 'Terrible names.'

'Is one of them Sir Saskia?'

Old Ryce let out a shriek and collapsed beneath his wheel.

'Sir Saskia, Captain Vileheart, the Lady of the Bloody Hand, the Swordmistress of Skynadar,' he gibbered. 'They're all her, and more besides. She'll come and kill us all!'

'She might well kill us – but not before we get rid of this dam and get the river back, I swear it,' said Odo, surprised by his decisiveness. Sir Saskia would not have her way this time! 'Eleanor, can you please keep watch?'

Odo started down the ladder. Old Ryce was still shrieking below.

Eleanor opened the door and went out on to the dam wall, just as the three guards Old Ryce had mentioned arrived. Two men and a woman in the dirty leather armour of Sir Saskia's brigand group. None of the three had weapons ready. The closest had his hands full with a loaf and a wheel of cheese, the second was drinking from a stone bottle of ale, and the third had her thumbs through her belt.

Runnel was already in Eleanor's hand, and her practice, first with Odo and Biter and then with the older sword, made the required movements second nature.

The enchanted sword cut across in a lightning move that sent cheese and bread flying. The brigand holding them staggered back, clutching a long but shallow wound across his chest.

The other two went for their weapons, and the stone bottle flew at Eleanor's head. She ducked beneath it, and moved in to strike as the second brigand tripped in his haste to attack and impaled himself on Runnel.

It happened so quickly that Eleanor didn't have time to react. Her enemy went down gurgling from a terrible wound to his throat.

The third raised her hands and cried, 'Quarter! Give quarter!'

Even with this traditional cry for mercy, Runnel went to lunge. Eleanor dragged her back, wrestling the sword to her side. She had seen plenty of blood before, from her father's patients, but never so much as a result of her own actions. Her gorge rose. She fought it back down.

Odo shouted something from inside and below. Eleanor heard it as if he were even further away. She was shaking, almost unable to comprehend that she had defeated three bandits. One wounded, one dying . . . maybe . . . and one surrendered.

This was knight's work. And she had done it.

'Are you all right? What's happening?' shouted Odo, and a few moments later he came panting out the door, having climbed back up the ladder faster than any mill rat ran up a beam to escape a ratting dog.

'Enemies,' said Runnel in Eleanor's stead. 'Bandits, who should pay the penalty for their foul misdeeds: death.'

'Yes,' said Biter, shifting in Odo's hand. 'Their lives are forfeit.'

'No,' croaked the man with the wound to his chest. He had both hands pressed against it, his fingers bloody. 'Not us. There's been some mistake. We serve Sir Saskia the knight.'

'You mean Captain Vileheart,' said Eleanor.

The two survivors exchanged a look of hopelessness.

'I never wanted to be a bandit,' said the woman. 'It wasn't my fault. The harvest failed –'

'Enough!' said Eleanor. 'We're not going to kill them, are we, Odo? I mean . . . I already . . . and if we have to, of course . . . but . . .'

'No,' said Odo, frowning. For all the talk of knights fighting, he'd never thought to see someone seriously wounded, maybe killed . . . someone who a few minutes before had been utterly unharmed.

He drew himself up to his full, quite imposing height, which seemed all the more considerable with the enchanted sword in his hand, the emerald in its pommel flashing green.

'Tend to your wounds, take the dead man, if he is dead, and go. But if we encounter you again in these lands, your lives will truly be forfeit.'

'Thank you, thank you, gentle sir, noble maid,' gabbled

the wounded man. He gestured at the woman, and they both picked up the fallen man.

'Leave your weapons,' Eleanor ordered. Runnel emphasised her words by darting forward.

A minute later, Eleanor and Odo were alone again on the dam wall, the only sign the brigands had been there three heavy and badly made swords, three daggers and a bloodstain.

'They'll go straight to Sir Saskia,' said Runnel. 'You shouldn't have let them go.'

'Maybe,' said Eleanor. She picked up one of the regular swords and hefted it, testing its weight. 'But unless they have horses it'll take them several days. Here.'

She gave the sword to Odo.

'We need no other swords, squire,' said Biter indignantly.

'He'll need it to get the chain off Old Ryce,' she said. 'I'm guessing you don't want to be used like a chisel on old iron?'

'No, indeed,' said Biter, shuddering from tip to pommel.

Odo sheathed Biter and swung the sword over his shoulder.

'First we release Old Ryce,' he said, nodding. 'Then we start a fire under that huge copper kettle. It's full of pitch and sulphur and who knows what else. The log wall will burn, the dam will collapse –'

Eleanor grinned. 'And then the river will be free!'

TWENTY-NINE

'It'll be a powerful big fire,' cautioned Old Ryce as they hurried along the broad path downstream from the dam. 'There's enough pitch, naphtha, and sulphur in my cylinder for nine dozen dragon breaths.'

'Good,' said Odo without pausing. After freeing Old Ryce, he'd used the brigand's sword to loosen some of the bronze plates to let the incendiary mixture in the cylinder leak out faster. He had left it pooling at the bottom. After climbing out he'd thrown a burning torch down into the pool. The pitch had caught immediately, though Old Ryce had assured him it would take half an hour or more before enough plates buckled and the whole lot went up.

When that happened, the dam would burn too, very quickly. The timbers were what kept the earth fill in place. Once enough of them burned, the dam would go, and the lake would empty back into the river.

There would be a flood. Odo was a miller's son, and knew a lot about sluices, mill ponds and winter floods.

He'd thought, looking at the complete emptiness of the river ahead and the size of the lake behind, that all that water gushing out would mostly go along the river rather than spread sideways and cause havoc.

Now that it was closer to actually happening, he wasn't so sure, and he also wasn't so sure about Old Ryce's timing. One thing he did know was that they wouldn't want to be inside the river gorge when the dam gave way.

'Faster!' he urged Eleanor and Old Ryce, taking a moment himself to look back. There was a bright glow in the middle of the dam, a very bright glow, and even more smoke then when the 'dragon breath' column of fire was burning. He turned and ran after the others, urging them to go faster still.

They had barely made it out of the gorge entrance when a titanic explosion came from behind them.

First, a flash so bright that everything was lit up as if it were day. A moment later, a savage shock of hot air that knocked them all down, accompanied by a clap of thunder so loud it left everyone's ears ringing.

'Never thought it would all go at once,' shouted Old Ryce as they shakily got to their feet. 'Under pressure, I s'pose . . . acts like the burning powder stuff the Karnickans have been mucking about with.'

'What?' shouted Eleanor. She was distracted by the earth trembling beneath her feet. Slightly addled by the explosion, it took her a full second to work out what was causing it.

'The flood!' she cried. 'Quick! To high ground!'

Odo pointed and ran at the same time, towards the slope of the nearer hill, some two hundred paces from the gorge entrance across entirely flat ground, extending from the low mound of the riverbank.

The dam, instead of slowly burning and opening up to allow a gradual flow, had been completely destroyed in an instant by that stupendous blast. Now all the water it had held back was coming down the gorge – all of it at once!

'Run!' Odo yelled.

Eleanor raced past him, always faster on foot than he was, despite her shorter stride. Odo glanced behind. Old Ryce was hobbling along, his legs weakened by his long imprisonment at the base of the tower in the dam.

Odo ran back, picked up the old man, threw him over his shoulder and started running again.

Behind him, a wall of water sixty feet high exploded out of the gorge, an enormous wave that immediately spread sideways, sweeping up everything in its path.

Eleanor made it to the hill, panting and entirely breathless. She ran up a dozen paces, climbed a massive stone and only then looked back.

Odo was thirty paces behind her.

Just that little bit too far. The sideways wave that caught him was only a fraction of the height of the great flood tearing deafeningly down the river channel, but it was still taller than the boy and immensely powerful.

'No!' shouted Eleanor as the flood picked up Odo and Old Ryce, turned them over and smashed them down, covering both old man and boy instantly in a tide of muddy brown water and debris, including broken timbers from the dam and entire trees wrenched out of the riverbank.

The wave broke at the foot of Eleanor's rock, and the flood turned to flow aside, seeking lower ground. Eleanor jumped down and waded in a few paces, but immediately had to retreat. The current was so incredibly strong she could barely keep her footing.

'Odo!' she called. 'Odo!'

No answer came. She couldn't see anything. The moon wasn't bright enough, the water was too muddy.

Odo had been wearing his hauberk. He had Ryce over his shoulder.

If she didn't do something immediately, he would be drowned for sure.

'Runnel, help me! I have to see!'

A flash of ruby light shone out over the water. Two shadows struggled under the surface. One of them, the larger one, held the other in a tight grip, but he seemed to be going in the wrong direction, deeper into the muddy water. On seeing the red flare, his direction righted.

A sword broke the surface of the water and rose high, Odo hanging on for grim life with Old Ryce under his arm.

Eleanor was there to help him. Slowly they waded through the churning waters, took two paces up the muddy slope and collapsed.

Odo lay weakly on his stomach, coughing up dirty water while Eleanor pounded his back.

'Ow! Not so hard,' he complained between coughs. 'I'm all right.'

'You could have drowned!' protested Eleanor.

'Especially me,' said the old man weakly. He rolled over on his back and looked up at the night sky with pale, rheumy eyes. 'Thanks to you for coming back, young knight. There's few indeed who would do such a thing.'

'𝕾𝖎𝖗 𝕺𝖉𝖔 𝖎𝖘 𝖆 𝖒𝖔𝖘𝖙 𝖛𝖆𝖑𝖎𝖆𝖓𝖙 𝖐𝖓𝖎𝖌𝖍𝖙,' declared Biter.

'A fairly stupid one,' said Odo. 'I was too eager to destroy the dam and free the river. There'll be a lot of damage downstream.'

'Most of the closer villages will be empty, scared off by the "dragon" and Sir Saskia,' Eleanor reassured him.

Old Ryce flinched as she mentioned that name.

'Yes,' said Odo, a troubled look settling on his face. 'Sir Saskia. We still need to do something about her. We must warn Sir Halfdan and the others at home particularly.'

'Home?' asked Eleanor. 'But our messages, the ones we sent from Hryding – they will be warned. Besides, she won't get there for weeks, not if she does her bandit trick in every village in between.'

'I think she'll head straight for Lenburh,' said Odo. 'She'll know it was us and will want revenge. Did you see, when we left the gorge? There was a tent and a hitching rail?'

'You mean . . .' said Eleanor with a sinking heart. 'The bandits we let go . . . they did have horses?'

'I'm afraid so,' said Odo. He groaned and sat up. 'At least one horse anyway. They'll tell Sir Saskia we were at the dam, and she'll wreak bloody vengeance on our home.'

'No one with honour would countenance such tactics,' said Runnel. 'To attack innocents is beyond reproach.'

'Sir Saskia is a wicked and most perfidious individual,' said Biter. 'She cannot possibly be a real knight.'

'We have to get there first and warn everyone,' said Eleanor, thinking of her father. He was a healer, not a fighter. He wouldn't last a moment against those fiends.

'How?' asked Odo. 'She'll get word in two days or less, and then if she hurries . . . How far did you say a laden knight could go in a day, Biter?'

'Six leagues,' replied Biter. 'On a path or road.'

Eleanor was looking over the floodwaters, glittering in the moonlight.

'There might be a way to beat her there,' she said.

Odo looked up at her, and then where she was looking. The waters were receding, ebbing back into the channel, though that still surged in flood and would do so for days yet.

'Oh, of course!' he exclaimed. 'The river! We can make a raft!'

He stood up, forgetting his weariness and many minor bruises, and clapped Eleanor on the back. She was knocked forward and turned to him with a scowl.

'Hey, just returning the favour,' said Odo.

'I didn't take in a lot of water and need my back slapped like a baby,' she griped.

'You're lucky,' said Odo. He was watching the water, and suddenly waded out to grab a long beam of good timber, once part of the dam. It was a little charred but sound.

'I *am* lucky,' agreed Eleanor. She thought about that for a moment, then drew Runnel half an inch out of her scabbard. 'Hey, Runnel! You hear that? I fought three brigands and won, and I survived the dam breaking and the flood. You can't be cursed at all.'

'Hmmm,' said Runnel, unconvinced. 'Perhaps it is a slow curse. Or delayed somehow.'

'And there was no dragon,' pointed out Odo as he dragged the beam out of the water and waded in to collect another, all raw material for the raft he was already designing in his mind. 'That's lucky too.'

'Perhaps,' said Runnel. There was a note of regret in her voice.

'Hey, help me with this,' said Odo. 'Get that small one there.'

Eleanor nodded, but paused to look down at her sword.

'There is no curse, Runnel,' she repeated. 'You were unlucky with your knights, that's all. There was never any curse.'

Runnel did not reply, or if she did it was so quietly that whatever she said was lost as Eleanor splashed into the water and grabbed a piece of floating wood from Odo's firm grasp.

By early morning, the full devastation caused by the destruction of the dam was clear to see. The raging floodwaters had ebbed all the way back to the river channel, which now ran full spate to the top of the banks, but did not overflow them. For half a league on either side, all that was visible was mud, toppled trees and debris.

There was also a massive cloud of black smoke still hanging over the gorge. A reddish reflection under the cloud suggested that some part of the dam still burned.

'The mixture will burn underwater,' said Old Ryce. 'Mayhap there's some left in the cylinder . . .'

The ancient artificer had proved to be very useful in making their raft. He'd built ships, he told them, and all kinds of terrible engines for use in war. Captain Vileheart had hired him in far-off Axim, across the sea, but had soon made him a slave. He didn't want to talk about that though, and every time they said 'Vileheart' or 'Sir Saskia' he would fall silent and begin to shake.

The first and most important piece of good advice Old

Ryce had given them was to start making the raft on the riverbank, even when it was still knee-deep in floodwater. This meant they only had to push it a few feet into the water, instead of trying to drag it across a broad expanse of very sticky mud. Which probably wouldn't have worked, because it was a heavy vessel, mostly made of beams from the dam held together with rope, nails, bolts and wire, all scrounged from the bandits' guard camp and the ruins of Hellmere. The scrounging had taken most of the morning, once the sun came up.

'You ready?' Odo asked Eleanor. She and Old Ryce were already on the raft. Its front quarter was in the river, the water rushing at it, trying to drag it away. One good shove from Odo and they'd be off. Without him, if he couldn't jump aboard fast enough. 'It's going to go very fast.'

Eleanor took a tighter grip on the rope they'd lashed across the raft for passenger support and checked to make sure their armour and the two swords were secure, tied down with another rope. Old Ryce changed his handhold and gave her an uncertain, largely toothless grin.

Odo pushed. The raft moved a few inches in the mud then stuck fast. He got down lower and heaved again, really getting his full strength behind it. His left shoulder, the one hurt by Sir Saskia, twinged. He grimaced, but didn't stop pushing.

Inch by inch, the raft moved out into the river. Water foamed up all along one side, splashing over Eleanor and

Old Ryce . . . and then suddenly the raft spun sideways and was away!

Odo, caught by surprise, hurled himself forward and just managed to grab hold of the stern rope and pull himself half onto the raft even as it rocketed down the river, wallowing and bucking with the force of the flood.

'Climb up!' shouted Eleanor. The raft was rocking so wildly and going so fast she didn't dare let go and move back to help Odo.

'That's what I'm doing!' Odo shouted back. 'It's harder than it looks!'

He got his right knee up and then the whole leg, and with a huge effort managed to roll completely onto the raft. But he knew he couldn't rest there. The raft was spinning and crashing into the riverbank every ten or twelve paces, and at this rate would be shaken to pieces long before they got to Lenburh.

Tucking his legs under the stern rope, he sat up and reached over to pull out one of the long poles from where it had been secured. Holding it with both hands, he used it to fend the raft off from the riverbank just as it went in for another collision.

Eleanor, up at the bow, was already doing likewise. She didn't have Odo's weight, but she was fiercely determined, which counted for a great deal.

Old Ryce cackled and threw his hands in the air for a

second, almost resulting in him going overboard.

'It ain't what I'd call shipshape and Jyllen fashion,' he announced, grabbing hold of the rope again. 'But it works.'

'We're going so fast,' said Eleanor, relishing the feel of chill air on her face. The sensation made up for being hungry. They hadn't gone back for their packs, high above the gorge, and though they'd taken the bandits' food and drink, that had all been consumed at breakfast. 'If this keeps up we might be at Lenburh by tomorrow morning!'

'The flood will slow as we get further along,' said Odo. But he grinned and added, 'It will certainly be a lot faster than walking. We'll beat Sir Saskia to Lenburh for sure.'

'Will we be able to stop the raft?' asked Eleanor as they pushed hard to avoid hitting the riverbank again and were suddenly carried out towards the middle, where the river flowed even faster.

'I, uh, hope so,' said Odo, realising only then the significance of her question. He had been so focused on making the raft and getting it going, he hadn't once thought about how they would stop.

THIRTY

Poling ashore proved to be much harder than either of them expected. They didn't even try for the first few hours, since it was obvious they would fail, the river foaming and roaring and carrying them along so quickly. Later in the afternoon the flood did seem to ease a bit, and they tried to pole for the riverbank several times, but still without any success.

'We'll be carried past Lenburh at this rate,' said Eleanor. 'Look, that's *Hryding* up ahead!'

'Pole!' shouted Odo. 'Pole hard!'

They pushed with all their strength. It was useless. Although the raft came close to the riverbank, it spun as it did so and was quickly carried back into the main flow despite everything Odo and Eleanor could do. To make matters worse, the raft was also slowly beginning to come apart, unable to withstand the many knocks and collisions with debris and the riverbanks.

'Eels,' said Biter. 'I feel I may soon be joining the eels again.'

'No, you won't,' said Odo, but not with complete conviction. Inwardly he was afraid the sword might be right. 'The flood will ease, I'm sure of it.'

He knew this was true. Eventually. But they might be well past Lenburh before that happened, if the raft lasted that long. Visions filled his mind of trudging back to Lenburh from the south, only to find it burning, Sir Saskia and her troops looting and pillaging and killing . . .

'The jetty,' said Eleanor suddenly. 'The jetty at Anfyltarn.'

Odo's waking nightmare disappeared.

'Yes!' he said. 'We should be able to steer into that at least!'

Eleanor was calculating.

'If the river keeps up this speed, I reckon we'll arrive about dusk.'

'We might be able to get a horse from the smiths,' said Odo.

'How far do you think Sir Saskia will have got?' asked Eleanor.

'I don't know,' said Odo. 'We'd better keep a good lookout.'

'The bandits you didn't kill would have reached her by now,' said Runnel. 'She will be forewarned.'

'They won't expect us,' said Odo. 'At least not on the river.'

'She sounds clever,' said Runnel. 'Perhaps clever enough to expect the unexpected. Remember what I said about people not guarding the unexpected ways? That doesn't apply to the really smart commanders.'

With those unsettling words sinking deep into their

thoughts, provoking a whole cavalcade of new worries, Odo and Eleanor resumed trying to pole the raft away from major collisions with debris, not get washed overboard themselves, and keep an eye out for any of Sir Saskia's soldiers on the riverbank.

They saw few people at all, probably because everyone who lived nearby had taken to higher ground in case of more flooding. Where everyone had been distraught about the lack of water in the river, now they were frightened of too much. Particularly as the flood had been announced by a deafening thunderclap, a gout of fire that reached to the sky and a vast black cloud that was only beginning to blow away.

One fellow who was wading about in a flooded pasture near the river shouted something as the raft passed, but they could only hear one word clearly. That was 'Dragon!'

'I suppose people think Quenwulf dried up the river, and Quenwulf flooded it too,' said Odo.

'They'll know the truth soon enough,' said Eleanor. 'No dragon needed. Just a black-hearted drassock and her minions.'

'We'll sort out Sir Saskia,' said Odo. 'Sir Halfdan can send word to the King's Wardens, and his nephews' manors are only a day's march south. There are three of them and they have squires and armed retainers. And with warning, everyone in the village can fight.'

It was a surprise attack he feared. Without time to prepare

and gather at Sir Halfdan's manor house, the villagers wouldn't stand a chance. It would be terrible – beyond terrible – if Odo and Eleanor succeeded in their quest to free the river only to come home and find out there was no one left to enjoy the return to a normal life.

Odo brooded on this as he pushed the raft away from the vast, tangled root-section of a fallen tree. *A normal life.* Did he really want to give up Biter and stop being a knight? Eleanor didn't need the sword now, since she had Runnel. Doubtless she would go on questing and become a knight herself. But what would Odo do?

Would he continue to be Sir Odo, or return to being Odo, the miller's seventh child? He'd been so sure when he set off that he didn't want to be a knight. Now . . . he was almost sure he didn't want to be a miller's son again.

'The jetty!' cried Eleanor from the front of the raft.

They'd made even faster time than she had thought. The sun was only just beginning to set, and there, only a few hundred paces ahead, was the Anfyltarn jetty. It looked totally different now, with the water right up to the planks, and even over them in a few places, as if it were an almost-submerged bridge jutting out into the floodwaters.

'We're going to hit it!' she exclaimed.

She was relieved, because if they didn't, the river was going to keep taking them along, and neither of them could find bottom to push against with their poles.

The raft hit hard, loosening more of its timbers. For a moment it seemed as if it might swing away and around the end of the jetty, but Odo leaned out and grabbed one of the posts and held the vessel in place. Old Ryce jumped off as best he could, considering his knees, and tied a rope to another post. Eleanor made a loop with her rope and caught a third, swiftly tying a knot.

'Quick!' she said, reaching across to grab Runnel in her scabbard. 'It's coming apart!'

The battered raft was disintegrating under Odo's weight. He threw Biter in his scabbard onto the jetty, and then their armour, and jumped himself only a few seconds before the raft broke into pieces and the pieces swirled away.

The jetty didn't feel all that solid under their feet either. It was swaying and groaning, the river tearing at it like a wild beast. Odo, Eleanor and Old Ryce snatched up their gear and ran for the riverbank, splashing through mud until they found the river road, which had not been reached by the floodwaters.

Only then did Eleanor's gaze rise to where she knew Anfyltarn was located, up the hill beyond the forest. There she saw columns of smoke, as there had been on their previous visit.

But there was a lot more smoke now, great billows of black-and-white smoke rising to the sky. Far more than could come from the forges of the smithy alone.

'Odo,' she said, 'I think Sir Saskia took a detour on the way to Lenburh.'

'Why would she do that?'

'Because I told Mannix about your armour. She'll want to replace anything lost in the flood . . . and to make sure no one else can do the same.'

It made a horrible kind of sense, given what they now knew about the villain. Help herself without caring about anyone else.

They put their armour on as quickly as they could, and with swords in hand began to climb up the hill. Old Ryce stayed behind. He'd started to follow, but only went a few steps before he had to stop, quivering and shaking at the prospect of being recaptured by Captain Saskia Vileheart.

Odo told him to hide and await their return.

'We definitely will return,' Eleanor told him. 'So stop your whimpering.'

'Old Ryce doesn't doubt it,' he said, clutching at their hands. 'He doesn't dare . . .'

They followed the same track as before, when they'd chased Toland. It seemed as if that had happened months before, Odo thought as they carefully moved to the fringe of trees. So much had happened since then, in only a short time. Now, as then, there was no possibility of turning back. Duty called him forward.

Through the forest they heard shouts and cries and the

clash of battle up ahead. Smoke was drifting through the trees. Hurrying to the edge of the cleared area, they saw that part of the palisade was on fire and soldiers were massed in front of it, ready to charge through when enough of it was burned away. But there were plenty of defenders behind other parts of the palisade, firing bows and crossbows and even throwing rocks, and several bucket chains of villagers were bringing water from the central well to throw over the burning timbers.

The besiegers were Sir Saskia's troops, as Eleanor and Odo had suspected. Sir Saskia herself was only a hundred paces away, standing some distance to the rear of her troops, safely out of bowshot. Mannix stood by her side holding a trumpet, but there were no others close by.

'Charge the miscreant knight now!' cried Biter, jabbing himself forward, Odo holding him back.

'Wait,' warned Runnel. 'Coolness in battle is essential. Assess the enemy, the lay of the land and the likelihood of the outcome.'

'If we can defeat Sir Saskia, the others will run,' Eleanor strategised. 'There's just her and Mannix. We can do it.'

'She defeated me easily before,' Odo pointed out.

'Well, she hasn't fought me yet,' said Eleanor, hoping she sounded as brave as she wanted to sound. There wasn't time for second thoughts. A section of the palisade fell in with a mighty roar and a huge billow of smoke. 'Look, they can't hold the wall for long, and once the enemy is inside, the smiths will be outnumbered.'

Odo nodded. He was staring at the battle, frozen in indecision. Ordinary people were dying there, being wounded, doing their best to defend themselves against coldhearted killers. Smiths and apprentices, villagers who had woken up that morning without fear, going about their normal business, only to be attacked for no reason save greed and viciousness.

All those ordinary people who would be killed unless someone helped them.

'I'll take Mannix,' said Odo calmly, bumping a fist against his chest as though clearing an obstruction. 'No mercy for either of them.'

Eleanor bared her teeth, raising Runnel high above her head, the ruby in the pommel catching the sunlight in such a way it bathed the whole blade in a bright red light. Then she broke into a run.

CHAPTER
THIRTY-ONE

Sir Saskia turned as Eleanor closed the last few paces. Amidst the noise of battle she hadn't heard the girl's approach until she was almost upon her, and even then it was only well-trained combat senses that raised the alarm. She ducked under Runnel's first, powerful swing and sprang away, drawing Ædroth. She managed this just in time to parry a series of blows, giving ground with each one.

Mannix had not been as fast as his knight. He managed to interpose the trumpet between Odo's first two-handed downward blow, but the impact sent him sprawling to the ground. He lay there, weaponless, and held out his hands.

'Chivalry demands you allow me to stand and draw!' he shouted as Odo furiously raised Biter above him.

Neither sword nor knight hesitated.

Biter came down point-first on Mannix's shoulder, shearing through his armour as if it were no more than river mud. Mannix screamed and swore and clutched at the wound with his left hand, his right arm now useless.

'Chivalry is wasted on bandits,' said Biter with uncharacteristic acid. The emerald in his pommel flashed. 'Come, Sir Odo. We must hold these others off the squire, who is showing uncommon valour.'

Odo looked around. He'd been totally caught up with attacking Mannix and was shocked to have won so easily. Eleanor and Sir Saskia were trading blows a dozen paces away, both dancing forward and back, swords flashing so fast he could barely see them.

Most of Sir Saskia's troops were trying to force their way through the smoking breach in the palisade and into a wild melee with the best-armoured smiths, who were fighting with massive hammers. But a group of six bandits had turned back and were coming towards Odo.

'Six!' muttered Odo under his breath. 'With spears!'

'Dare I suggest a frontal assault?'

Before Biter could finish the sentence, Odo charged at the enemy, screaming a wordless cry of rage.

Eleanor saw Odo's wild charge out of the corner of her eye, but could give it no thought. Every part of her being, mind and muscle was focused on fighting Sir Saskia. Runnel was doing much of the work, but Eleanor had to anticipate what the sword wanted to do, and go with her, rather than against her, and for the first time she was really managing to do all of that at the same time.

'Six!' shouted Runnel, and Eleanor rolled her wrists over, carrying out her training perfectly, one foot sliding forward, her short but whip-fast arms bringing the sword back up, slicing under Sir Saskia's attempted block, encouraging her to retreat. This time, the false knight didn't counterattack but kept backing off.

Sir Saskia was trying to get closer to her troops, Eleanor realised, and began to circle around to cut her off.

'Imp!' spat Sir Saskia. 'Chilblain! Surrender and I will let you live!'

Eleanor didn't waste breath answering. She sprang forward, stabbing at Sir Saskia's left armpit from below. The woman reeled from the sudden attack, feinted with her sword to Eleanor's right and kicked her hard under her left knee.

Sir Saskia wore steel-clad boots. The pain was like fire. Eleanor's leg collapsed and she fell sideways, Runnel desperately moving across her body to parry a stab at the girl's face.

Then it was Eleanor's turn to counter as Sir Saskia leaped forward and raised her sword for a two-handed blow that would have separated Eleanor's head from her shoulders if it had landed. But Eleanor rolled aside and reached out with Runnel, slicing Sir Saskia across the back of her knee, where she had only leather armour. The false knight roared in pain, hopped back and fell over, landing heavily in the earth, her sword flying out of her hand.

Eleanor crawled on her elbows in a frenzy, and pushed Runnel ahead to the full extent of her arm. The very sharp point of the sword pricked Sir Saskia's throat, just above the top of her hauberk.

'Yield,' said Eleanor, her voice very calm.

Odo was never really sure what happened with the first two bandits. He just let Biter do whatever he was going to do, tried to twist and jump out of the way of the thrusting spears, and a few seconds later those two bandits were down on the ground and he was rushing past, apparently unhurt and screaming his very first battle cry:

'For Lenburh!'

The four bandits who were strung out in a line ahead of him thought it was a horrifying battle cry. When two of their number fell almost instantly, and then the huge warrior with the sword that glowed a ghoulish green continued to thunder towards them, they all came to the same decision at the same time. They were used to frightening peasants and small skirmishes. Already unnerved by the defiant smiths in their fine armour, wielding huge hammers, Odo was too much for them.

They threw down their spears and ran for the forest.

This was the beginning of the end for Sir Saskia's forces. The troops on the wall looked back and saw Mannix writhing on the ground, Sir Saskia held at sword-point by a girl equipped with an enchanted sword, while another knight wielding his own sorcerous weapon chased two of their number towards the trees.

The attackers broke. The cry 'Save yourselves!' went up, and within a few seconds there were dozens running for the forest. The smiths pursued them for a dozen paces, caught several with hammer blows to their backs and let the others go.

Odo too stopped pursuing at the edge of the trees. He was completely winded and not really sure what had happened, save that he was alive, Eleanor was alive and Sir Saskia was captured.

'We did it!' he exclaimed, holding Biter high. 'We've won!'

'See?' Eleanor told Runnel delightedly. 'I told you that you weren't cursed!'

But even as she spoke, the setting sun was blocked by a sudden shadow, and a great wind blew across the battlefield.

Odo looked up and slowly lowered his sword.

Eleanor's triumph cooled instantly to ashes.

An enormous golden dragon, easily twenty times the size of Odo's water mill, came to a crashing, earth-shaking landfall in the clearing between palisade and forest, incidentally crushing several of the slower bandits beneath its massive feet, each of which was equipped with claws twice the size and breadth of Biter.

Everybody stopped. Everybody stared. There was total silence, save for the quiet sobbing of the wounded.

'The beast,' said Runnel in an awed voice. 'The mighty Quenwulf!'

As if in answer to her name, the dragon lifted her massive head towards the sky and, with a sound like a thousand blaring trumpets, let forth a great blast of fire – red fire that was far hotter than Master Fyrennian's old forge, so hot that even though she aimed upwards, everyone around had to shield their faces and duck down. A pure, white smoke billowed out after the flame, spreading across the battlefield like fog, redolent with the scent of a burning forest of tall pines.

Then the dragon spoke, and her voice was a thousand great drums all beaten at once, the earth shivering with the vibration. Everyone in earshot felt that voice in their bones.

'I am Quenwulf. Who calls me from my rest?'

THIRTY-TWO

'Impossible!' Saskia Vileheart gasped. 'It can't be . . .'

'It is if Runnel says it is,' said Eleanor bleakly. She straightened up, favouring her injured leg. She stared at the dragon and thought of Runnel's sketch in the dirt – the spots where a dragon was vulnerable, the eyes and under the jaw and wings. None of that would be any use. Not against this mighty creature, not against that flame. And those jaws couldn't just bite a horse in half, they could swallow one whole and not even feel it going down.

'Who calls me?' roared the dragon again. 'Who kindled the great fire to summon me from my sleep?'

Eleanor looked across at Odo, where he stood near the trees. She made the 'run away' signal he'd done before, when they first found Biter, but it was his turn to ignore her.

Odo cleared his throat and stepped forward into the dragon's shadow and towards its head, the source of that all-consuming fire.

'I lit the fire, oh Mighty Quenwulf!' he shouted, his voice only quavering a little. 'Though I did not mean to wake you from your rest.'

Quenwulf moved her head to face him, and one great black-pupilled golden eye followed him. Odo noticed a heavily armoured eyelid blink across for a second. Perhaps the eyes of smaller dragons were vulnerable. Quenwulf's certainly were not.

'And I helped light the fire!' shouted Eleanor. She moved to stand next to Odo, Runnel held down at her side.

Their shoulders touched.

'At least we won a battle,' he whispered. She smiled weakly up at him.

'Few in their right minds do mean to wake me,' said Quenwulf. The dragon's eyelids closed again, halfway, and stayed lidded. 'I see that you bear enchanted swords. Tell me your names, all of you.'

'Odo,' said Odo. He hesitated, then added defiantly, 'Sir Odo of Lenburh, and this is –'

'Hildebrand Shining Foebiter, Dragonslayer and Scourge of . . . Scourges!' shouted Biter, attempting to come up and lunge forward, even though he was at least twenty paces from the tip of the dragon's nose. Odo wrestled him back down and sighed. It was one thing to be killed by a dragon, but he hoped he could at least do it with dignity.

'Dragonslayer?' said Quenwulf. 'I think not. Perhaps

scourge of your own knights though. Or merely nuisance to your bearers. And you?'

'I am Sir Odo's squire, Eleanor,' she said, standing as tall as she could.

'And I, Reynfrida Sharp-point Flamecutter,' said Runnel, very respectfully. 'Sometimes known as the Sorrowful Sword. Mighty Quenwulf, I beg a boon.'

'Speak, little sword.' The dragon's voice rumbled warningly. 'Take care what you ask of me.'

'I ask that you forgive your untimely waking, and let Sir Odo and Squire Eleanor go free,' said Runnel. 'They have true and noble hearts, and do good in the world. And the sword Biter, my youngest brother, he has long slept, with dreams of eels. He does not know what he is about. Let them go, and destroy me in your fire.'

'You seek an ending from Quenwulf?' the dragon asked.

'I am cursed,' said Runnel. 'I have been the death of three knights, and wish no more to fall because of my burden.'

'I told you, you aren't cursed,' said Eleanor, under her breath.

'Who brought the dragon?' countered Runnel. She spoke very softly, but still Quenwulf heard.

The dragon laughed, a laugh that sent a gout of the white, pine-smelling smoke across Odo and Eleanor.

'You did not bring me here. The great fire in that foolish dam woke me, but not before time. What is it you think you know of dragons, Sir Odo? Squire Eleanor? What do you know of me?'

'Little,' said Odo.

'Very little,' added Eleanor.

The dragon raised one eyelid in a questioning way. 'Tell me all.'

'Uh, the stories talk about you . . . er . . . razing towns and . . . um . . .'

'Eating heroes,' said Eleanor. 'Burning villages . . .'

'I concede that this is true,' said Quenwulf. 'Except perhaps the hero part. I would not have called them "heroes" myself. Did you ever wonder why I did these things?'

'Because you're a dragon?' said Odo.

'I am a judge,' said Quenwulf. 'A most terrible judge. Though a fair one, I would say. The towns and villages I razed were empty. I must keep my eye in, after all, and also maintain my reputation. I do not take lives unless I find it necessary.'

Eleanor's gaze slid to the remains of a bandit still visible under one of the dragon's claws and then hastily back to the dragon.

'For those I have judged and found guilty,' said the dragon with an unflinching rumble, 'I am also the executioner. Now you have summoned me by fire, and I will again sit in judgment.'

'Who are the accused?' asked Odo. He felt strangely calm now. The dragon was not the unthinking beast he had always thought she would be. He already greatly preferred her to Sir Saskia.

'I will judge all of you present,' said Quenwulf. 'Gather around. In front.'

'I and my soldiers may not be tried by you, dragon!' said Sir Saskia. She had got up, and was slowly backing away, with Mannix drooping at her side. 'I answer only to my liege! We will withdraw, and you may deal with these others as you see fit.'

The dragon's long, spiky tail slowly slid across the ground and curled behind Sir Saskia and Mannix. They stopped and both looked nervously about. The tail slid in closer, spikes towering above them. Sir Saskia and her squire reversed direction, stumbling forward as the dragon's tail almost swept them up, and hurried as best they could to join Odo and Eleanor in front of Quenwulf's maw.

'I *will* judge you,' said Quenwulf, 'for I met an old man down by the river while I was following the smell of smoke from my summoning. He was less frightened of me than I expected, and that told me much, but now I wish to know more. When I call your name, step forward and open your eyes wide. Attempt no nonsense or dissembling as I look into your mind, or it will be extraordinarily painful. For you, that is. Sir Odo and Biter, to me!'

Odo stepped forward and opened his eyes wide, and the dragon looked at him, really looked at him. He felt her ancient, knowing gaze penetrate into the very depths of his being.

'Hmm,' said Quenwulf. 'Interesting. A little too cautious. You didn't want to be a knight, and yet . . . you have the makings of a great one.'

Odo felt her gaze leave him and focus on Biter. He trembled, but he forced himself to stay upright.

'Foolish sword,' said Quenwulf. 'You have learned little, and forgotten what little you knew. It was ever thus. You may step back, Sir Odo.'

Odo stumbled backwards, ending up having to crouch down on one knee. This felt strangely natural, so he stayed there, with Biter stuck in the ground. The boy leaned on the sword's hilt. Biter was, for once, completely silent.

'Eleanor and Runnel.'

Eleanor stepped forward and met the dragon's gaze with her chin up and head held high. Her bruised knee almost gave way again, but she locked it by force of will. Like Odo, she felt Quenwulf peer into her mind, as if a light was examining every tiny corner of not just her head, but also her heart.

'You are brave,' said Quenwulf. 'Ambition, now tempered by the reality of killing. Do you still wish to be a knight?'

'Yes,' said Eleanor, unable to be anything but honest with the dragon looking at her still. 'But I know I have much left to learn.'

'That is for others to decide,' said Quenwulf. Eleanor felt the dragon's unsettling gaze move to the sword. 'Runnel?'

'Eleanor is a knight in all but name,' said Runnel. 'Yet

I would not want her knighted, for my curse –'

'You are not cursed,' Quenwulf proclaimed. 'And never have been. It is possible, however, that one or more of your knights may have been.'

'I am truly not cursed?'

'You have been a little mad,' said Quenwulf, leaning back and huffing in a deep breath. 'I find the ignorance of both you and your brother startling, and I recommend you address it. Enchanted swords should know more of their making. You may step away.'

Eleanor stumbled back and also ended up kneeling.

'Squire Mannix,' said Quenwulf, 'also known as Strangling Jack and Osric Keynton – branded murderers banished from their supposed homelands, according to my old friend.'

'No, that's not me!' protested Mannix, looking futilely about for any means of escape.

'Again, I refute your right to judge me or my squire –' Sir Saskia started to say, but she choked into silence as the dragon's tail moved again, whipping around like a scorpion's, the long spike on the end stabbing Mannix right through the middle and then flipping him back into the dragon's mouth. It happened so quickly he didn't even have time to scream.

Quenwulf swallowed.

Odo and Eleanor gaped at her with a mixture of horror and awe.

'Sir Saskia.'

The armoured woman limped forward. On her second step she suddenly jerked her arm forward to throw a hidden knife at Quenwulf's eye. The armoured eyelid flashed shut as the knife struck, bounced and skittered down the dragon's snout.

Eleanor and Odo held their breath, waiting for the tail to strike again, for the dragon to snap Sir Saskia up in a single gulp. But Quenwulf merely opened her eye again and focused the full weight of her stare at the rogue knight, who, whatever her other faults, was not lacking in courage. She opened her eyes wide too, and stood there, a defiant sneer on her face.

'A knight turned to evil is among the worst of things to walk the earth,' said Quenwulf distantly. 'Yet there is some small flickering of light . . .'

'Do what you will, dragon,' sneered Sir Saskia. 'I do not fear death!'

'No,' said Quenwulf. 'That is why I will not give it to you.'

She reached out with one huge forefoot, flicked out a claw and with great precision cut the armour from Sir Saskia, leaving her standing in her gambeson. Then the claw flickered once more, tapping her precisely in the centre of her forehead.

'I have placed a doom of banishment upon you,' said Quenwulf. 'You will walk east for one thousand days and never turn back, unless I tell you to.'

Sir Saskia's legs stepped out from under her. One step, then another, like a marionette. 'No!' she cried, fighting the dragon's will with a mighty effort.

'East, I say. Do not go south, north or west. I will know where you travel, and if you stray you will see me again.'

'With a lance in my hand and a fearless destrier beneath me!' Sir Saskia snarled. Her feet carried her another three steps. Then five.

'I order you to go!' Quenwulf roared.

Sir Saskia's will failed.

'A lance for the dragon,' she cried to Eleanor and Odo over her shoulder as her legs carried her away. 'For you two, your deaths shall not be so swift!'

Then she was gone, vanished into the forest.

Not one of her soldiers followed.

'You set her free!' protested Eleanor.

'I have found very little of interest to the east,' said Quenwulf. 'She'll die from thirst or starvation, most likely.' The dragon didn't sound as if she cared all that much. 'I believe that there is some hope of her redemption however – a very slight hope. Perhaps if the liege she betrayed yet lives . . . I did not tell you to get up!'

Odo had begun to stand. He went back down on one knee as Quenwulf spoke, suddenly afraid again.

'Listen to me, Odo,' said Quenwulf. 'You are not really a knight. It is not within a sword's rights to grant that privilege, no matter how much it might wish its wielder to be so.'

'Oh,' said Odo. He wasn't a knight? He thought he'd be relieved, but he wasn't. He realised now that he didn't want to go back to the mill. He wanted to do all the things a proper knight was supposed to do, a real knight: help people, protect the weak, fight against injustice . . . everything except slay dragons. The stories seemed to be wrong about that part.

'However, it is well within *my* rights,' Quenwulf went on. Extending her forefoot again, one sharp claw came down upon Odo's right shoulder and then his left, touching so slightly that even the bruised one felt only a brush of air. 'Rise, Sir Odo.'

Odo stood, shaking, and immediately looked at Eleanor. She stayed exactly where she was, staring up at the dragon, hardly daring to hope.

'Fate favours the bold, I have often heard said. Usually just before an incineration. Perhaps you are also ready, Eleanor. I am not entirely certain, however. But as it may be long before your worth can be adjudged by a true knight or another dragon, I will take matters into my own claws. Bow your head before me.'

Eleanor did as she was told, her mouth hanging open in sudden hope. Quenwulf's claw brushed with surprising delicacy across her shoulders, and she heard the dragon's words boom out across the battlefield:

'Rise, Sir Eleanor!'

She obeyed, feeling a full inch taller even though both her knees were weak.

'My judgment is given,' said Quenwulf. 'Knights be true, and swords . . . attend to your natures rather than scourges and curses lest I be sterner with you when next we meet. Do not grow rusty, in mind or steel. Farewell from the mighty Quenwulf!'

With that, the dragon launched herself upwards, wings extending as she leaped. An enormous downdraught tumbled Odo and Eleanor end over end and enveloped them in dust. When it was past, they slowly staggered to their feet, coughing and choking.

'Sir Odo,' said Eleanor, with a small laugh that hinted at the potential to become a sob.

'Sir Eleanor,' croaked Odo.

'Our knights!' chorused Biter and Runnel, flinging themselves together with a clash of steel that made their wielders wince, both at the suddenness of the movement and the sound it made.

'What do we do now?' asked Odo. He looked around the battlefield. The sun was just dipping below the horizon, and under its last red light there seemed to be no living or even wounded bandits in the immediate area. Quenwulf had slain all that remained. The fire on the palisade was almost out, the bucket brigade now reinforced with all the former defenders as well as the unarmed villagers. They hadn't spared a moment to do more than glance warily at the dragon as she passed judgment. One perfectly natural fire was enough to worry about.

'Round up the ones who got away?' suggested Eleanor,

not very enthusiastically. She was exhausted, but the bandits would be trouble and needed to be dealt with. It was knights' business, and she would do what had to be done.

Odo started to nod, then shook his head.

'We have to,' said Eleanor wearily. 'They'll attack another vill—'

'Look behind you, Sir Knight.'

The first of the bandits had stepped out of the forest, holding his hands above his head. He was followed by several others, and then more, all of them trudging along with their heads down and their hands up.

Behind them, keeping to the forest shadows even in the twilight, came many urthkin, their sword-knives out and ready. At the treeline, their leader bowed low, to touch the earth.

Sir Odo and Sir Eleanor returned the gesture, then saluted with their swords.

'The voice of the dragon was felt in the earth, Sir Odo,' said the leader. 'We always come when called.'

Smiths came out of the gate bearing chains to bind the captives, Master Thrytin leading them with Toland at his side. They too bowed before the weary knights, though not to the ground.

'This is the stuff of legend!' cried Thrytin. 'You have saved Anfyltarn, the river, all of the north! And Great Quenwulf, creature of ancient tales —'

'I saw her speak to you!' babbled Toland. 'The dragon!'

'Whatever we can do for you, Sir Odo, Sir Eleanor, we shall do! What is your need?'

'Food,' said Odo.

'Water,' said Eleanor. 'And a bed.' With Sir Saskia disposed of, going home could wait one more night.

'You shall have it!' exclaimed Master Thrytin. 'And your swords will be cleaned, oiled and burnished. I will do it myself!'

'No,' said Odo, gripping Biter tightly. 'We look after our swords, as they look after us.'

EPILOGUE

A month after their victory at Anfyltarn, Eleanor was standing knee-deep in a strong current of clear, pale brown river water. Eels darted to and fro in front of her, seeking somewhere to hide, but there was no escaping her aim, which had always been mostly lethal but was now entirely so after hours of training under Runnel's direction. Boredom and frustration further made her the terror of all nearby river creatures.

One eel's life was saved by her best friend's hail. Eleanor looked up hopefully to see Odo coming along the path from Lenburh, but he shook his head and her face fell.

'How long does it take to pack a travelling chest?' She stabbed at another, less fortunate eel. 'That ancient, one-footed, cross-eyed, barrel-bellied –'

'Sir Eleanor!'

Odo shared her annoyance with Sir Halfdan's tardiness, but felt it beneath their newfound dignity as knights to be cursing another knight. Particularly as Sir Halfdan might hear about the indiscretion through village gossip, if overheard, and he *was* offering to personally, and proudly, introduce them to the court of the king – who would, he assured them, have many tasks for the kingdom's newest knights. All they had to be was patient.

'Don't fret on it,' said Odo.

'I can't help it. I'm *bored*.'

Time passed slowly, even with memories of their accomplishments to mull over.

'A knight's work is not made entirely of adventures,' said Runnel from where she watched on the grassy bank, point thrust firmly into the ground.

'Just one more would be good . . .'

Odo stuck Biter next to Runnel, far from any possibility of coming into contact with water or eels, and picked up the wicker basket. There would be many murdered eels today, judging by Eleanor's mood, which was fine from Odo's perspective. He liked eel pie.

'Why don't we make our own adventure?' Odo asked her as he joined her out in the river. The water was cold with the coming winter, but not yet icy.

'How?'

'I don't know. Hold a tournament perhaps, on the green. Offer a prize or something?'

'A test of skill,' called Biter approvingly. 'An excellent idea!'

'One that would serve well to advertise your considerable prowess,' Runnel agreed.

'Why would anyone come to Lenburh?' Eleanor said disconsolately. 'It's leagues from anywhere.'

'They might,' Odo said. 'Better than just practising though.'

Eleanor was about to answer when both knights heard a hue and cry rising up from along the path.

'Sir Odd! Sir Eel! Come quickly!'

Eleanor sighed. It was the baker twins, Aaric and Addyson, whose demeanour around Eleanor and Odo had been only slightly improved by the knights' triumphant return to Lenburh. Apart from the nicknames, the twins were now the source of an incessant stream of requests to deal with minor irritations and slights, far below a knight's calling.

'What is it this time?' asked Eleanor wearily. 'Pickles the cat hissed at you? A malevolent tree root tripped you?'

'No! No! This is real,' protested Aaric, coming to a panting halt on the shore. He did seem to be actually frightened, not pretending. 'It's the village — We're under attack!'

'By an army of frogs?' scoffed Odo.

'No, a blind king has come,' said Addyson. 'Pursued by bilewolves close behind! You must help!'

Eleanor and Odo burst out laughing. This was the most absurd attempt to rile them yet.

'Begone, gang-toothed squiddlers!' barked Biter, launching himself out of the grass and into Odo's hand, making him slash a threatening line through the air. 'Ere you find yourselves bisected!'

'Trisected!' added Runnel, flying to Eleanor's grasp and adding her own flourish to her brother's. The swords shone brilliantly in the afternoon light, polished and oiled to a state of perfection.

Ordinarily this would be enough to send the twins off at speed, but not this time.

'We aren't joking,' gabbled Aaric. 'The blind king, he's real, and Silbey the shepherd has been bitten – it's horrible, her flesh eaten away. Your dad's there, Eleanor, seeing what can be done but –'

'We need your help!' exclaimed Addyson.

Eleanor lowered the eel-spear. Odo could see now that Addyson's face was deathly pale, and not from flour. Aaric's hands trembled, clasped before him in apparently sincere pleading. Eleanor glanced at Odo, who was no longer smiling.

In the distance, there came a long, howling cry. It rose and fell, the sound sending shivers up everyone's spines.

'Bilewolf,' said Runnel. 'Sounds like a big one too.'

Eleanor looked at Odo. He nodded. Aaric and Addyson parted as the knights ran through and past them, heading to the village, straight towards where the howl had come from.

'For Lenburh!' Odo cried.

'For Lenburh!'

Want to find out what happens next?
Read on . . .

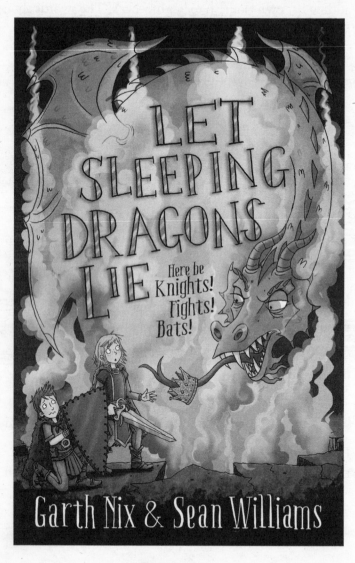

LET SLEEPING DRAGONS LIE

Here be
Knights!
Fights!
Bats!

Garth Nix & Sean Williams

Piccadilly
PRESS

ABOUT THE AUTHORS

Garth Nix and Sean Williams first collaborated on the Troubletwisters series, which they followed with a book in the Spirit Animals series, *Blood Ties*. Garth is also the bestselling author of the Seventh Tower series, the Keys to the Kingdom series, the Old Kingdom series and *Frogkisser!* Sean's bestselling novels include those in the Twinmaker series and several in the Star Wars® universe. Both Garth and Sean live in Australia – Garth in Sydney and Sean in Adelaide. This is their first book featuring Odo, Eleanor and Biter . . . but it won't be their last.

Thank you for choosing a Piccadilly Press book.

If you would like to know more about our authors, our books or if you'd just like to know what we're up to, you can find us online.

www.piccadillypress.co.uk

You can also find us on:

We hope to see you soon!